End?

The End?

"Without you, it's like a flower without its buds..."

Sadab Mahir

ISBN 978-984-35-1042-6 (Paperback)

First Edition: 2021

To everyone who indeed seeks to venture onto the path of fantasy, reality, justice & humanity.

CONTENTS

"Life's a risky rollercoaster; going through various phases, ups and downs, which you have no choice but to ride..."

— KELVAC

1

Cold Strikes

"Hello everyone! Today had been a tough day for the New York citizens as the autumn started alongside tornados, and people struck the storm to go to their work..." as the reporter in the T.V. spoke through.

It was the time of the day Eliott loved the most. Yet he wasn't feeling the normal enthusiasm he does on the usual Saturday nights.

Stella was out on the street, wind blowing with a cold breeze, she tightened herself into her trench-coat broadening her scarf over her neck and abdomen. Streets were darker than usual; street lights held dimmer than normal.

"Jennifer Studfort, please do a favour by explaining all the scattered books, would you?" Miss Winsent spoke interrogating.

It wasn't that late at night as the darkness made it seem; evening had barely finished.

"How should I explain if the scattered books never belonged to me..." Jennifer answered harshly.

It was getting colder as night was turning darker; "trring" rang the cordless landline; Minsie quickly left the utensils; she had been cleaning with a towel, and rushed to answer, it didn't seem to be the hour which would bring any good news.

"She's still missing."

"Who is? And who are you even?" asked Minsie in confusion.

"Wait, you don't know yet?"

"Know what...? No, I don't know about anything." answered Minsie as she hadn't heard about anything at all.

"Well, then I think it isn't me you should hear it first from."

"Wait, no tell..." Minsie demanded confusedly, but the call was already hung up.

"What a strange call at this hour." thought Minsie to herself, "probably was a wrong call." but taking to mind, all the things that took place that week it seemed that wasn't one to Minsie.

"Then, why does all of the information lead to you as belonging the mess?" questioned Miss Winsent interrogating.

"How am I supposed to answer any of that while I have had no idea about any of this until now!" replied Jennifer Studfort.

"Well I don't think I have to know any of that; you either prove yourself innocent to me within hours or I take you as the culprit of all this mess." backfired Miss Winsent in the hardest of the tones.

"Well, I sure will as this is questioning both my loyalty and respect!" back-shouted Jennifer Studfort.

"You sound promising but not quite..." said Miss Winsent lowering the tone but still keeping up with the harshness.

"It will, just wait till I prove." answered Jennifer Studfort in irritancy.

The night turned darker and darker as the hours passed, Jennifer had already left off to proving herself innocent; Stella was still out on the streets; Minsie resumed cleansing the utensils; Eliott was in a cozy comforter on his couch still not feeling what he normally did...

As the sky turned pitch black, the birds went into their shelters and the owls woke up staring into the darkness. She is still onto searching the missing girl, nowhere to be found; she had looked into every corner of everywhere she had thought it was worth looking, but as the night turned darker her panic was intensifying, alongside the fright of being out alone that late at night.

"Would I be safe out here?" she thought to herself "Or should I return?".

"But if I return what will happen to her?" she thought in terror.

She headed back to where her car was parked; even though she was worrying about the missing girl, she decided to go back home, because if something happened to her there won't even be a slight chance of the missing girl surviving.

She drove through the dark, empty highway; not a single car to be seen in miles. "Deashh!" something hit her car, although she would've thought of slowing down and seeing what happened; she struck the speed to the highest she could reach; she was sensing pure danger.

"Good morning, Ms. Jennifer." greeted Mr. Spencer enthusiastically.

"Good morning" replied Jennifer

"How may I help you?" asked Mr. Spencer kindly.

"Well, there're tons of things I will need help from you with..." replied Jennifer in a joking tone.

"And what are they?" asked Mr. Spencer.

"Well, can we sit down somewhere first?" requested Jennifer.

"Sure, let me arrange us a seat..." offered Mr. Spencer.

"No, not here please" denied Jennifer.

"Cafe?" offered Mr. Spencer.

"Yeah, a coffee shop would be the best!" agreed Jennifer.

Mr. Spencer and Jennifer walked to a coffee shop nearby; a typical coffee shop, but with the minimalist customer was what they sought and went to.

Minsie woke up and the first thing that came up to her mind was that the caller had mentioned about a missing female, and she was wondering who it could be, so she decided to contact each and everyone in her knowledge who could go missing.

As Minsie was freshening up, she made herself a mug of coffee - her usual morning thing- she sat cozily on her couch comforting herself, along with the mug of coffee.

She started calling one by one, she decided to contact from low to high chances of the person going missing. She had already thought of making the conversation casual; without telling anything about the unknown call.

Sun had gone more than halfway down, the sky started to turn dark as usual, but as it was autumn; each and every passing moment turned the sky towards a higher tone of pitch black; darker and darker.

Eliott's day had been passing all usual, still something was -even if slightly- different. He brew himself a cup of coffee which he loves on the Sunday evenings, along with any web series, which to him is the best combo ever! Well even though everything else seemed a bit different and he was being a bit less enthusiastic but one thing he could never be less enthusiastic on is his usual Sunday combo.

"Will it be possible to collect all of the information by today?" demanded Jennifer over the phone call.

"I assume not, it usually takes about a week to retrieve all of those information, but some could be collected by today; I am verily sorry, and I have been trying the best from my part." replied Mr. Spencer.

"Alright, though thanks a lot for helping out..." replied in sorrow and disappointment.

"I am happy I could have tried helping a person like you; kind and generous." replied Mr. Spencer generously.

The night was turning darker and deeper, the skies were on the highest of tones of pitch black.

Minsie had contacted almost everyone she thought could go missing, all were well and safe. She was starting to get a bit relieved knowing almost everybody was safe and sound. But one thing was still circulating through her mind, the fact that the caller recognized her; if it was a wrong call, the caller was supposed to not recognize her. The bad thing was that Minsie couldn't recall the voice of the caller at all.

At the end of the day, Jennifer was left with nothing but disappointment; she could not think of another way of collecting the information; worst of all was that she had given her word to Miss Winsent of proving herself innocent; within hours, and not days.

She had been worrying the whole day, thus she was having severe headaches, so she had took some pills to relieve her for the time being, which would normally put her to sleep within an hour or so.

Minsie had thought of going to sleep and continue contacting the people the next day evening, cause the next day was Monday and she will have to go to work.

Eliott was going throughout his presentation which he would be presenting the coming day; to that far his presentation seemed excellent to himself; he had already corrected almost all of the typos, and was just about ready for the coming day.

The night turned even more darker as the owls woke up and the birds returned to their nests.

"Had she been found?" she asked the police personnel.

"Sorry, but not yet." answered the police personnel in a soft tone.

"It's the second night of her going missing, when will she be found?" she demanded in sorrow & hopelessness.

"We're trying the best from our part; it has to be the fortune for us to find her." answered the police personnel.

"Well, I hope it is no far till she being found." she replied.

"Hopefully..." sympathized the police personnel.

As the wind blew and stars started appearing; the dark hours of the night came close by.

Stella hadn't returned yet; she then was just writing a simple poem on her diary -she isn't a frequent diary writer but amuses to write sometimes- which stays with her all now and then; a simple small vintage type diary.

The night went colder as it turned darker; the streets were empty, no one to be seen in sight; the cold breeze made the night seem like one in the lands of Antarctica.

As the sun appeared, Jennifer went rushing to her car as if she were a maniac, she had never been that anxious about being late; she had been extremely worrying ever since she had woken up.

"One Frappuccino, please." requested Jennifer

"Sure, here you go." replied the Starbucks staff humbly

As she couldn't sleep well last night, she had to take a dosage of caffeine, so that she doesn't go snoring in front of Miss Winsent, which would bring her more trouble.

"Good morning, Ms. Jennifer." greeted Miss Winsent arrogantly (her usual way of talking).

"Good morning." replied Jennifer in a low tone.

"So, how did you plan to prove yourself today?" questioned Miss Winsent sharply.

"Well, you see retrieving information from certain sources take much more time" replied Jennifer.

"Do you try to mean; you weren't able to collect enough evidence?" asked Miss Winsent.

"Yes, I suppose." replied Jennifer in hesitance.

"Well anyways, to your surprise you have already been proven innocent to me..." said Miss Winsent.

"Wait, what?" shockingly asked Jennifer along with a bit of relief.

"Yes, you heard me right, you have already been proven innocent." replied Miss Winsent.

"Wow!, glad to hear that, and do take my apology for not keeping my word." replied Jennifer.

"Sure, but here's the deal, as you haven't kept your own words, you will have to help find the culprit at any possible way." demanded Miss Winsent.

"Sure, would be glad to be of your help." generously replied Jennifer.

"Well, thank you, but I would suggest you to think twice before giving your word." answered Miss Winsent with a bit of harshness

"I would put that into action in the very future, thank you." replied Jennifer in a hard tone.

Even though, Jennifer was relieved by being proved innocent, she still was a bit irritated to have to work alongside that issue which doesn't even relate with her in any manner.

The birds were out in the sky flying and chirping, as the sun appeared fully along with it's shine.

"Good Job." complimented Mr. Malcof.

"Thank you!" replied Eliott in happiness.

"Well, I think we're done for today." mentioned Mr. Malcof.

"Yes I believe." replied Eliott in a funny tone.

Eliott was successfully done with his very perfect presentation, which he had put time on. He was happy that the presentation had went pretty well, some had also noted his perfection over it; even if not directly. To him it seemed that was worth putting time on. As the C.E.O had mentioned; he was done for office that day, which he couldn't be more happy on.

As the sun had rose up to it's highest level, the birds went into their nests along with the food they had collected.

She had been out all night the previous day; still worrying about the girl who was gone missing since three days then; nowhere to be found, she had asked about the girl to the police last night, yet no information at all was provided. Though she had tried her best to find information herself all night but nothing to be found. She was only left with tension and worry.

The sun had moved down from its highest level, the birds went back chirping into the sky; while the owl was still sleeping.

Minsie had finished her work and then was returning home, as she had half-day that day. It wasn't an awful day nor of the best days either, Minsie had been thinking of the unknown call the entire day, not even a moment was spared. Minsie had decided to resume contacting the rest of the people, as soon as she reached home; if all went okay then she would be relieved of that.

As the sun was setting down, the owls woke up and the birds returned to their nests.

Eliott was already home, he had prepared himself a cup of coffee and some snacks for the evening. Although he was happy that his day went well, he was still worried about some stuffs.

As the sky turned dark, the wind blew harder than it had all day, along with a cold breeze making it necessary for people to cozy up with something warm.

Minsie had contacted everyone she had in mind, trying to not forget any, yet she was still worried of forgetting anyone, also by the possibility that the person she forgets be the very person that is in trouble, which exactly was what she didn't wish at any all.

The night deepened, and the sky darkened to a tone of pitch black, darker than dark.

Stella was out walking through the cold dark night streets, covering herself into a trench-coat and sweatshirt; her usual winter-wear. She was a very free spirited person, along with generosity, which wasn't quite liked by some.

2

Fog Starts to Clear up

The dark hours of the night came close by, as the cold breeze surrounded all over the world.

All of a sudden, Stella came to Minsie's mind, although they had a fight last week, it wouldn't be alright for her to let any of her friends be in danger, seeing how nice of a person she was. She hadn't contacted Stella ever since they fought, she immediately grabbed her phone and called Stella.

"The person you are trying to call isn't reachable right now." phrased the digital voice

Exactly what she thought was happening, it was Stella's mother that day, who she thought was a wrong caller; was actually Stella's mother. When she came back home that day after the fight; she had decided not to contact Stella as long as Stella didn't contact her.

The night was colder than any before that winter, the owls stared right into the dark deep sky.

The lady searching for the missing girl received a phone call, she hesitated to answer it but she did.

"Hello, Ms. Franklin speaking." said the lady as she answered the call.

"Hello, how are you? This is Minsie." replied the caller

"I am alright, I know it is you, Minsie, speaking; but why did you mind to call?" demanded Ms. Franklin in disappointment.

"I am really sorry to not have recognized you, and I couldn't call back either as you had called over my landline that day, so it was all unknown." replied Minsie in guilt.

"Well, I am glad at least you tried and figured out then called back." replied Ms. Franklin in appreciation and relief then; that she was not alone anymore.

"Thanks, I wanted to ask if Stella is alright or not?" asked Minsie

"Well you see, as I mentioned earlier she had gone missing, and hadn't been found yet." told Ms. Franklin

"Not even now?!" asked Minsie tensed.

"No, not even now, I have tried in every possible way but…" hesitated Ms. Franklin.

The night went colder and colder as it went darker, streets held quiet, streetlights hung dim, silence present everywhere.

"Trring!" rang the house-bell, and to Jennifer's surprise it was Eliott Walfador.

"At this hour of the night!" first thing that struck Jennifer's mind.

"Hello" greeted Eliott.

"Why are you here at this hour?!" demanded Jennifer without even noticing Eliott's greeting; simply because no one at all was welcomed at that hour to her home.

"I can explain but can we sit down and talk?" replied Eliott.

"Well, I can't make you leave from my doorstep..." answered Jennifer.

Eliott walked in, and Jennifer followed by, after closing the door.

"Would you like a cup of coffee?" offered Jennifer.

"Sure, thank you." replied Eliott

Jennifer then made themselves two cups of coffee, and she also arranged a plate of biscuits, she set all of those into a tray and carried it to the mini-table in her finely decorated drawing-room. Then she sat onto the modernly set-up couch.

"Well, now can I know what brought you here?" asked Jennifer frankly.

"Well you see, I have to give you some synopses before moving on to the main story..." answered Eliott.

"Sure, sounds like time to me..." replied Jennifer.

"Sure is." answered Eliott.

"Well, if it is important then I would rather listen." affirmed Jennifer.

"Well, I assume I should begin..." offered Eliott making it clear that it was important.

"Please." insisted Jennifer.

The night turned darker and deeper, as silence spread everywhere.

"Hello." greeted Ms. Franklin

"Hello, good to see you!" replied Minsie.

"Well, thanks for inviting me over." thanked Ms. Franklin as she moved into the house.

"Don't mention, it is my duty." affirmed Minsie.

"So helpful of you." replied Ms. Franklin in appreciation.

Both Minsie and Ms. Franklin moved into the living room, as Minsie offered a cup of tea.

"So can you tell me everything, starting from the beginning?" demanded Minsie.

"Alright, so see it was this typical Saturday afternoon, I was sitting over near to the counter-top in our kitchen, then as usual Stella notified me about going out and as she normally goes out alone; I didn't ask much about where she was going, why she was going, or when she would be back, also cause I was busy studying some documents." told Ms. Franklin.

"Oh I see." replied Minsie alongside the event-telling.

The night was darker than ever as the darkest hours had already arrived, birds asleep in their nests, dogs growling, owls staring deep into the dark sky.

"I knew she would at most be back by two o'clock, but she wasn't, so I immediately called the police and reported Stella as being missing, cause I definitely knew any minute more than two o'clock would be an alert towards some sort of danger." told Ms. Franklin as she finished the 1 hour long story-telling.

"So, that was pretty loose right there..." said Minsie as she sought deeper into the situation.

"Yeah, pretty loose, I had no idea any of such would happen…" replied Ms. Franklin as she took the last sip of her tea.

"I assume something bad had happened earlier that week, as she hadn't been acting well with me either." told Minsie.

Minsie was a friendly and goofy kind of person but when it came to serious matters; she was quite mature.

"Well…" nodded Ms. Franklin.

"Did you seem to notice anything?" asked Minsie.

"Not really, but she surely wasn't on the good side of the moods." replied Ms. Franklin.

The night was in it's deepest and darkest position; as it came nearer to its end.

Ms. Franklin and Minsie discussed about the situation all night long until the sun rose and they went back to their own works, but they had already planned how the day will work out; what they're supposed to do.

The sun had risen with it's ultimate shine, but the sky was still foggy as before, which made the shine a bit blurred.

"One coffee latte, please." asked Eliott.

"Sure, sir." replied the Starbucks staff

Eliott took his coffee and set off for work, that day was going to be a stressful day for him as he had already planned a lot of things to do the very day.

"Good morning!" greeted Eliott as he walked in to his workplace.

Everyone in there greeted him back as he moved inside.

Stella had been out all night until she decided to rest. She had again went back to her personal diary, but that time she had written how her days were going in-place of the poems; her days had been rough but still pleasant; then that no one was there to interrupt her freedom or peace.

"Hello." noted out Miss Winsent.

"Good morning." greeted Jennifer as she walked in.

"Good to see you here." mentioned Miss Winsent.

"Well, I had to come here; simply cause I don't hang loose on my words." pointed out Jennifer.

"Yeah, I can see it all." noted Miss Winsent.

"Crystal clear, isn't it." mentioned Jennifer.

"Well, let us move on to the main reason you are here for." said Miss Winsent.

"Sure!" replied Jennifer.

"Well then, I believe we should begin." said Miss Winsent.

"But, to mention I have some other works to do, so I wouldn't be here for much long." told Jennifer.

"Taking the 'other works' as important, I wouldn't mind." replied Miss Winsent.

"Glad to hear." said Jennifer.

Jennifer had visited Miss Winsent, because of the incident she was asked to help Miss Winsent on.

Sun couldn't be clearly seen due to the foggy atmosphere, but seeing the time of the day, it could be noted for lowering down from it's highest level.

"Hello, good afternoon." greeted Ms. Franklin.

"Good afternoon." greeted back Minsie.

"Well, where are we off to?" asked Ms. Franklin.

"Let's grab some coffee, then we'll decide, alright?" suggested Minsie.

"Starbucks?" offered Ms. Franklin agreeing to Minsie's idea.

"My favourite!" agreed Minsie.

Ms. Franklin and Minsie were set off for the day; they had already decided where they were off to that day, but the question here was which one to go first.

On that typical Tuesday, Starbucks was all so quiet, since everybody was onto their work; usual working day early-afternoons. Minsie and Ms. Franklin decided to sit down and discuss so they moved to a coffee table on the corner and sat to discuss the day's plan.

"Should we contact the FBI too?" asked Minsie.

"What brings that to your mind?" replied Ms. Franklin.

"Well you see, they can help us track where Stella's last location was, as to where her phone network was last seen." replied Minsie.

"That is a great thought, but do you think they'll prioritize a typical teen leaving home mad?" questioned Ms. Franklin.

"Well, fun fact; I have a friend working in FBI, so I am quite sure she'll help out…" told Minsie.

"Wow, that is great!" replied Ms. Franklin as her mood uplifted along with a bit of relief by having somebody of known in that department, which ought to be the most helpful seeing the situation they were in.

"Where should we put that in today's plan?" asked Minsie.

"I suggest putting it to the very last." suggested Ms. Franklin.

"Huh, why?" asked Minsie in confusion.

"See that thing is going to help in any way; it is an absolute solution, so saving it as a last option would be something keen to do." explained Ms. Franklin.

"Oh, I didn't view it that way, great thought though." replied

Minsie as she understood the concept.

"Well, should we get going?" offered Ms. Franklin.

"Sure, the rest we'll sort out in the car, while we're on the road." replied Minsie.

Minsie and Ms. Franklin left their chairs and set off to the parking lot to where their car was parked. They already had in mind how the day was going to go, so they decided to sort things out on the road.

"May I come in?" asked Eliott as he knocked the door.

"Please." replied Mr. Malcof

"Thank you." said Eliott as he walked in.

"May I know what brought you here?" asked Mr. Malcof frankly.

"Well, I am done with all my work for today over the project."

"Great to hear." complimented Mr. Malcof.

"So I wanted to leave early today, if that would create no issue." mentioned Eliott.

"It sure wouldn't, keeping into mind about all your effective contributions." replied Mr. Malcof along with a simple compliment.

"Thank you, meet you tomorrow." said Eliott as he walked out.

The sun was about to its mid-level, slightly warm was how the weather seemed.

"I think that's all for today, you can take a leave now." said Miss Winsent as she caressed the documents into the file.

"Should I?" asked Jennifer gently.

"You may, as you mentioned earlier about having some important work." replied Miss Winsent kindly.

"Thank you!" said Jennifer as she left.

The day seemed to work good with Jennifer, she was done before time, which made her a bit relieved from that long day. She thought of grabbing some coffee on the way.

"Sure, why not." replied the young policeman.

Ms. Franklin had mistakenly asked the police about whether or not they could track Stella's last location, which didn't seem to bother Minsie much about, seeing how much of a friendly person she was.

A hour or half had passed since the policeman went to check the information. Minsie and Ms. Franklin were waiting outside; sitting onto the chairs.

"Well, we were successfully able to retrieve the information in a short time." said the young policeman as he walked towards them, along with some documents on his hands.

"Oh great then!" replied Minsie and Ms. Franklin nodded with a smile.

"Ok so, it says Victoria Avenue, Riverside, California." said the young policeman as he read the location on the document.

"I don't seem to recall anybody in that specific location nor do I think there's any reason Stella would be there." mentioned Ms. Franklin as she got confused.

"Eliott!" slightly screamed Minsie as she recalled the location.

"Eliott?" questioned Ms. Franklin.

"The guy with those good looks, you must have noticed -even if for once- with Stella." quickly answered Minsie.

Minsie almost knew everything of Stella, taking in to mind how long they have been best friends, it was pretty normal.

"Oh that guy." replied Ms. Franklin shortly.

"Yes! yes, it's his house address." mentioned Minsie.

The sun has come down to a lower position, releasing a cold breeze into the air.

Stella could feel the chill cold wind blowing over her, she had always loved sitting by a fireplace in that type of weather. She was walking over a bridge, it was quite foggy out in there making it not quite easy to see the far end of the bridge.

"Don't you think the fog started to clear up." said Ms. Franklin as she and Minsie moved into the car.

"Yes, it sure has." replied Minsie alongside Ms. Franklin's words.

Minsie and Ms. Franklin had already left the police station and were off to some other place they had decided to go, then their schedule had totally changed as they had gotten some hints onto the incident.

The wind blew, making it seem like it was whispering; the sun had set while moon welcomed the evening.

3
FIGURING OUT STELLA

"Well, can you take a moment to describe what sort of a person this guy is?" requested Ms. Franklin.

"Umm, based on every point I have seen him in and the behaviour he had shown, I could say he is a pretty nice person." replied Minsie.

"Any specific reason why you would refer to him as being nice?" questioned Ms. Franklin.

"Umm, if you see one of the situation, where Stella and I were getting followed by two creepy guys on an empty street; Eliott joined us over, probably just in case if the creepy guys posed any threats we three could very well outnumber them." told Minsie.

"Oh, that sounds protective of him." exclaimed Ms. Franklin.

"Kind of." replied Minsie.

It was more than halfway through evening, the weather was much colder than at the beginning of the day.

"So what about Stella?" asked Ms. Franklin.

"You mean?" questioned Minsie.

"Did she seem to like Eliott?" asked Ms. Franklin.

"Umm, that can be considered a personal thing but yeah as I seem to notice, she did have an affection towards him..." replied Minsie.

The sky had darkened, into a deeper tone of black, changing the chill evening into a cold night.

Stella had decided to rest somewhere, she had written a lot on her diary lately; which seems like her only companion.

"I think we can now rest, now that we know Stella didn't get kidnapped or something." said Ms. Franklin.

"I think too." replied Minsie.

"But we have to definitely keep in mind, that she might still be in danger though." mentioned Ms. Franklin.

"We definitely should." replied Minsie.

"So, let's go to my place?" insisted Ms. Franklin.

"Oh, no you are already in so much trouble, I don't want to trouble you any further…" replied Minsie.

"You don't say it that way; you visiting my house wouldn't be any trouble; after all you're just like my daughter…" said Ms. Franklin sincerely.

"Aww, thank you!" replied Minsie as she agreed.

Ms. Franklin and Minsie headed towards Ms. Franklin's home, they had thought of discussing about the situation over there while having dinner prepared by Ms. Franklin.

"Hello?" said Stacy as she answered the phone call.

"Hello, how are you?!" replied the caller.

"I am alright. Just to mention I may have not recognized you…" said Stacy.

"Sad to see how fast you forgot me…Jacob" replied the caller.

"Oh come on, Jacob you must know I am bad at remembering voices and you had called my landline so…" replied Stacy.

"Funny…" said Jacob in an angry tone.

"But I have to mention, I was like woah, who's this person with this nice voice calling at this hour…" said Stacy.

"Nice voice?" pointed out Jacob as his mood uplifted.

"Yeah, honestly…" said Stacy in a mischievous tone.

"Yeah totally honest!" replied Jacob in a sarcastic tone as they both laughed quietly.

The night deepened as it darkened, owls stared right into the sky, birds resting in their nests

"Ok, so what do you think Stella disappeared for?" asked Ms. Franklin as she arranged the cutleries onto the dining table.

"Well, I can't say anything specifically…" replied Minsie.

"But like, any guesses?" asked Ms. Franklin as she put the plates onto the table.

"Umm if you see, Stella was acting unusual last week…" said Minsie as she sat onto one of the chairs.

"Yeah…" said Ms. Franklin alongside Minsie's words.

"So I must assume something had happened earlier that week other than our fight…" mentioned Minsie in awkwardness.

"Oh, you two had a fight…?" questioned Ms. Franklin.

"Yes." replied Minsie.

"Was it too serious of a fight?" asked Ms. Franklin as she served the dishes to Minsie.

"No, not that serious, just a fight over some simple stuff." replied Minsie.

"I can assure it wasn't the reason Stella disappeared." said Ms. Franklin frankly.

"Yeah, I hope so." said Minsie hesitantly.

Both Minsie and Ms. Franklin sat onto the chairs by the dining table to have their dinner, which was finely prepared by Ms. Franklin upon their arrival.

The sky darkened to a deeper tone of pitch black, the cold breeze was let out along with heavy winds.

"So any advices over it?" asked Stacy as the two came near towards the end of their conversation.

"Not really much, I think just figure out a way to work it out…" replied Jacob.

"Ok, I guess I got to go sleep, you know tomorrow I have to go to work, so…" mentioned Stacy.

"Well, bye then!" said Jacob.

"Bye!" replied back Stacy as she hung up the phone call.

The streets were quieter than usual, silence present throughout the atmosphere as the night deepened.

"I can see it crystal clear; the difficulty in figuring out Stella…" pointed out Ms. Franklin.

"Yes true, she is a person full of mysteries and surprises." replied Minsie as she gave out a little laugh.

"Yes, I have to agree on that." replied Ms. Franklin as she smiled.

"I think pretty much everyone who knows her closely would agree..." said Minsie.

"But, in the current situation we are in, we must figure out Stella..." mentioned Ms. Franklin.

"As in?" asked Minsie as she focused onto the topic.

"If we can figure out what Stella does normally in these type of situations, as in if we could figure out where she would go usually in these type of scenario, then it'll be easy for us to reach her." explained Ms. Franklin as she got serious over the situation.

"Yes, I agree. We will have to work on that though..." replied Minsie as she sought deeper into the topic.

"Maybe, let's take a break till tomorrow morning, then meet up again; with fresh minds?" suggested Ms. Franklin.

"Oh, yes that would be great, and I'll take leave from work tomorrow..." mentioned Minsie as she agreed.

"Well, then you'll be free of any tension." replied Ms. Franklin.

"Yes, absolutely. I think I should say bye for today..." said Minsie.

"Oh, sure. Bye then, stay safe." replied Ms. Franklin as they moved towards the doorway.

Minsie took a leave, and drove to her home to get a good night's sleep, after-all she hadn't slept the previous night.

Ms. Franklin closed the door after following Minsie to her car.

"The house feels so empty now…" thought Ms. Franklin.

Stella wasn't there to accompany Ms. Franklin and thus the house felt quite empty, after-all nobody likes a house empty of their family members.

The night deepened to the darkest tone of pitch black, birds resting in the peace of the ultimate silence.

"Good morning!" said Minsie as her phone call got answered.

"Good morning, Ms. Minsie." greeted Mr. Monzelle.

"Sir, I wanted you to know; I've some work today." said Minsie.

"Important, I assume." questioned Mr. Monzelle

"Sure is." answered Minsie.

"If you want to take a leave for today then it's totally fine as you stated it to be important." replied Mr. Monzelle.

"Well, thank you!" exclaimed Minsie.

The sun had just risen, birds woke up and readied to go find food, owls went to sleep.

"Hello." said Ms. Franklin.

"Hello, see you in that Starbucks?" offered Minsie as she answered the call.

"Sure, I will be there in ten minutes." agreed Ms. Franklin.

"Okay then, bye." replied Minsie as she hung up the call.

Minsie got up to get readied, she had woke up quite early, so she had thought of discussing everything over in Starbucks; a chilly cozy environment, along with coffee to keep them awake.

Ms. Franklin had arrived to Starbucks, and as just she entered she saw Minsie ordering coffee, she was happy to not be late.

"Oh hello, I ordered you a Mocha." said Minsie.

"Oh thank you very much!" appreciated Ms. Franklin.

"Let's sit over to the corner." suggested Minsie as she handed Ms. Franklin the coffee.

"Alright, sure." replied Ms. Franklin as she took the coffee.

Minsie and Ms. Franklin walked towards a table at the corner, along with their coffee; usual mornings.

"Ok so where do you two normally go?" asked Ms. Franklin as she pulled a chair.

"Me and Stella…we usually meet up in coffee shops." replied Minsie as she sat onto a chair.

"No, like I mean like take yourself with Stella in this situation where you two would disappear; where would you go?" questioned Ms. Franklin as she took a sip of her coffee.

"That's critical right there." answered Minsie.

"We have to think critically…" replied Ms. Franklin.

Minsie took a sip of her coffee as she tried to think of an answer to that question, she hadn't given that a thought anytime before.

The sun had appeared fully along with its shine, birds flying chirping; in the bright sky.

"I think she's a pretty independent person, and she wouldn't go asking for help to anybody at all." pointed out Minsie.

"Hmm." noted Ms. Franklin

"So she probably didn't go to anybody's house" said Minsie as she finished her answer.

"Well, nice concept, but give it a second thought." replied Ms. Franklin as she sought deeper into the answer.

"Alright." agreed Minsie politely.

"See I get what you tried to mean, but I can assure you Stella would never go to a Hotel so I think we should check out her friends' houses, because there's still a possibility." elaborated Ms. Franklin over her point.

"I think you're right, we should now go check on." agreed Minsie as she understood the idea.

"But would they be at home now?" asked Ms. Franklin.

"Oh yes, I forgot it's a Wednesday morning…" replied Minsie.

"I think let's meet up at evening then?" offered Ms. Franklin.

"Oh, sure. See you at evening then." said Minsie as she got up.

Both Minsie and Ms. Franklin got up from their chairs and left towards their cars on the parking lot of Starbucks.

Hours passed, sun had started lowering down, ending the afternoon while starting the evening; cold and dark.

"Hello." said Minsie as she took her car keys.

"Hello, Minsie." replied Ms. Franklin.

"I'll am getting out now…" informed Minsie closing the door.

"Ok I'll be out now too." replied Ms. Franklin.

"Ok so we'll head to Stacy's place first?" offered Minsie.

"Sure, I'll be right there, but we should go inside together…" agreed Ms. Franklin.

"Sure I'll wait at the parking lot, but do you know where Stacy lives?" questioned Minsie.

"As far as I remember it's Hellman Avenue, Riverside, California." replied Ms. Franklin in confusion.

"No, it is the 3rd alley on the Hensler Avenue, Riverside, California." corrected Minsie.

"Oh alright, I couldn't recall. By the way, whom are we visiting today?" questioned Ms. Franklin.

"Jacob and Stacy…" replied Minsie.

"Only Jacob and Stacy?" asked Ms. Franklin as she closed her door and walked towards her car.

"Yes, you see we have a small group of friends and I know only Jacob and Stacy are reliable in this situation." answered Minsie as she gave out a little laugh.

"Oh alright, that would save us some time." replied Ms. Franklin as she laughed along.

"Ok so, see you over on Stacy's." said Minsie as she got into her car.

"Alright, see you." said Ms. Franklin as she hung up the call.

Minsie and Ms. Franklin both got onto their cars as they left towards Stacy's house on Hensler Avenue, Riverside, California.

The sky deepened as the moon appeared, along with a cold breeze: making it a chilly winter evening.

4

UNDER THE SPOTLIGHT

"Three young people were found dead today evening near Riverside, California, their identities are still being searched." said the reporter through the radio.

"Wait, what?!" screamed out Ms. Franklin to herself.

"I must hurry before it's too late, what if one of the three is Stella, I will regret all my life for her death." thought Ms. Franklin as she drove faster

Minsie had already reached at Stacy's house and was waiting outside over on the parking lot for Ms. Franklin.

Ms. Franklin mistakenly was on the 4th alley of the Hensler Avenue, and was moving back to the 3rd alley.

"Hello, over here." called out Minsie loudly from a distance as Ms. Franklin came near sight.

Ms. Franklin parked beside Minsie's car and waved to Minsie.

"Hello." greeted Ms. Franklin as she got out of the car.

"Ok, so we go inside now?" asked Minsie.

"Yes, let's go in." replied Ms. Franklin.

They two walked towards the entrance as Ms. Franklin nodded.

"By the way, have you heard the news?" asked Ms. Franklin.

"Which news?" replied Minsie.

"Three people were found dead this very evening!" told Ms. Franklin in a tensed tone.

"What!" screamed out Minsie facing towards Ms. Franklin.

"Yes, you heard me right." replied Ms. Franklin.

"That sounds terrifying, I think we should probably hurry before Stella's in any danger." mentioned Minsie.

"Yes, we definitely must." replied Ms. Franklin.

Minsie knocked Stacy's house door while Ms. Franklin stood behind waiting for the door to open.

"How may I help you?" said Stacy as she opened the door.

"Oh, it's you Minsie." said Stacy just as she noticed Minsie.

"Yes it's me, and Ms. Franklin is here too." pointed out Minsie.

"Oh, good evening, Ms. Franklin. How are you?" said Stacy as she faced Ms. Franklin.

"Good evening, I am alright." replied Ms. Franklin.

"Let's go sit inside…" insisted Stacy.

"Alright, thank you though." replied Ms. Franklin as she and Minsie walked in.

Stacy led them into the living room, while she went to the kitchen to prepare them coffee and some cookies.

"Oh god, why did you trouble yourself to arrange these?" said Ms. Franklin as Stacy served them the coffees.

"Oh come on, it's no problem." replied Stacy as she sat on the couch taking a cup of coffee.

"So may I know, what brought you here?" asked Stacy in a friendly tone.

"Ok, so Stella has been missing, so we wanted to check if she was here or not." mentioned Minsie.

"Oh she's been missing! But she is apparently not here." told Stacy.

"Oh well." replied Minsie.

"It's been four days since Stella left home and went missing." mentioned Ms. Franklin in a tensed tone.

"Oh god! that long, I think we must find her before anything bad occurs…" said Stacy.

"Yes absolutely; we're trying our best right now. By the way, we'll be heading to Jacob's to check if Stella is there." informed Minsie as she put the empty coffee-cup onto the table.

"Can I join?" asked Stacy trying to help find Stella

"Sure, but if it wouldn't trouble you." replied Ms. Franklin.

"Helping friends is a pure duty." replied back Stacy.

Ms. Franklin smiled to Stacy's words, and Minsie smiled along.

The sky darkened as the evening slowly changed into the night.

Ms. Franklin, Minsie and Stacy all headed towards Jacob's house in hurry, for it was getting too long for Stella to be gone missing.

"Hello." said Minsie as the door opened.

"Oh hello!" greeted Jacob as he faced the three.

"Really sorry; to bother you at this hour." apologized Ms. Franklin.

"It is no problem, but is everything alright?" replied Jacob.

"Umm, not really, Stella's been missing since four days now." said Minsie; emphasizing "Is she here?"

The night deepened as the sky darkened; the birds went back to their nests while the owls woke up.

"Four days!" screamed out Jacob in shock.

"Yes, four days!" said Stacy alongside.

"So, is she here or have she contacted you?" asked Ms. Franklin.

"No…" answered Jacob lowering his voice.

"Well, what can we do now?" asked Stacy.

"This was the last place to search anyways…" replied Minsie.

"Wait no, remember the police said her phone's last location was at Victoria Avenue…" pointed out Ms. Franklin.

"Oh yes!, so Eliott's house!" mentioned Minsie as she screamed.

"Well, can I come with all of you?" asked Jacob politely.

"You sure can." replied Minsie.

"But wait, we all go in my car." mentioned Ms. Franklin.

"Sure but why?" questioned Stacy.

"Because the news said there were three dead bodies found this very evening, and it's getting late at night, so I think we should stick together so we're safe." explained Ms. Franklin; gently.

"Well, then let's go!" exclaimed Minsie.

The owls stared right into the dark sky as the night deepened.

"Who is it?" said Eliott politely as he opened the door.

To his surprise it was Ms. Franklin, Minsie, Jacob and Stacy; he hadn't expected all of them together there in any manner at that hour, if not any of them at all.

"Is Stella here?" asked Minsie moving forward.

"No, sorry?" replied Eliott.

"She had been missing since four days…" mentioned Stacy.

"And her last location was here…" added Jacob.

"Would you mind to explain us?" demanded Ms. Franklin; politely, facing Eliott.

"Umm, what?!" replied Eliott in absolute shock and confusion.

The drawing room was neat and clean, a movie was being played on the T.V.

"So, we had a fight…" said Eliott.

"Fight!" responded Minsie.

"What sort of fight?" asked Stacy.

"Umm, an argument…" answered Eliott hesitantly.

"For?" asked Jacob.

Ms. Franklin sat and listened quietly while the others questioned.

"Something personal…" replied Eliott.

"Hmm, so was it serious." asked Stacy.

"Quite serious." answered Eliott as he leaned forward.

"So, do you have any idea where she had gone?" asked Minsie.

"Not really." replied Eliott.

The moon glowed like a star in the deep dark night sky.

"Well, I think she might have went to the mountains, it isn't quite far, and it is a silent environment." suggested Stacy.

"And over there it is good for camping…" added Jacob.

"Oh, wait yeah…" replied Minsie as she sought deeper.

"That is quite possible, because Stella also had a large bag on her back when she left as far as I remember." responded Ms. Franklin as they got near their car.

The four had already left from Eliott's place and were walking towards the parking lot to where their car was parked.

"We shouldn't waste a single second to go check the mountains." advised Minsie.

"But we need flashlights before we go there…" added Stacy.

"Let's hit a super-market then?" suggested Jacob.

Minsie grabbed some cold coffee while Stacy and Jacob took some flashlights and snacks; Ms. Franklin waited outside the store, in the car, looking at the maps.

"Done." said Minsie, as the three got in.

Ms. Franklin drove the car fast on the empty road under the deep dark night sky.

"I think it'll be better to split into separate teams, for it to be quick…" suggested Stacy, as they got out of the car.

"I think too." added Minsie, as she opened the trunk.

"Well alright, if that's what you all think." agreed Ms. Franklin.

Stacy & Jacob went into one team and Minsie & Ms. Franklin went into the other.

"We head two different directions." told Ms. Franklin as she handed the flashlights to everyone.

"Stella!, are you out in here?" screamed Stacy as they moved deeper into the mountain woods.

"Stella, are you here!?" screamed Minsie.

The sky turned darker and darker as the night deepened making nothing but the silence the loudest of all.

It been hours searching for Stella, Stacy and Jacob decided to sit down for a while, and drink some coffee.

"So!, what do you think of life?" asked Stacy.

"It's like the sky, it goes higher and higher but you have only tiny bit of it within sight's reach…" replied Jacob as he leaned onto a tree.

"Wow, I like your concept!" complimented Stacy.

"What about yours?" asked Jacob staring right into the deep sky.

"Stella!!" screamed out Ms. Franklin loudly.

"I think we should sit down for a bit, we've been walking for a while…" offered Minsie.

"I wouldn't love to but we have to…" replied Ms. Franklin.

"It's all dark; with some directory markings which could only be viewed if one strains their eyes." told Stacy.

"That is deep right there." responded Jacob.

"Yeah, true." said Stacy as she stared deeper into the dark sky.

"Kcshha!" a sound of footstep onto the grass-ground came from a distance.

"Who is there?" asked Stacy and Jacob as they stood up and turned their flashlights on.

"Who's it?!" demanded Minsie as Ms. Franklin and she turned their flashlights towards the figure.

As all of the four flashlights fell on the figure, it made the figure seem like it was under the spotlight.

As the four focused onto the face of the person, to their delight it was Stella!; they had finally found Stella after such a long search.

The four started from opposite directions and they had ended up colliding in the middle where their search finally ended.

"Oh Stella!" screamed out Ms. Franklin as she ran and hugged Stella tightly.

"Mom…" cried out Stella as she hugged Ms. Franklin back.

"Are you alright…?" asked Ms. Franklin in lovely tone.

"Yes I am, now better than ever…" replied Stella as she cried.

"Have you taken your meals properly, I mean did you even eat?!" questioned Ms. Franklin in a hard tone.

"Yes I have!" answered Stella along with a smile.

"Thank you to everyone of you for coming to search for me, I couldn't be any happier to see you all. It feels the stars are straight down on earth's surface…" said Stella, as tears showed on her eyes along with a smile.

"Aww, welcome…" replied Stacy.

"Don't mention, what are friends even for, huh?" replied Jacob

"My duty! mate!" replied Minsie.

Everyone present there at the moment; gave out a laugh, followed by smiles.

The stars glowed in the sky as if diamonds shining, while the night deepened.

"But I expected somebody else too…really expected that person and it breaks my heart to not see that person…" said Stella as tears fell down from her eyes.

"Expectations, never are reality, huh…" added Stella.

"Who?" asked Ms. Franklin.

5

CONFRONTATION OF STELLA AND ELIOTT

"Things don't go the way you ever plan it to…" sighed Stella.

"Yes, true." responded Jacob.

"Yeah, but would you tell us whom you expected to be here along with us?" asked Stacy in curiosity and confusion.

"Ok everyone, probably Stella is in a shock by us being here to take her home at this hour, so let's go home then we can all sit down and sort things out, alright?" advised Minsie.

"Sure, let's go to our house…" told Ms. Franklin.

"Yes please." replied Stella.

The sky turned darker to a rich tone of pitch black as the night deepened.

"Let's have dinner first, then we'll sit down and talk." told Ms. Franklin.

"And let's all get freshened up before we get to the dinner table?" suggested Stacy due to that tiring day.

"Yes please." replied Ms. Franklin.

Ms. Franklin had prepared dinner for everyone as soon as they arrived at the house, she had arranged the table with cutleries, plates and glasses on it. She placed water and some cold drinks for everyone, on the dinner table.

"How do you come to cook such delicacies!" complimented Jacob, as he finished freshening up and sat onto a chair by the table.

"And in no time…" added Stacy, as she smiled at the two.

"Yeah; such a mysterious suspense." added Minsie, as she laughed walking towards the table from a distance.

"Oh god, I can't even tell if you're joking or not." replied Ms. Franklin, as she gave out a little laugh.

"No, we're saying for real." told Stacy.

"Oh please don't…" replied Ms. Franklin, as she smiled harder.

"So why not let's start" offered Stella holding up her cutleries.

"Sure, why not!" replied Minsie taking on her cutleries.

All of them sat onto the chairs and started their dinner; Ms. Franklin had prepared the dinner so finely that there was no room left for any manner of complain.

"May I help you with the dishes?" asked Jacob politely.

"How much more gentle could you be?" pin-pointed Stacy.

"May I please?" asked Jacob again, as he smiled to Stacy.

"Alright sure, thank you though." replied Ms. Franklin as she agreed, after-all she was out all day too.

Everybody there helped Ms. Franklin clean up everything, because she had already been troubled preparing the dinner.

The night deepened as the sky turned even darker and darker.

"So would you please tell us who it was that you expected to be there with us so badly?" asked Ms. Franklin gently.

"Yes please." added Stacy.

All of the five had moved to the living room; they all sat over on to the couches; everybody facing Stella.

"If you want to take some time to answer, then it is totally fine." said Minsie trying to not pressurize Stella.

"Eliott." answered Stella as tears filled into her eyes.

"Why?" questioned Ms. Franklin calmly.

"I mean why did you even disappear?" corrected Ms. Franklin.

The room was silent for a moment, felt as if it was a courtroom.

"Uh, Eliott, I had a fight with him…" replied Stella.

"Just simply that?" asked Ms. Franklin in a harsher tone.

"Not just…" mentioned Stella, as her eyes drowned in tears while speaking.

The room was more than just emotional; silence everywhere.

"What happened dear, would you please explain?" asked Ms. Franklin in an emotional and soft tone.

"A lot has happened, everything which nobody would ever want to take place." said Stella trying to stop her tears but failing.

"Oh please Stella don't cry." said Stacy trying to calm Stella.

"Why should I not." said Stella out loud as she cried harder.

Minsie went rushing to Stella, and hugged her tight.

"I had seen dreams, which were shattered into pieces in just a matter of moments." told Stella as she cried even harder.

"Don't cry, please don't. Everything will be alright, sooner or later." said Minsie as she hugged Stella even tighter.

The room was way more sentimental than it ever possibly had been.

"I suggest leave the questions, for now." suggested Jacob.

"Yes please, you can see in what situation Stella is currently going through." added Stacy.

"Yeah, I am thinking that, too." agreed Ms. Franklin.

Ms. Franklin, Stacy and Jacob had moved to the kitchen while Minsie remained in the living room with Stella; trying to calm her down and give her company.

"Should we continue?" asked Jennifer.

"Yes please; thankfully we are running constant." replied Miss Winsent, as she entered the room, closing the door.

"Yeah, and we are halfway there…" added Jennifer.

"Yes, yes, hopefully we are whole way there in no time." said Miss Winsent, as she walked further inside.

The sun had rose with its magnificent shine brightening the atmosphere.

"I'll be off there soon." said Minsie.

"Alright." replied Stacy.

"See you there." said Minsie, as she hung up the phone call.

Minsie and Stacy were off to the Starbucks, for a simple chat with Ms. Franklin and Jacob on the current situation.

"I'll be there in just 4-5minutes." told Ms. Franklin.

"Fine, Jacob is already there and Stacy and I will be there in just some moments." replied Minsie.

"Alright, meet you there." said Ms. Franklin as she hung up.

The sun was at it's highest peak, birds in their nests; resting.

"Good morning." greeted Eliott as he started his presentation.

"Good morning." greeted back the audience.

Eliott had gone early to work, because he was due an important presentation, and he didn't want to be delayed at such situation.

"I think it should just be one of us asking or none." stated Stacy.

"Yes, I guess you're correct." agreed Minsie.

"Because see, a person feels way more frank if it's just one person listening rather than more; it's harder to feel free speaking to a larger audience." added Stacy

"I think Stacy is on point." mentioned Minsie.

"Well then, whom?" questioned Jacob.

"I also think Stacy's on point, and Minsie would be the right one, if you all agree." told Ms. Franklin.

"Yes absolutely." responded Jacob, as he agreed.

"Honestly I was going to suggest that if you didn't." said Stacy, as she agreed, smiling in a funny manner.

"Well, I go up by your opinion..." agreed Minsie with a mischievous smile, while she put her empty coffee cup down.

"Alright then, it's fixed." pointed out Ms. Franklin.

The sun started lowering from it's highest peak as the birds flew.

"Thank you." said Eliott as he put an end to his presentation.

"That was perfect." said one of the audience.

"It was informational and truly on point." said another audience.

"Yes, in simpler terms; it was worth listening." said Mr. Malcof.

Eliott was allowed to leave early as he was done with the week's last presentation, and so he had nothing else to work on.

"Hello!" greeted Minsie, as the door opened.

"Hello, good to see you." greeted back Stella.

Stella seemed quite happy to see Minsie there at that hour.

"I think let's wait here until Minsie calls back." said Stacy.

"Yes, I assume that would be right." replied Ms. Franklin.

"I do too." added Jacob.

The three were still at Starbucks, while Minsie went to see Stella.

"See a lot has happened, you weren't there either for me to share all this, so I remained all quiet." told Stella.

"Stella, I'm sorry to have not been there when you needed me, but would you specify when all this occurred and where I was." asked Minsie as Stella started to open up.

"As I mentioned a lot had had happened, it simply didn't take place in a matter of moments." elaborated Stella.

"Oh well." responded Minsie as she listened closely.

The sun was getting lower to it's midway height as the air started to turn slightly colder.

"Alright, I think it's enough for today." said Miss Winsent.

"Well then." replied Jennifer as she caressed the documents into a file, facing up towards Ms. Winsent.

"I think it will be better if we continue tomorrow." told Miss Winsent.

"Sure, then may I take a leave." said Jennifer; getting up.

"You may." replied Miss Winsent.

The two were more than halfway done from their work.

"I'm glad, at least the hunt is now over." pointed out Jacob.

"Technically the hunt towards the reason isn't." added Stacy.

"Yeah, I think you're right." replied Jacob.

Stacy and Jacob got out of Starbucks and were walking towards the parking lot; Ms. Franklin had some work so she had to leave, so the two left as well.

"Ok so, it was one early morning, I had went to the University early even though I had a class quite late that day. I was there trying to create an eye-catching poster for the charity of the poor people." started Stella as got more emotional.

"Mmhmm." responded Minsie as she listened closely.

"I was there just to help people in need." phrased Stella.

"But, Casey created this huge issue just to showcase me wrong. She literally put nausea-creating pills into people's food, and put a whole bunch of empty packets of those pills inside my bag with labels, which made it seem I put them for people to get dizzy and to do that I had went early that day which was simply false." elaborated Stella.

"All that just to create a meaningless fiasco!" screamed out Minsie as she got a bit heated up onto Casey's actions.

"I mean she definitely had a deeper intention other than just a fiasco." exaggerated Stella.

"Seems so." replied Minsie.

"I honestly didn't even notice because I was so focused into the poster. Then after a few hours I just got called out of the class and was humiliated in front of everybody." told Stella.

"Oh god…that's too bad." sympathized Minsie.

"It didn't even start onto getting worse." said Stella sarcastically.

"Woah, that sounds troubling, carry on." insisted Minsie.

"Alright so, out of all the people, I thought Eliott would trust me, I mean I trusted him so badly onto trusting me, but what really came to sight was he going with the majority." elaborated Stella, as tears filled her eyes.

"Ah, I am sorry for you." said Minsie sorrowfully.

"I had not only trusted him but loved him and I couldn't even think he'd do such a thing, I mean he went into Casey's team afterwards, like literally when I needed him so badly at such a situation. He wasn't there when I was down and not only that he literally went with Casey and Melson to the protest, the thing I and him together planned." told Stella stuttering, tears kept falling from her eyes as the room got more and more emotional.

"We had planned all of the things we were supposed to do in the protest. He did all the exact things, but with Casey. She had literally won everything putting me into the black-hole." added Stella, as she cried harder.

"A Queen stays queen even if the crown isn't with her for the time being." quoted Minsie.

Stella cried harder and harder; she couldn't stop her tears from falling like waterfalls.

"That's not only it, a lot more happened." added Stella.

"I had gone early another day. I literally saw Eliott throwing away our friendship bracelet that I gave him while Casey was wearing one that seemed like she just got." stopped Stella; drowning in tears.

Stella was crying so hard that it started to get hard for her to even speak

"Oh please don't cry, please." said Minsie, as she patted Stella.

"We'll continue later, alright…" told Minsie, as she sympathized.

The sun was down to it's midway position, birds back to their nests having their lunch.

"Trring!" rang the phone.

"Yes, whom?" answered Ms. Franklin.

"Minsie it is." said the caller.

"What happened?" questioned Ms. Franklin tensely.

"I think it's too personal and I wanted to suggest if I alone could help Stella sort this situation out?" asked Minsie.

"Yes absolutely, thanks for helping." appreciated Ms. Franklin in an emotional tone.

"She'll be alright, but she's been through a lot and it'll take time to sort things out." replied Minsie empathetically.

The situation had gotten more emotional than it was thought it would be; more serious as well, but Minsie took the lead to sort things out, after all somebody had to help Stella out of the situation she was going through.

"Sad to hear, can we help?" asked Stacy.

"No it's alright, one will be enough to help." said Minsie.

"Alright, take care." greeted Stacy as she hung up the phone call.

"I mean now I could say it's pretty normal for anybody to disappear, and/or distance themselves from this cruel world even if it's for a short time being." commented Jacob.

"Well yeah, I think too." replied Stacy.

"Even though we don't know what specifically occurred, we could still tell by the general explanation Minsie gave, that things weren't alright at all." added Jacob.

Jacob and Stacy were just about to get into their cars, when the phone call had arrived.

"Stella, let's go to Starbucks…" offered Minsie as she went up.

"Sure." told Stella.

Stella had calmed down from the crying during the sentimental conversation.

"Two chocolate macchiato, please." told Minsie.

"I want it bitter." added Stella.

"Alright, is that it?" asked the Starbucks staff.

"Yes." replied Minsie.

"Let's sit at the corner…" demanded Stella.

The two went to a corner table, and sat onto the high-chairs.

"So, have you confronted him?" asked Minsie softly.

"Whom, Eliott?" replied Stella.

"Yes, have you?" asked Minsie.

"Umm not really, but I did went to…" told Stella.

"I think you probably should." advised Minsie.

"Well…" replied Stella.

"The sooner the better." pointed out Minsie.

"That needs a second thought I assume." commented Stella.

"No, I am telling nothing is assured unless made clear with the person who the misunderstandings are with." explained Minsie.

Stella was confused on that point onto if she should or shouldn't confront Eliott.

"Hello." said Stella in a harsh tone.

"Hello…" replied Eliott irritated by Stella's voice tone.

Silence was present for minutes as the two stood there staring at each other's eyes; eye contact was hard and painful for both.

"I…" hesitated Stella.

"Y-y-you…?" stuttered Eliott.

"I am mesmerized by seeing how easy it was for you to move on with the lie without inspection." said Stella sarcastically.

"I moved on!?" screamed out Eliott.

"Yeah you!" replied back Stella.

"Wasn't it you the whole time who didn't even want me to bother." exclaimed Eliott.

"No, it had been you the whole time who had accepted the lie unseeing the truth." back-shouted Stella.

"Yes I am wrong, I have always been wrong in your eyes, haven't I?" demanded Eliott.

"I should be the one saying that!" replied Stella.

"Yeah absolutely!" responded Eliott sarcastically.

Eliott slammed the door close as tears started to fill his eyes, while Stella ran towards her car crying hard. Both of them were equally emotional; Eliott was rather more sensitive.

It was hard on both of them, all the things that had took place in the short period of time; had broken both of them down very badly.

6

Misunderstandings Blemished

"Hi." greeted Minsie, as the door opened.

"Hello!" greeted back Stella.

"I am really excited!" mentioned Minsie.

"Yeah today's sleepover would be lit!" responded Stella happily.

"Woohoo!" exclaimed Minsie in excitement.

Days had passed in misery and sorrow since Stella confronted Eliott, things were quite back to normal except their hearts.

"Mom is out today for an important business trip so it's just two of us!" told Stella.

"Cool." replied Minsie as she wore the house-slippers.

"Oh yeah! and-" added Stella.

"And whom?" asked Minsie.

"And the movies!" told Stella along with a mischievous smile.

"Uh you…" sighed Minsie as the two walked inside.

The evening was calm and peaceful, winds blowing softly.

"Yes, please." said Jennifer.

"Ok so we're all set!" told Stacy.

"Alright, see you." said Jennifer, as she hung up the phone call.

"Ok, we'll watch movies later at night, alright?" confirmed Stella, as she sat onto the couch.

"Yeah sure." agreed Minsie as she returned after freshening up.

Minsie turned the T.V on, as she sat onto the couch cozily while Stella took out some novels to read.

"The identity of the new dead body found was just revealed by police today." told the reporter.

"It's getting quite risky in town, now that there's been four dead bodies found." pointed out Stella.

"Yeah…" replied Minsie.

"The name of the respected person was told to be Eliott." said the reporter.

Stella turned towards the T.V; shocked, as the book in her hand fell off.

"Eliott!" exclaimed Stella in shock.

"What on earth am I hearing!" exclaimed Minsie.

Stella rushed towards the door as she put on her trench-coat; tightened it, grabbed the keys, and slammed the door shut.

"Oh goodness, what's happening…" thought Minsie in worry.

"Eliott Hencshmet, precisely." mentioned the news reporter.

"Thank god, it's at least not Eliott Walfador." sighed Minsie out loud in relief.

Stella drove the car faster than ever; she wouldn't be able to stop the guiltiness if something had happened to Eliott in any manner, taking all those to mind; she drove faster and faster.

"Hello." greeted Mr. Wilfindor.

"Oh, hello, good to see you." replied the boy.

"How may I help?" asked Mr. Wilfindor.

"I mean, I was told that you wanted to meet me…" added Mr. Wilfindor.

"Yes I did, so I had some really serious things to mention…" told the person.

The evening deepened as the sky turned darker, while the birds returned to their nests.

"I think this is legit!" exclaimed Stacy.

"Yes I assume." replied Jennifer.

The two were out onto some important works on their own.

"Thduk Thduk!" a sound came as the door banged.

Stella banged Eliott's house door harder than ever; but no one was there to answer.

"So what is it specifically that I may be of help on." asked Mr. Wilfindor as he became a bit confused.

"Casey…it had been Casey who had been doing all this, not Stella at any all." told the person hesitantly.

"What!!" screamed Mr. Wilfindor in shock.

"Yes you heard me right, I had wanted to mention earlier but some things didn't let me." said the person lowering their voice.

Hours had passed, the door hadn't yet been answered; Stella got more and more worried and thus she didn't leave.

"Oh goodness, who is it!" asked Eliott as he walked nearer to the door in horror.

Stella had been drowning in tears leaning to the wall.

"Are you ok, Miss?..." asked Eliott.

"Oh you are here!" exclaimed Stella.

"Where else was I supposed to be...?" questioned Eliott softly.

"No, never mind." replied really soft and emptily.

"No, it's ok tell, please..." insisted Eliott as he patted Stella on her left shoulder as he sat down beside her.

"Umm, I heard a news that said a dead body was found and the person was Eliott and..." Stella was explaining as tears filled her eyes as she stared at him.

"And?" asked Eliott in a soft, confused and emotional tone.

"I was just really shocked and would have regretted all my life if anything had happened to you..." added Stella in a soft tone.

Tears filled Eliott's eyes as he got to know how much Stella really cared for him.

"I am sorry." said Eliott softly with tears falling off his eyes.

"Huh?" asked Stella in a soft and confused tone.

"I am sorry; for everything I have done." elaborated Eliott.

"No I'm sorry too for being so harsh on you." said Stella, as she turned her head; staring up to the open sky.

"I just couldn't see how much of a diamond you are... your pure heart..." added Eliott as tears kept falling off his eyes.

"I am sorry too, I should have had sort things out with you instead of creating a fiasco." replied Stella.

Both their eyes were filled with tears as they got more and more sentimental while the two opened up emotionally.

"I just can't tell how much I have had fell for you." told Eliott.

"I can't either." added Stella.

"Without you, it's the same as the night sky without the moon or the stars…" said Eliott as she stared at the sky with tears.

"It's like a flower without it's buds…" added Stella.

"I someway thought you were into Casey…" mentioned Stella.

"How did you think I would let the ladder set up by us to be used by someone else…" quoted Eliott.

"I don't know, I was just all so frustrated at that moment and all confused. I was so breaking down." said Stella as her voice cracked with a soft cry.

"Oh Stella… I can't figure out what made you feel that way… in any manner." sighed Eliott.

"I think; I was too scared to lose you…" told Stella crying.

"Oh Stella… that's not possible…" replied Eliott.

"How can you be so certain?" asked Stella in a soft tone.

"The much I am in love with you; the love has bound me to never let go of you. I just can't explain how much I am attached to you, what just your presence means to me…" said Eliott as tears filled his eyes red.

The evening had turned into a deep night as the sky darkened.

"Oh, god, this is tensing me a lot…" said Minsie to herself.

"It's been quite a lot of time since Stella left, god is she in trouble or something?" thought Minsie worrying.

Minsie had been worrying ever since Stella left, but then she was even more worried; seeing how long it was since Stella had left.

"Ok, so I have put the details up." said Stacy.

"Alright, I'll check." replied Jennifer.

"Ok so be on time huh." told Stacy.

"Sure, will be." replied Jennifer.

"Yes, and be sure to keep the details on mind." added Stacy

"Yeah, yeah I sure will." assured Jennifer.

The night deepened as the sky darkened while the moon and stars glowed like diamonds in the night sky.

"I am in the same position, I have loved you ever since, and I can't resist. I can't even tell how much precious you and just your existence is to me…" told Stella with tears in her eyes.

"Things had all changed ever since…" sighed Eliott.

"Everything had happened in just a matter of moments but the effect it had put feels to have been forever." sighed Stella.

"Sadly just slight misunderstandings created all this fiasco and disaster…" pointed out Eliott sentimentally.

"Yeah just slight things brought huge issues…" agreed Stella.

The conversation of the two had turned deeply emotional.

"Good morning to everyone present here." said Mr. Wilfindor.

"There is an announcement." told Mr. Wilfindor.

The place silenced; as all heard about having an announcement.

"It had been Casey since the first who had been creating all this issue." mentioned Mr. Wilfindor.

The people present there were shocked to hear all that suddenly.

"Sadly, Stella had been blamed, and even humiliated by some, which I would like to apologize for." told Mr. Wilfindor.

Stella had then been honored with her respect back, she was happy to get proved innocent and free of any blames.

Finally, the right was being seen rather than the very wrong; clearly in everyone's eyes.

"Forgive me for what I've done and I give my word that I would do none of that ever again…" said Eliott deeply as he walked nearer to Stella.

"You too, please forgive me as well." said Stella lightly.

"Can we be the forever, if it's ever possible?" asked Eliott turning his head towards Stella as his eyes turned red and filled with tears as he got more emotional.

"I suppose we can…" replied Stacy staring right into his eyes.

"But from now on, we sort things out with ourselves if there are any misunderstandings, we don't sink it inside ourselves and die from the inside…" told Eliott as he smiled softly, eyes still filled with tears, and as deep emotions became clearly visible.

The two were then even more sentimental as they got more emotionally attached to each other.

"Yes absolutely." cried Stella with a light smile.

7

Finally Stelliot

"Minsie I've got to tell you a lot; everything, I mean." said Stella in excitement; as her happy mood reflected.

"Yeah I know!! And I would murder you if you didn't want to tell me!" replied Minsie; excited to hear.

Till the bright sky had appeared Stella and Eliott had stayed up out; staring at the stars; chatting with each other. and it wasn't until the morning that Stella met Minsie and were able to talk.

"Ok so we're officially together now!" told Stella.

"Yayy, finally Stelliot!" replied Minsie out loud.

"Oh god yeah actually…" said Stella shyly as she laughed.

"It took a while though." pointed out Minsie broadening her eyes.

"I mean we went through storms to reach our destination" told Stella with a mischievous smile.

"At least the flower bloomed after the storms." said Minsie

"I mean, I can't be more happy, yeeh!" mentioned Stella happily.

"Yeah obviously!" pointed out Minsie.

"I mean…" said Stella, as she smiled.

"I just hope the storms don't ever return!" told Minsie.

"Aww, thank you! And yeah me too!" replied Stella.

The two were sitting chillingly at the canteen of their University.

"I think it'll be a good idea to not get too personal over here…" told Minsie as she looked around.

"Yes I think too…" agreed Stella.

"But by the way, how did Mr. Wilfindor get to know all this?" pointed out Minsie; suspiciously.

"What do you mean?" asked Stella; confused.

"Like it was Casey and not you…" explained Minsie.

"Right. I didn't even think of that." told Stella suspiciously.

"I mean it's pretty suspicious…" mentioned Minsie.

"Yeah, exactly. Like I don't think anybody knew that Casey had been doing all this or if someone did; who is it?" Stella raised a question, getting suspicious.

"Actually that's worth looking upon." told Minsie.

"Drring!" rang the bell.

"Oh god, I have to go to the class, let's discuss about it later on, when the classes are over…" told Minsie.

"Yeah sure, I got to go too, see you." replied Stella as they got up from their chair taking their bags.

"Yeah see you!" said Minsie as the two changed directions.

The classes started normally as all students were present in their own subject classrooms.

Minsie couldn't focus onto the lesson properly, as all going in her head was; who and how someone got to know all about that.

"Was he or she stalking Stella? Or Was he or she just accidentally present there at the moment where Casey brew the trouble spells?" all those questions unraveled in Minsie's mind.

"Minsie!" called the professor.

Minsie didn't respond as she was on her own world of thoughts.

"Minsie!! Are you present here with us or not?!" demanded the professor as he got heated up.

"Ye-y-yes sir?" replied Minsie as she got shocked by the scream.

"You better pay attention." ordered the professor as he turned.

"Sorry sir…" said Minsie confusingly.

"Why am I thinking all that now, I actually should better pay attention onto my studies…" thought Minsie in her head.

Stella was also a bit distracted but not much; she was a pretty participative student by nature.

"Ok so I think that is it for today, we'll do further discussions next class. Class dismissed." told the professor.

"Thank god…" thought Minsie to herself.

Both Minsie and Stella didn't have class for the following period so they moved into the canteen; recess-time zone.

"Ugh Stella…" said Minsie as she walked nearer to Stella.

"Huh?" responded Stella as she sat onto a chair.

"I am literally so distracted…" told Minsie.

"I'm more of insecure right now than distracted…" told Stella.

"I am rather distracted by all that…" told Minsie.

"Like for the whole class time, I couldn't at all concentrate onto the lesson; thinking all those stuff…" added Minsie.

"I can understand it's all messing up with our minds." said Stella as she put her bag off her shoulder.

"Yeah exactly…" agreed Minsie as she sat down properly.

"Do you think somebody was stalking?" asked Minsie.

"Not stalking, but more of spying…" said Stella.

"Stella?" a voice called out.

"Yes?" said Stella as she turned her head.

"Umm, are you free; to talk?" asked Eliott.

"Umm yeah…" said Stella hesitantly, looking at Minsie asking if she was ok, by eying her.

Minsie nodded as she agreed and let Stella know it's fine.

Stella got up and took her bag as she started walking with Eliott.

"So how's your day been?" asked Eliott cutely.

"It just started…" replied Stella laughing.

"I mean still it's been hours since we communicated…so just checking up if you're okay." added Eliott.

"Aww, how cute!" mentioned Stella smiling.

"Thank you…" said Eliott blushing.

"By the way, you're making me feel how much of uncaring I am…" said Stella making a cute-angry face.

"You're just making me more obsessed with you…" told Eliott.

"So, do you like roses or jasmines?" asked Stella.

"Roses, why though? Are you going to gift them to me or something?" asked Eliott blushing with a mischievous smile.

"If you want I may, though why roses?" replied Stella.

"Umm… because roses are the perfect example of that nothing good comes without hardship…" told Eliott.

Just only their words could tell how sacred their love was; unbreakable bond and ultimate care; deep and pure…

"Honestly, that is really an amazing thinking…" said Stella.

"So, why do you like jasmines?" asked Eliott.

"I mean you already guessed I like jasmines…lol, it's because it shows how a simple thing can be more attracting than any gorgeous could… sometimes it's the smell of beauty not the look." explained Stella.

The sky was brightened by the sun as the clouds added contrast.

"Stacy, are you free right now?" asked Jacob.

"Yeah, is everything alright?" asked Stacy worried.

"Yes, yes. Just wanted to chat…" told Jacob shyly.

"Sure, am here…" replied Stacy.

Birds were flying round and about, in the empty sky; chirping.

"Hi" said Minsie.

"Hello, how are you?" asked Lesohn.

"Haven't seen you in a long time…" told Minsie.

"Yeah it's been a while. Life is like that, you see somebody for days and somebody not at all..." said Lesohn.

"Yeah I agree too, it's all about destiny...every meet has a meaning and a purpose..." said Minsie.

The wind blew, giving life to the nature and the atmosphere.

"What's your type of music?" asked Jacob.

"Classic, sad yet dark..." replied Stacy loving the question.

"Musical Instrument?" asked Jacob facing the sky.

"I like ukulele but piano has more life in it..." explained Stacy.

"Agreed, I also think pianos are the best; their tunes are mesmerizing and it flows well." told Jacob as he agreed.

"What about you; what sort of music do you like?" asked Stacy.

"Something that flows well, goes high in the middle then back down; classic yet bold; peaceful yet full of life..." told Jacob.

"Imagine we're laying on the grass, and there is a piano piece playing in the background..." said Stacy closing her eyes.

"A night sky; dark yet full of bright stars; the moon glowing beautifully at the corner..." added Jacob deeply imagining.

Just imagining such a peaceful scene felt mesmerizing...

"I have a great plan, will you be free tonight?" asked Eliott.

"Yeah sure will..." replied Stella smiling, as she blushed.

"So I'll pick you up after evening, alright?" told Eliott

"Yeah alright..." agreed Stella.

Birds flew freely in the bright sky, while owls slept peacefully.

"Drring" rang the bell.

"Ok, I'll have to go now." said Stella getting up.

"Alright, see you later..." replied Eliott.

All the students were rushing to their subject classrooms just as the bell rang; forming a crowded and noisy environment.

"Minsie?" called the professor; as he took attendance.

"She isn't here..." told a student.

"I think she isn't coming because she usually isn't late to class..." assumed the professor looking around the classroom.

"Yes, I think so too..." told another student.

The teacher stopped the simple matter there and continued with the lesson for the day.

"So sir, the presentations will be held next week?" asked Stacy.

"Yeah, you're right, it's due for next week" told the professor.

The class behaved a bit shocked and confused hearing that.

"Minsie, don't you have any class right now..." asked Lesohn.

"I do but I don't want to join..." told Minsie.

"Umm, are you sure?" asked Lesohn to confirm.

"Yes, anyways I won't be able to concentrate..." told Minsie.

"And I am feeling good; talking..." added Minsie.

"Oh, good to hear that..." replied Lesohn along with a smile.

"So do you like night sky with moon and stars or a morning sky with birds and butterflies…?" asked Minsie.

"That's a hard choice right there, but I may say night sky with stars as it has a deeper beauty and is peaceful & soothing to look at, yet dark." explained Lesohn.

The time passed by; as the two kept talking about deep stuffs…

"Shh-shrhh" a sound came as a car stopped by.

"Would you please enter, Mademoiselle." insisted Eliott.

"Thank you…" said Stella; as she got in.

"By the way, where are we going?" asked Stella just as she got in.

"You would see, and I'll have to put up a blindfold on you." replied Eliott politely facing Stella.

"Umm, I am honestly nervous and confused." told Stella.

"So, may I?" asked Eliott, in a very gentle manner.

"Yes, you may." said Stella, as her excitement and curiosity rose.

Eliott then put a blindfold on Stella; she was dying in curiosity.

"Stacy, have you prepared everything?" asked Jennifer.

"Yes I have!" said Stacy in an enthusiastic tone.

"So, that's great, thank you." appreciated Jennifer.

"What are friends for…" replied Stacy giving out a little laugh.

"Yeah, yeah, alright bye." said Jennifer as she laughed along.

"Yeah bye." said Stacy as she hung up the phone call.

The two were planning something exciting; in the deep secrecy.

"Seriously?" asked Minsie in a shocked tone.

"Yeah, seriously." replied Lesohn.

"Drrr." a vibration interrupted their conversation.

"Oh I think somebody's calling, I have to hung up." said Minsie.

"Oh, alright. Talk to you later." said Lesohn, as the call hung up.

"Hello?" said Minsie.

"Hello, Minsie." replied the caller.

"I'm sorry, who's it?" asked Minsie.

"It's me; Ms. Franklin." said the caller.

"Oh, How are you?" said Minsie as she got to know the caller.

The night deepened, as the sky darkened, while the birds rested.

"Umm, have we reached?" asked Stella.

"Close but not yet." replied Eliott.

"I can't hold back my excitement." said Stella in a dramatic tone.

"Yes I can guess, I am thrilled too." replied Eliott.

"Thrilled? Why?" asked Stella in confusion.

"Umm, thinking you would like the surprise or not." said Eliott.

Stella gave out a little laugh knowing what Eliott was thrilled for.

"Oh alright, great!" said Ms. Franklin.

"Thanks, hope you find it mesmerizing too." replied Minsie.

"Don't worry, I can predict, I will." said Ms. Franklin laughing.

They gave out a few little laughs as the night kept deepening.

"I can wait no more…" said Stella dying in curiosity.

"I hope you like it." said Eliott, as he pulled over.

Eliott got off, and went on to hold the door open for Stella.

"Here, take my hand." told Eliott putting his hand forward.

"Should I take the blindfolds off?" asked Stella taking his hand.

"No, no." said Eliott.

"Alright." replied Stella; agreeing quickly.

Stella got off the car, as if a princess getting off her carriage holding onto the prince's hand under the night sky, just as in the older times.

The two walked further as Eliott guided the path for Stella.

He took off her blindfolds, as the moonlight beamed onto Stella's eyes just as she started opening her eyes.

"Wow!" screamed out Stella sweetly; as she fully opened her eyes.

"This is mesmerizing, I am more than just shook." added Stella.

Owls were awake while the birds slept in the deep dark night.

"Oh, that's very stunning to hear." complimented Ms. Franklin.

"I guess so…" said Minsie as she laughed.

"You probably could, anyways I think it's getting late; you should go get some sleep…" said Ms. Franklin.

"Yeah, bye talk to you later." replied Minsie; looking at the time.

"Yeah, alright bye…" said Ms. Franklin, as she hung up the call.

The two would have had talked longer if it wasn't late.

"Do you like it?" asked Eliott nervously in a cute soft tone.

"No… I absolutely love it." said Stella.

"Nothing could be more peaceful than laying down on a grass-field looking at the stars…" elaborated Stella.

"Though something can…" said Eliott deeply.

The night sky was deep dark, as the moons and stars glowed.

"Hello." said Lesohn blankly.

"Hello, How are you?" said the caller.

"Fine, is everything alright?" asked Lesohn.

"No, just wanted to ask if we could meet up tomorrow?" asked the caller, looking forward for an answer.

"Yeah, sure." replied Lesohn in a sweet tone.

"Thank you!" said the caller in a happy tone.

"Alright bye, see ya." said Lesohn.

"Yeah bye, see you tomorrow." replied the caller hanging up.

Lesohn put the phone down, and went to bed reading his book.

"What?" asked Stella looking up at the deep dark sky.

"Your presence…" told Eliott looking at the bright stars.

"Aww." replied Stella smiling hard.

The night deepened as the two smiled at each other lovingly.

8

Darkness Unraveled

"Hello." greeted Lesohn as he entered, and sat on a chair.

"Hello!" greeted Stacy.

"Nice to meet you!" added Stacy.

"Here is your order Miss." said the Starbucks staff placing a tray.

"Thank you." said Stacy.

"I've ordered you a Mocha." said Stacy handing the coffee cup.

"Thanks, Stacy." replied Lesohn taking the coffee cup.

"So, anything specific we are here for?" asked Lesohn.

"Yeah, yeah." said Stacy as she opened her bag to search.

"What is it?" asked Lesohn.

The sun was shining brightly on the open sky, as the clouds scattered around.

"Alright, see you later." said Stella.

"Yeah, bye sweetie." replied Eliott, closing his car window.

The two had laid over the grass-field all-night watching the stars.

"Honey, where have you been?" asked Ms. Franklin.

"Umm, I was out on the grass-fields watching the stars." said Stella hesitantly in shyness.

"I was so tensed, you know." told Ms. Franklin, as she put the teabags into the warm milk cup.

"I am sorry. By the way, Eliott was with me too." replied Stella.

The birds were seen flying and chirping all around the open sky.

"So..., we had this assignment..." said Stacy broadening out a document on the table.

"We two are teamed together..." added Stacy.

"Oh alright..." said Lesohn hesitantly smiling, as he looked on the opened document over the table.

"I thought you would know..." said Stacy.

"No, I didn't..." replied Lesohn.

"It's fine, now you do..." said Stacy smiling.

Stacy and Lesohn put their coffee cups farther away, so that it doesn't get spilled over the document.

"Oh really. You two are back together?" asked Ms. Franklin.

"Yes, mom..." said Stella in a shy smile.

"I am happy to hear that." told Ms. Franklin smiling sweetly.

"Thank you..." replied Stella.

"So, when did you plan to go watch the stars at night?" asked Ms. Franklin as she took out some panna cottas from the fridge.

"It was a surprise..." told Stella pouring water into a glass.

"Oh really. He seems to be a sweet guy...his choice of a surprise is really cute..." commented Ms. Franklin placing the dessert onto the table.

"Mr. Monzelle, I think the event should take place on Wednesday." suggested Minsie analyzing her schedule.

"Alright sure, I will contact them right away." replied Mr. Monzelle, as he dialed the number to call.

The call was received right away and he told everything in detail.

"Oh..., alright." said Mr. Monzelle over the call, as he hung up.

"What did they say?" questioned Minsie in a tensed tone.

"Umm, sorry Minsie, but they said for the event to take place on Thursday..." replied Mr. Monzelle hesitantly.

"Oh, alright." said Minsie not getting disturbed but a bit tensed.

"Yeah, I hope you have no problem and do attend on Thursday timely." told Mr. Monzelle softly.

"Sure." replied Minsie lowering her tone.

Minsie knew her schedule would be totally messed up due to that change of plan.

"Yes he is..." replied Stella smiling.

"Alright honey, I have prepared breakfast, sit down and have it..." told Ms. Franklin, gesturing her hands over the dishes.

"Alright, thanks." greeted Stella as she sat on the bar-stool.

Ms. Franklin closed the door by, and left for work by the car.

"Hello?" said Minsie receiving the phone call.

"Hello." greeted Stella over the phone call.

"How are you Stella?" asked Minsie looking at her documents.

"I am fine, what about you?" replied Stella.

"I am fine too…" said Minsie reading a document in her mind.

"So, I was thinking of meeting up…" told Stella as she ate.

"Oh, sure. I'll try to leave early." told Minsie looking the phone.

"Alright then, meet you." said Stella pointing as a bye for then.

"Yeah alright, see you." told Minsie, as she hung up the call.

Stella continued having her breakfast, while Minsie relied onto a cup of coffee as she went through her documents.

"Ah, finally." said Miss Winsent in her fine accent.

"Yeah, finally we are done…" added Jennifer.

"Now, all we have to see is how this works out…" pointed out Miss Winsent as she went through the plan thoroughly.

"Yes absolutely…" said Jennifer alongside.

The two were finally over planning some stuff to solve a mystery they had been swirling into, for a while.

"I am heading to Starbucks, alright?" informed Minsie.

"Yeah alright, I'm on my way too." told Stella.

"Alright, I think that's pretty well planned…" said Stacy.

"Ahead of time." mentioned Lesohn, as he took a sip of coffee.

"Yeah, but let's go through it for one last time…" told Stacy.

"Yeah sure…" replied Lesohn putting his coffee down.

Stacy and Lesohn were almost done planning their assignment. Minsie and Stella were heading to Starbucks for some chit-chat.

"So may I leave?" asked Jennifer lifting her bag.

"Yes, you may take a leave." replied Miss Winsent.

"Alright, bye." said Jennifer.

"Bye." replied Miss Winsent softly.

Miss Winsent went back to some other work as Jennifer left closing the door by.

"Alright, I think that's all for today…" said Stacy facing up.

"Yeah, that's pretty much it." replied Lesohn looking at Stacy.

"Then, I think we should leave…" said Lesohn gesturing Stacy.

"Yeah, yeah; let's leave." replied Stacy getting up from her chair.

"Alright, then." said Lesohn getting up with his coffee in hand.

"Oh, hello Stella." greeted Minsie as she entered.

"Hello." replied Stella in a sweet and joyful tone.

"Sorry, if I may have been late…" apologized Minsie.

"No, no. I just came." replied Stella facing sideway to Minsie.

"And by the way I ordered you a Frappuccino." told Stella.

Stella handed Minsie the coffee and the two started to walk in.

Stacy and Lesohn were walking out together chit-chatting.

Lesohn was facing Stacy as he walked. Right then, he crashed into somebody splashing his coffee.

"Oh, oh; sorry." apologized Minsie looking down to the spilled coffee on the shoes and the floor.

"Y-y-y-you?" said Minsie as she looked up to the person's face.

"Minsie?" said Lesohn; noticing her as he faced her.

"Stacy?" asked Stella as she noticed Stacy beside Lesohn.

"Stella." replied Stacy as she faced Stella hearing her name.

Minsie kept staring right into Lesohn's eyes; deeper than deep.

"Sorry, I think I should clean up." said Lesohn pointing out.

Minsie kept silent as she used a tissue to clean the spilled coffee off the floor. She didn't utter a single word while Stacy and Stella talked on…

"Alright, see you." said Stacy, as she left by the exit.

"I should go too, bye…" said Lesohn waving quickly as he left.

Stella held Minsie's hand pulling her to near a table to sit.

"Minsie?!" called out Stella in confusion, as she sat properly.

"Y-y-yeah?" replied Minsie as she got out of her thoughts.

"Where are you?" asked Stella broadening her eyes.

"Uh, here…" replied Minsie, half there and half not.

"So, remember yesterday we were talking on who told the truth about Casey and how they knew…?" said Stella to remind her.

"Yeah, yeah…" replied Minsie as she tried to recall.

"Actually, who could it be?" wondered Minsie out loud leaving aside her thoughts that unraveled in her mind.

"I have no idea." told Stella stretching her legs out.

The sun was down to the mid-way, changing the day to a noon.

“I think that’s enough…” said Ms. Franklin in a hard tone.

“Uh, as you say…” replied the person in front.

“But take in mind this might cause issues later on.” told the person gesturing using their face.

“It’s fine I can handle them…” replied Ms. Franklin softly.

The noon had begun normally, as the birds went for their lunch.

“We have to check on anybody concentrating either on you or Casey.” explained Minsie as she sought deeper into the situation.

“Yeah I guess…” replied Stella sighing.

“And we must see if somebody is acting weird.” added Stella.

“More of being nervous…” pointed out Minsie

“Yes, yes…” replied Stella; as she thought of it quickly.

Minsie and Stella were fully focused onto the topic; they kept the conversation going on as time passed by.

Days were passing as Stella and Minsie kept their eyes onto anybody suspicious; they were fully determined to find the person who had told Mr. Wilfindor about the incident. The two were worrying about if somebody was spying them or not, which indeed would mean a larger trouble than Casey’s petty issues; she usually caused.

“Minsie? May I have you in my cabin, please?” told Mr. Wilfindor gesturing with his head.

“Yes sure, any problem…?” replied Minsie; facing backward.

Mr. Wilfindor had called Minsie from behind as she and Stella were walking out chatting to leave; as their classes had ended.

"Is this an alert of some sort of trouble?" questioned Minsie in her head to herself as she faced back to see Mr. Wilfindor.

"Should I wait?" asked Stella generously, facing Minsie.

"Umm..." said Minsie as she was about to answer.

"You may leave." told Mr. Wilfindor facing Stella.

"Wait, why would he ask me to leave in that manner? Is this a sign before a storm?" asked Stella to herself in her head.

"Alright sure..." replied Stella nodding to Mr. Wilfindor.

"Take care, see you..." said Stella as she turned towards Minsie.

"This seems worse by being alone right now..." thought Minsie.

"We're going to be halfway done!" exclaimed Lesohn gesturing.

"Yes we will be by today..." replied Stacy as she looked up.

"Hopefully..." added Lesohn as he broadened his eyes.

"Isn't he so sweet?" asked Stacy in her head as she smiled.

"Stacy, aren't you going?" asked a student from her class.

"No, I will probably be late today..." told Stacy facing her.

"Oh alright, see you later then." said the girl as she walked away.

"Yeah, see you." replied Stacy facing in the opposite direction.

Stacy and Lesohn were sitting outside under the open sky.

The weather seemed to be chilly yet bright that morning.

"Alright, thank you." said Minsie as she closed the glass-door.

All of a sudden it started to rain, as students exiting, ran back in.

"Oh my god!" exclaimed Minsie as she ran inside putting her bag on top of her head so that her head doesn't get wet.

"Why now!" exclaimed Minsie out loud to herself.

It was Thursday and Minsie had an event on her workplace which ought to be really important and she had to attend it; there were no other choice then to attend.

Minsie thought that the rain might stop in no time; as it seemed to not be that heavily raining, thus she was less worried.

"Omg, we have to take all these in before these get wet." told Stacy, as she tried to grab everything as quickly as she could.

"Yes, or all of our time into this would be wasted." said Lesohn.

The two tried their hardest to grab everything off the table as it rained on them. They ran in as soon as they were done taking the belongings into their hands and arms.

The rain became heavier and heavier as it sounded harder.

Minsie was standing by the glass wall near the exit, waiting for the rain to stop; so that she could go attend the event.

"Ugh…" sighed Minsie in irritancy.

Minsie had nothing to do other than to wait. She was looking around the exit hall as everybody waited for the rain to stop; two people just came running inside by the door.

"Lesohn! and…" said Minsie as she looked closely.

"Stacy!" exclaimed Minsie as she looked more closely.

The thunder struck with the loudest of the noises.

"What are they two doing together again!" thought Minsie.

It had begun storming heavily as thunder struck with it's enormous sound which created an intense environment.

Lesohn was helping Stacy dry herself from the rainwater that dropped onto her, while running inside.

"You alright?" asked Lesohn offering a couple more tissues.

"Yeah, yeah. Are you?" replied Stacy placing the stuff onto the table from her hand.

"Yes I am…" nodded Lesohn putting down his overcoat onto the leaning part of a chair; to dry out.

"I don't think this storm is ending anytime soon." told Stacy.

Minsie stood there staring silent; she was confused and shocked.

"Yeah, me neither…" replied Lesohn looking around.

"Minsie?!" exclaimed Lesohn noticing her from a distance.

He walked towards her seeing that she had been wet by the rain.

"Where are you going?" asked Stacy as she got confused.

"Oh, Minsie?!" said Stacy noticing her from far distance.

"Hey, you alright?" asked Lesohn as he neared Minsie.

"You seem to be all wet in rainwater…" said Lesohn looking.

Minsie didn't utter a single word and walked out of there as tears filled her eyes, she went out despite the storm. It was raining heavily but she couldn't feel anything, to her it was all silent as she was in deep shock, while tears fell off her eyes, as she walked slowly not bothering the heavy rainfall.

"What happened?" asked Stacy as she came near to Lesohn.

"I really have no idea. She just left, without uttering a single word…" told Lesohn as he looked out the glass door.

For Minsie, everything stopped; all the noise and the rainfall, it went all silent as she walked empty.

"Trring!" rang Minsie's phone soft and subtly.

"Yes?" said Minsie answering the call without noticing the name.

As the phone had rang, the ringing sound broke her shock and brought her back to the world.

"Minsie, where are you?!" questioned Mr. Malcof.

"Sorry, I won't be able to attend…" told Minsie in an empty tone.

"Why though?" demanded Mr. Malcof.

"I can't explain right now, I will explain later." told Minsie.

"Alright, perhaps take care, you sound empty." told Mr. Malcof.

"Yeah I will." told Minsie, as she hung up the phone call.

She was standing in-front of an empty bench, she sat onto it falling, as she leaned backwards. She had no idea of anything at all.

"What's wrong with me?" asked Minsie to herself in her head.

The storm was even heavier and louder than ever. The lightning struck as the sound of thunder occupied everyone's ears.

9

As the Storm darkened

"Minsie!, are you alright?" asked Stella running to Minsie.

"Why are you sitting here without any shield?!" demanded Stella.

Minsie had been drowning in rainwater, she had been sitting in the bench for hours and was fully wet.

"What happened?!" asked Stella, as she sat beside Minsie.

"I don't even know myself." replied Minsie looking downwards.

"Have you gone insane?" screamed Stella softly, as she pulled Minsie up to stand.

Stella then dragged Minsie to her car. She handed Minsie a towel that was in the trunk of the car, back from when they had gone to the beach earlier. She helped Minsie dry the hair, and then commanded her to sit.

"I feel you aren't even in your senses…" told Stella angrily.

Stella turned the car heater on as she closed the car door sitting.

"Did anything wrong occur?" asked Stacy in confusion.

"No…" told Lesohn in a soft yet confused tone.

"As I mentioned she didn't utter a single word." added Lesohn.

"Did you have any sort of argument or something earlier?" asked Stacy as her mind was swirling up in confusion and worry.

"Would you please tell me what happened." said Stella driving.

"At least now!" added Stella as she slightly turned her head towards Minsie quickly, and back on the road..

"Stacy..." uttered Minsie in an empty tone looking downwards.

"Stacy?" asked Stella in confusion.

"Yes Stacy..." replied Minsie quickly, in a low volume.

"Stacy what?!" demanded Stella gesturing with her head.

"Stacy and Lesohn are together..." told Minsie.

It was still storming badly; outside, as it rained heavily...

"Coffee?" asked Stacy raising her hand which held a coffee cup.

"Sure..." replied Lesohn softly, as he swirled into his thoughts.

"Take it..." said Stacy handing the coffee.

"Thank you." replied Lesohn, as he leaned back.

"No arguments at all, like nothing. I am just so weirded out by such a behaviour." told Lesohn to Stacy's earlier question.

"I know Minsie well, there must be something up, or she wouldn't act in that manner in any way." told Stacy as she sat.

They both were equally confused on why Minsie acted that way.

"Wait, you like Lesohn?" asked Stella in surprise.

"I mean..." said Minsie as she hesitated to answer.

"Well, I take it as a yes... I am surprised though." told Stella.

Stella had never been interested into the tea as most other people do. She had been focused into studies, life; living it fully; she had always been into much more serious topics...

"But what made you say Stacy and Lesohn are together?" asked Stella in mere confusion.

"Umm, remember that day in the coffee shop?" asked Minsie.

"Yes…" replied Stella, thinking why she would ask that.

"What was Stacy and Lesohn doing?" pointed out Minsie.

"But what is up?" asked Lesohn in a quick pace.

"I have literally no idea." told Stacy not knowing anything at all.

The storm had no sign of stopping; the sky was deep and dark.

"Obviously not dating…" replied Stella in a loud tone.

"If they weren't, why and what were they together in the hall for?" Minsie raised a question.

"I have no idea." said Stella without even thing.

"Okay leave all that and tell, did Lesohn know?" asked Stella.

"He probably noticed but I am not sure…" replied Minsie.

Stella took that as a good point against the probability of Lesohn and Stacy dating, which she ultimately didn't want occurred.

"Hello?" said Jennifer as her call got answered.

"Yeah, hello." greeted Mr. Wilfindor as he picked up the call.

"Umm, I needed some information…" told Jennifer.

"I should probably go check with Stacy; if she likes Lesohn or not…" thought Stella to herself.

Minsie sat there in the car with her forehead leaned on the window looking outside in complete silence.

"No that might not be a good idea…" thought Stella.

"It is strange how everything changes in just a series of moments…" thought Minsie to herself in pain.

"But at least I should try asking…" rethought Stella to herself.

The storm was calmed down a bit, but the sky was just as dark.

"Alright, thank you…" said Minsie as she opened the car door.

"Should I help you to upstairs?" asked Stella facing Minsie.

"No, it's ok. I am totally fine…" replied Minsie.

"Alright then, see you later." said Stella as Minsie got off.

"Yeah, see you…" said Minsie quickly as she ran to the house.

Minsie ran as quickly as she could to her house due to the rain.

"Oh god, where is this thing!" said Stella as she hit her hands over her legs as she sat looking at the messy room.

"Mom, have you seen my file?" asked Stella softly shouting as she was upstairs, while Ms. Franklin was downstairs.

"Drring" rang the house bell.

"Stella would you please check the door?" told Ms. Franklin.

"Oh god where did this file go!!!" said Stella as she walked.

"Yes?" asked Stella as she opened the door looking up.

"Searching for this?" asked the person as he showed a file.

"You're such a creep!" said Stella snatching it from his hands.

"I came to give this; you left it at the classroom and now you were shouting so loud that I heard you were searching for a file, so…" explained Eliott shrugging at Stella.

"Oh." replied Stella, while Eliott looked at Ms. Franklin waving.

"Anyways, you want to go together?" offered Eliott as he waved back with a smile facing towards at Ms. Franklin.

"Umm, I would have, but I have to go pick up Minsie, there's been a problem going on…" explained Stella.

"Oh…" said Eliott facing towards Stella.

"Anyways, you go, I'll catch up later on." told Stella smiling.

"Alright, see you then…" replied Eliott.

"See you." replied back Stella waving, as Eliott got in the car.

Stella closed the door caressing the file as she hurried upstairs.

"Hi Stacy!" greeted Jacob as he neared to Stacy.

"Hello, how are you?" asked Stacy as the two walked.

"I am fine, haven't seen you in a while…" replied Jacob.

"Oh, just busy with some projects…" told Stacy.

The two chatted as they walked along to their classroom.

"I am coming, I'm coming!" said Minsie as she closed the door.

"Alright I'm waiting…" replied Stella, as she hung up the call.

"Here I am." said Minsie as she knocked on the car window.

Stella opened the door and Minsie sat fixing the position.

"See you in the canteen?" asked Stella as they walked outside of their classroom together with books in their hands.

"Sorry, but I have another class…" told Minsie turning to Stella.

"Right now?" asked Stella to confirm.

"Yeah, no time off in between…" told Minsie sighing.

"Alright, see you later then." said Stella as she turned around.

Minsie also turned around walking towards the direction of the next class's room as she put her books in her bag.

"Let's go hit the canteen?" offered Stacy in a jolly mood.

"Yeah sure, why not…" replied Jacob as he agreed.

Stella went to check onto Eliott into his classroom; dawdling.

"Let's sit on that table by the wall?" suggested Jacob; analyzing.

"Yeah sure." replied Stacy quickly, without hesitating.

"Problem?" asked Stacy turning to face towards Jawdnie.

"Not at all." replied Jawdnie friendlily gesturing with her hands.

"Alright, I'll just head to the canteen…" thought Stella.

Stella couldn't find Eliott at all after searching him for a while.

"My class will start right away…see you later!" said Jawdnie.

"Yeah see you." replied Stacy as Jawdnie left for class rushing.

"Do you've any classes?" asked Jacob trying to recall if he had.

"Not in a while, you?" replied Stacy recalling her schedule.

"Me neither…" replied back Jacob recalling that he had none.

"Alright I've got to tell you a bunch of stuff..." told Stacy.

"Sounds curious!" replied Jacob focusing onto the conversation.

Stella was dawdling in the past few minutes, but then she'd been walking normally, and was just near the entrance to the canteen.

"I am about to reveal some stuff..." told Stacy excitedly.

Stella was about to enter the canteen, but she backed up and hid by the wall of the canteen as she heard Stacy saying that she would reveal some stuff...

"Phew... I was about to be in there!" thought Stella in her head.

Although even if Stella jumped in onto them, the conversation would still continue as Stella is also a friend of theirs...

"It's better if I listen from a distance, cause if there's something to be told to Minsie; I won't get blamed and involved in the mess." thought Stella deeply as she looked at the consequences.

"Ok so first of all, I have been assigned to lead the project, that I have been wanting to do ever since..." told Stacy excitedly.

"Wow!" exclaimed Jacob; getting to know such a great news.

Stacy have had been talking about that project since forever, she truly showed great interest into it in every manner possible.

"But, are you alone or do you have a partner in it?" asked Jacob.

"I do have a partner..." told Stacy increasing the suspense.

"Who?" thought Stella in curiosity as the suspense increased.

"Who is that?" asked Jacob right away as he held on the coffee.

The suspense had been created to such an extent that both Stella and Jacob were dying in curiosity to know who it really was.

"Give it a guess…" replied Stacy making things more curious.

"Who can it even be?" thought Stella as her mind couldn't recall onto anybody who Stacy would be working with.

"Umm, Minsie?" guessed Jacob in an extremely uncertain tone.

"Minsie?!" thought Stella in her head in confusion and shock.

"No… she's in a different department…" told Stacy.

"Knew it!" thought Stella priding herself as she knew it early.

Jacob tried as hard as he could to guess who that really was, but was unable to recall anybody even working in that department…

"Anyways, I'll tell, since you're such a bad guesser" said Stacy.

"Yes, alright whom?" replied Jacob staring at Stacy for the reply.

"Whom???" though Stella in irritating and extreme curiosity.

Stella and Jacob were in such an intense moment that they couldn't hear anything around them nor notice.

"Lesohn!" told Stacy loud and clear, breaking the ice.

"Oh!" said Jacob as he hadn't even guessed anybody, let aside Lesohn.

"Uh oh…" thought Stella as she was relieved and surprised at the same time as she heard Stacy reveal whom.

"I knew Stacy and Lesohn weren't dating, they were just doing their assignment…" thought Stella as things cleared out.

"Nice…" added Jacob as he got to know which person.

Stella was about to turn around and leave, but right then she heard Stacy adding something to what she had said.

"He is nice of a person…" said Stacy moving into her thoughts.

"Cool…" said Jacob in hesitancy and awkwardness.

"He is indeed such a sweet person…" told Stacy as she detailed.

"What!!!" thought Stella in shock as things took a turn…

"Oh." said Jacob alongside Stacy's saying as things got awkward.

"I think…" said Stacy, as she paused for a bit hesitantly.

"You think?" asked Jacob as the conversation steered to a serious turn as Stacy's tone got serious than goofy.

"I think I am falling for him…" told Stacy hastily and happily.

"No!!!! What!" screamed Stella in her head as she was shocked.

Meanwhile, Jacob was traumatized by the news he had just heard. He didn't think things would go to such an extent. He had always been secretly…

"W-wh-why…" thought Jacob in extreme trauma.

"Why did it need to steer that way…why!" sobbed Jacob inside.

"Why did that had to happen!" questioned Jacob in his head.

"I-i-it's…," thought Jacob painfully "all over…".

"Oh god!, the thing that was supposed to not to happen has took place!" screamed Stella in her head; as she got tensed.

"Why did I even have to hear this…" sobbed Jacob in his head; struggling to keep the cry inside him.

"In which manner would I even face Minsie to say all this..." thought Stella in extreme worry as the tension rose.

"Maybe destiny had designed it this way..." thought Jacob; tears filling his eyes, as he couldn't keep his tears inside anymore.

"I was the one who asked Minsie to take all this positively, and now how would I be able to tell this extremely negative news..." thought Stella as her worry kept rising

"Me and her are never going to be us in any way." thought Jacob as pain rose over him heartlessly.

"Our friendships will be destroyed..." thought Stella deeply.

"It will never be the same in any manner..." added Stella.

"I think it's time to take a permanent leave..." thought Jacob.

He had always been secretly in love with Stacy; true and genuine love nothing fake nor pretention.

"What are you doing here?" asked a person from behind.

Stella had still been hiding by the wall and secretly listening.

The voice was up to her nerves, she had goosebumps, right away

Stella was freaked out to be found spying and secretly listening.

"Uh oh..." thought Stella inside her head in fear.

She had never been so afraid of facing someone, she was fearing to turn and face the person.

Stella collected all the courage she could, and turned around...

"Y-y-you?..." said Stella as she turned around facing the person.

10

LIFE CONTINUES DESPITE THE STORM

The sun was shining held high in the broad bright sky.

Jacob was there sitting in the very position he would never ever want to be in; learning that someone that the person loves, loving somebody else is actually extremely painful.

"Yes me…" replied the person right away as Stella turned.

"Eliott!" hesitated Stella as she threw her hair to the back.

Stella stood right there empty minded; she completely didn't know what she was supposed to say or how she would explain.

"Yes. But the question is what are you doing here; hiding by the wall?" demanded Eliott gesturing with his hands.

"I t-th-think my class is about to start so I would have to leave…" told Jacob in a cracked voice as he got up.

"Umm, I was just…" said Stella, as she hesitated.

"You were just?" asked Eliott right away; in confusion.

"Alright…" replied Stacy as she got a bit weirded out.

"I was just texting leaning by the wall." told Stella fake smiling.

Stella was lucky that she had her phone in her hand, and not only that; she was actually about to text Minsie and she have had texted Eliott earlier in the very place, so she wasn't really lying.

"Weird..., he never ever left in such a way." thought Stacy.

Jacob usually never leaves when they talk about those types of cheesy topics, so then when he did leave, it seemed strange.

"Oh...alright" replied Eliott as he fixed his hair.

"Anyways, I have to go..." said Stella as she sought the way.

"Yeah sure." replied Eliott as he gave her the path to go.

Stella rushed right after Eliott moved from the way.

"That was pretty strange..." thought Eliott entering the canteen.

"Oh goodness..." thought Stella sighing as she was out of Eliott's sight, while walking as she rushed.

"That felt intensively frightening... I couldn't think at the moment. I have had never felt that afraid..." thought Stella.

Stella had never hid and secretly listened to somebody or something like that ever before, and she had been frightened for being seen in such a state and then being taken wrongly.

"Can I meet you tonight?" asked Jennifer, while she walked, as her heels made loud sounds; tapping on the floor.

"Yes sure, see you then..." replied the person on the call.

"See you, bye." replied Jennifer, as she hung up the call.

Jennifer walked and got in her car as she sat fixing her posture.

"Class dismissed." said the professor, as students got up to leave.

"Sir?" called out Minsie as she neared the professors' table.

"Yes, Minsie?" asked the professor, right away; as he heard her.

"Do I have to stay late today as well?" asked Minsie standing.

"No, you don't have to..." replied the professor as he turned to turn off the projected smartboard and the computer.

"Alright then." said Minsie, as she walked out of the classroom.

Stella was hurrying to Minsie's classroom to tell her everything; Minsie's class was far from the canteen thus it was taking time.

Minsie wasn't feeling the mood so she just quickly walked to the parking lot and was almost quite near her car.

"Sir?" called out Stella as she stopped at the classroom door sketching with her shoes; as she had been rushing.

"Yes, how may I help?" replied the professor right away.

"Did you see Minsie?" asked Stella seeing no one in the room.

"Yeah, she just left." answered the professor as he turned.

"Where?" asked Stella thinking Minsie was still in the University.

"Towards the parking lot, I believe..." told the professor.

"Oh god!" exclaimed Stella as she turned rushing to the exit.

Stella ran as quickly as she could, and was just right near the exit to where the parking lot is, but she stopped there to check where Minsie's car was, so that she could be quick to go there.

"Bzzz-bzz-bzzzz." vibrated Minsie's phone in her pocket.

"I'll take it once I'm in the car..." thought Minsie to herself.

"OH NO!" said Stella with her reflexes; just as she saw Minsie opening her car door to get in.

"What if Stacy herself tells it to Minsie." thought Stella horrified.

Stella ran right away as she saw Minsie getting inside the car.

"Or what if Jacob tells exaggerating; by a bit…" thought Stella.

"And this is definitely not something to be said over the phone call…" thought Stella in terror as she ran as quickly as she could.

"Bzzz-bzz-bzzzz." vibrated Minsie's phone again as she took it.

"Hello." said Minsie grabbing the phone as she answered it.

To Stella's horror, Minsie was already out of the lot her car was parked as she reared it out, while Stella ran as fast as she could.

"Minsie!, Minsie!" shouted Stella calling out Minsie, to stop.

"Minsie!" shouted Stella with all the force she could gather.

Minsie was focused onto the phone, and she couldn't hear her name being called nor see Stella run; as her car was quite far.

Minsie accelerated as her car speeded up and she left the place.

Stella fell onto her knees seeing the car leave, as she took deep breaths due to running so fast with all the strength she had.

"Oh goodness!" said Stella with her reflexes, in despair.

"Would you please meet me at the evening?" asked the caller.

"Yeah sure…" replied Minsie in confusion as for why.

"Alright then…" replied the caller; about to hung up the call.

"Wait, but why though?" asked Minsie with a blank mind.

"Oh, nothing serious, but important…" told the caller.

"Oh, alright, see you…" replied Minsie, as she hung up the call.

"Drring" rang the house-bell with some knocks on the door.

"Who is it?" asked Ms. Franklin as she walked towards the door.

No one answered Ms. Franklin, but she seemed to have a visitor of hers coming that evening, so she guessed it might be them.

"Hello." smilingly greeted the person at the door as it opened.

"Oh you! Minsie." replied Ms. Franklin as she opened the door.

"Yes, me." replied Minsie smiling as she was offered to get in.

"Sit down, I'll brew you some coffee…" told Ms. Franklin.

"Isn't Stella here?" asked Minsie as she sat onto the couch.

"Drring!" kept ringing the doorbell with several knocks.

Stella stood there without getting the door answered; she had been waiting since quite a long time, as she kept tapping the bell.

"Oh goodness, please answer…" said Stella in her head.

"Here, take your coffee." said Ms. Franklin handing the coffee.

"Oh wait." said Minsie taking the coffee as she searched the bag.

"Come on, pick up the call!" said Stella calling a number as she dialed it onto her phone; quite quickly as her fingers trembled.

"Oh wait, I have to go to my car…" told Minsie as she got up.

"Why?" asked Ms. Franklin as she also got up putting the coffee cup onto the tea-table in her living room; where the two were in.

"I forgot my phone in the car…" replied Minsie taking her bag.

"Oh alright." replied Ms. Franklin; walking Minsie to the door.

"For Goodness's sake, please answer!" said Stella as she constantly kept on calling Minsie's number; with her phone.

Minsie reached her car as she unlocked the doors. She opened the front driver's seat door, and bent on to look for her phone.

Stella had tried calling Minsie's number a million times, but none of the calls were answered thus she was quite frustrated; she had stopped calling and left Minsie's place as she entered the car and drove leaving that area. Stella was still just as worried as before.

"Oh my goodness, what on earth is this?" said Minsie expressing her astonishment; to the thousands of missed calls and text messages by Stella, which was awfully high in amount.

"I'm at your place, waiting for you…" read one of the messages.

Minsie jumped into her car; on the seat, as she started the car.

"Sorry, I have some other work so I'll be heading elsewhere." wrote Minsie and sent it to Ms. Franklin immediately; due to leaving without properly telling that she was.

"Hello?" said Stacy as her call got answered.

"Hello." replied the answerer as he picked up the call.

"How are you?" asked Stacy right away as she got replied.

"I am great. What about you?" asked Lesohn taking his car keys.

"Yeah, I'm fine." replied Stacy as she poured water into a glass.

"Great then. By the way, what was it that you called me for?" asked Lesohn as he opened his door getting into his shoes.

"Oh, I was just thinking if we could continue our assignment?" asked Stacy hesitantly as she lifted the glass to drink water.

"Yes that assignment; how much were we done?" asked Lesohn.

"Not much, about twenty-five… percent done." assumed Stacy.

"Shh-shrhh" a sound produced as the car wheels sketched onto the road; as the car stopped at the red light.

"Damn " said Minsie braking the car as she noticed the red light.

"Thank goodness..." said Stella getting a green light just as she came; despite she having seen the red light from a distance.

Minsie was irritated to get a red light despite having seen a green light until she reached there and the green light switched to red. A car came from the opposite direction, which Minsie thought was lucky at the moment not getting the red light despite having seen it; on which she was a bit irritated.

"Oh, then it means a lot has to be done..." said Lesohn.

"So..., let's meet up today?" suggested Stacy; holding the glass.

"Umm...sure, I mean we don't have a long time to finish it, cause the deadline is not far away." said Lesohn as he agreed.

"Yes we definitely got to finish by the threshold." replied Stacy.

"Oh wait, am I seeing something wrong?" thought Stella.

Stella was slowing her car down moving towards the side of the road, in order to get a proper view from her car.

The red traffic light changed to green enabling Minsie to go.

"It is Minsie's car." thought Stella looking on the number-plate.

Stella was happy to find her on the way, but just as she was confirmed; the car started accelerating as it moved forward.

"Vzz-vzzh." vibrated Minsie's phone as she looked down to see.

Minsie picked up the call right away; putting it on loudspeaker.

"Hello, Minsie?" said the caller confirming the person he called.

"Yes Minsie speaking, how may I help sir?" replied Minsie.

"I wanted to handover a task, do you mind assisting?" asked the caller in a requesting tone but keeping the honor-worthy profile.

"Yes, I'd be happy to assist." replied Minsie instantly afterwards.

"Glad to hear. Ok, so I want you to give the previous week's documents to Lesohn, alright?" said Mr. Wilfindor; explaining.

"Dang it why!!!" thought Minsie in her head in irritancy.

"Hello?" said Mr. Wilfindor; by not receiving a reply afterwards.

"Yes…, yes alright." replied Minsie unwantedly; forcing herself.

"Alright then, thank you." said Mr. Wilfindor, as he hung up.

"Destiny never let's you move on…ugh." said Minsie to herself.

Minsie was quite irritated by having to go meet Lesohn as she didn't at all wished to do so in her current situation, cause she wanted to move on and forget what had happened earlier.

Stella had steered her way to the other side of the road as she followed Minsie's car; she was fortunately able to catch up on Minsie as Minsie drove slowly due to talking over the phone call.

Minsie instantly switched routes as she already had the documents in her car; inside a bag; on the backseat, so she didn't have to go back to her house in order to take the documents.

Stacy had suggested meeting in a cafe to finish the assignment, which Lesohn agreed and was on his way to there.

Stella saw Minsie's car accelerate to a higher speed; she did the same yet maintaining a distance in order to not freak Minsie out.

"Oh wow…" said Minsie to herself laughing at the coincidence.

Minsie had noticed Lesohn's car appear on the same road from a distance, seemingly going towards the nearby cafe.

"Seems like fortunately I can finish the task in a matter of moments." thought Minsie sighing happily.

Stella kept sticking to Minsie's car as Minsie changed directions. Minsie took a turn, but just as Stella was about to turn; another car blocked her by entering between her and Minsie's car.

"So my guess was correct, wasn't it…" thought Minsie looking forward at Lesohn's car parked in front of the cafe.

"Oh god, hopefully Minsie's doesn't go too far…" wished Stella.

Minsie neared the café, but a car overtook hers and parked behind Lesohn's car, disabling Minsie to park there.

"Oh wait, no!" shrieked Stella in terror noticing something.

Stella recalled whose car it was that just got parked as Minsie moved forward searching for a spot to park at.

"I-i-it's Stacy's car! I'll have to hurry!" thought Stella; terrified.

Stella had been following Minsie in order to provide her with a piece of information, that she didn't want Minsie to hear from someone else and definitely not from Stacy or Lesohn.

Stella drove as quick as she could, and parked her car within seconds. Time was going slow as she rushed towards the entrance, where Minsie was already at; about to open the door.

Minsie hurried, because she wanted to finish that task, that included Lesohn; as fast as possible…

By the time Stella reached the entrance, Minsie was already in.

Minsie went in with the documents held in her hands. She turned left just to see Lesohn was sitting with a girl.

"Hello…" said Stacy as she sat down properly onto the chair.

"Hello!" greeted back Lesohn facing her.

"Why should I care…" Minsie kept telling herself in her head.

Stella entered through the door and turned, to her terror i-it was Lesohn and Stacy sitting, while Minsie walked towards them.

"Again…?" thought Minsie as her heart broke into pieces, while she tried with all her force to stop tears from filling her eyes; as she saw the two; Lesohn and Stacy sitting together.

"Uh-oh…" said Stella; as a reflex action as she neared them.

All of that took place in just a matter of moments, bad takes no time to take place at all; just as in that scenario.

"I failed…oh god!" blamed Stella herself as she stood still, after reaching near them; Minsie, Lesohn and Stacy.

It seemed like the typical love triangle with an additional person trying to save a heart from breaking into pieces, but being late.

"Wrong time…right?" said Minsie sarcastically smiling with tears filling her eyes, which she was abstaining from happening.

Lesohn and Stacy looked up facing Minsie; all so confused as the two had no idea what was happening -particularly to Minsie- or was about to happen; just what secretly loving someone does.

Minsie was unstable from what she was seeing again. That time it just got so confirmed, breaking even the littlest of the hopes.

11

TIME FLEW AS THE CLOCK TICKED

"Good morning!" greeted Minsie as she stirred the coffee.

"Good morning…" replied Dexzart as he got off of the stairs.

"Sit down, I made you coffee." said Minsie gesturing with hand.

"Thank you." replied Dexzart as he sat down by the table.

Minsie then took out some cupcakes out of the oven, and sat down too, in order to eat breakfast; specially prepared by her.

"Trring!" rang the landline seeming to pierce through the ears.

"Oh gosh! Who is it?!" said Stella rhetorically as she ran.

"Hello, Stella?" greeted as the call was picked up by Stella.

"Hello, Minsie?" greeted back Stella instantly as Stella heard her.

"Yes, I wanted to ask if you could help out?" said Minsie.

"Sure, but help with what though?" asked Stella in confusion.

Three months, had passed; since the day when Minsie and Lesohn had met in the cafe. Things had took turns as time went by… nothing was the same anymore; everything had changed with the flow of time.

"Umm, I have some work to finish, but if I go, then Dexzart would be all by himself, so I was asking if you could accompany him, while I'm gone?" asked Minsie hoping for a yes.

"It's ok if I'm by myself…" said Dexzart along with a laugh.

"If I am free by the time you are leaving, then yes I could accompany; is that alright?" replied Stella waiting for an answer.

"No it's obviously not ok!" said Minsie rolling her eyes.

"Sorry?" asked Stella in a harder and a bit irritated tone.

"No, not you Stella. I was saying that to Dexzart…" told Minsie.

"Oh, sorry. But what's the answer to me?" asked Stella laughing.

"Yeah, it's alright; after-all I am leaving in the afternoon." told Minsie, as she took a sip of her coffee raising the coffee mug.

Stella felt a bit hesitated to accompany a guy, and that too when he's alone; yet she couldn't deny the request from her best friend; in any way…

"Alright then, let me know that you are leaving, a while before you do, as it would take time for me to arrive." said Stella.

"Yeah, sure." replied Minsie; instantly after Stella finished

"Alright, bye then." said Stella in a cheery positive tone.

"Yeah, bye!" replied Minsie, as she hung up the phone call.

Dexzart stared straight at Minsie expecting her to tell the reply.

Minsie gestured using her head to Dexzart as to asking what he was staring at her for, cause she didn't get it.

"What'd she say?" simply asked Dexzart vibrating his head.

"Oh that. She said she'll be coming over." told Minsie laughing.

"Oh alright, great." simply said Dexzart taking a bite of the deliciously made cupcakes which Minsie was widely known for.

"Battery very low." read a notification on Stella's phone.

"Oh god, I can't even seem to find my charger." said Stella.

"Stella!" a voice called from downstairs of Stella's house.

Stella ran down the stairs half ready to go out to Minsie's place.

"Can you please help me down here for a while?" requested Ms. Franklin as Stella went to her over in the kitchen; half dressed.

"Yeah, sure mom." replied Stella as she began helping her mom.

The day seemed busy for everyone yet it was cheering, as one happily helped the other out in doing various things.

"I am about done, I'll be leaving in a while." informed Minsie.

"Oh alright." accommodated Dexzart as he grabbed a bowl of salad to eat.

"Please don't mind me not hospitalizing you enough…" said Minsie giving out a little laugh, feeling a bit guilty.

"What should I do to you! You have been hospitalizing me since the beginning and it's not just enough it's way more than just enough!" said Dexzart in a soft shocked tone as he laughed rolling his eyes, as he faced back towards Minsie.

"Alright?" asked Eliott as he smiled facing upwards.

"Yes totally!" replied the other person smiling as he understood.

"Eliott?" asked a person as she turned around noticing Eliott.

"Yes." replied Eliott casually as he faced her turning around.

"How are you?" asked Casey in a happy and uplifted tone.

"Am fine, what about you?" replied Eliott returning the smile.

"Bzz-zz-vzz" vibrated the phone slowly moving; over the table.

"Oh, I got to go!" said Stella softly, making a sorry face.

"Where up-to?" asked Ms. Franklin, as she turned to face Stella.

"To Minsie's." said Stella as her voice lowered, while she exited.

"Today feels like a new start." said Casey to herself in her head.

"I am great as well." replied Casey putting her bangs backward.

"Yes?" said Stella picking up the call, closing the house-door.

"Just to let you know, I'm leaving right-away…" told Minsie.

The day was bright yet cloudy; silence and mind music playing.

Stella was driving in hurry, as she suddenly noticed Casey and Eliott through the glass door, while they were facing each other.

Stella didn't ignore it nor make a mess out of it; as she was in a rush to Minsie's house in order to reach on time.

"Alright bye, Stella would be here in a while." told Minsie.

"Alright, no problem, bye!" replied Dexzart as he slightly waved.

"I think maybe it's time I should start getting up…" told Eliott.

"Yeah." said Casey hesitating, as she unwantedly put up a smile.

"It was a good time talking…" said Eliott as he subtly smiled.

"Yes absolutely, but I think bye for now." replied Casey smiling.

"Yeah bye! See you later." said Eliott opening the glass door.

"Ouch, sorry." said Stella accidentally striking into someone.

"No, it's okay." said the other person as she looked upwards.

"Minsie." said Stella as Minsie faced her looking upwards.

"My bad, I was in a rush." apologized Stella with a smile.

"It's alright I was in a rush too. And by the way, I've prepared the ingredients for lunch; all you have to do is mix and bake to eat. Really sorry; I couldn't serve you the food." replied Minsie.

"It's totally fine, you already did the hardest part." said Stella.

"Thank you! Okay I am running out of time, bye." told Minsie.

The sky seemed a bit cloudy yet wonderful with the dark tones.

"Hello?" said Eliott instantly as the phone call got picked up.

"Yes, Franklin speaking." told the person answering the call.

"Could you bring Stella on the call?" requested Eliott politely.

"Sorry dear, she isn't at home." told Ms. Franklin in a soft tone.

"Oh she isn't at home…" rephrased Eliott understanding.

"Could you tell me who you are?" asked Ms. Franklin steadily.

"I-I am Eliott." said Eliott hesitantly in a soft and polite manner.

"Do you have any idea on where Stella might be?" asked Eliott.

"She said that she'll be heading to Minsie's." told Ms. Franklin.

"Alright, thanks a lot for helping." replied Eliott smiling.

"You're most welcome." said Ms. Franklin hanging up the call.

The sky had an unusual hue giving soft subtle yet dark chills.

"A lot has occurred in the past few months." sighed Casey.

"It feels like something drastically changed." replied the listener.

"Well, life definitely didn't remain the same." said Casey in a soft tone, which perfectly went with the weather over there.

"Drring!" a loud alerting sound came; as the doorbell rang.

Stella was mixing the batter and her hands were all dirty so she went to wash her hands real quick. In the meantime, Dexzart was coming downstairs and the two crashed as Stella's hands unlatched the doorknob. To their surprise. It was – Eliott.

Eliott was unable to utter a single word as he looked at the two.

It was a moment of pure silence; as Stella was surprised to see Eliott, while Dexzart didn't even have any idea who Eliott was.

"E-E-Eliott?" said Stella clenching her teeth in absolute astonishment seeing Eliott; breaking the silence.

"Really?" demanded Eliott, as he turned around and left sighing.

"Huh?!" said Stella harshly in annoyance and anger.

Even though Stella was hinted that Eliott might had taken her and Dexzart wrongly; what really was swirling up her mind was that she saw Casey and Eliott so close to each other, and that too at an event planner's place, yet he still reacted that way then.

The sky was in one of it's darkest tones with storms swirling; up head, while their thunderclaps made a different environment.

The rain started to fall making the roads wet, while Eliott turned his car on with tears dripping from his eyes as he tried his best to soak the tears in, but failed badly at doing so.

Eliott didn't expect that from Stella even by a bit, but that did occur, which disappointed him making him break down badly.

Stella absolutely didn't know how to react as she was badly hurt.

"Who was he?" asked Dexzart casually; as he was too confused.

Stella wasn't really in the condition to answer anything at all. She just had no idea; what to do or what to say at the moment, and stood there all silent, as tears dripped off her eyes unintendedly.

Sky darkened as the day changed into a dark stormy evening.

It rained heavily, as Minsie ran to the car, trying not to get wet.

"Dh-dhak!" a knock came on the door; in the stormy evening.

Stella slightly opened the door to check onto who was knocking.

"Casey?" asked Stella in astonishment; to why Casey was there.

"Yes me; Casey. I came here to give some documents, Minsie asked me to collect for her." said Casey handing the files.

"Thank you for helping out." said Stella in a confused tone.

"Yeah, and also Minsie asked me to make sure that no one takes a look at the documents." said Casey indicating her; not to look.

"Yeah sure, my task now." replied Stella smiling in irritancy.

"Alright then, bye." said Casey as she turned, and left the place.

Stella shut the door in extreme annoyance and straight away went upstairs to Minsie's room, and threw the files on the desk.

"Umm, Stella?" called Dexzart just as Stella came downstairs..

"Yes?" replied Stella, asking if he needed help on anything.

"Would you like to go walk to the Cinema Theatre with umbrellas under the rainfall, and also watch a movie together?" offered Dexzart in a very friendly approach to Stella.

Stella felt like denying, but then she's there to accompany him.

"Yeah sure, why not?" said Stella in a dim yet positive tone.

"Alright then, let's go." said Dexzart, as he grabbed an overcoat.

Stella put her overcoat on and grabbed two umbrellas for them.

"Eliott?" Casey let out a light scream, and ran towards Eliott.

"Are you ok?" asked Casey bending down to face Eliott directly.

"Yeah I am absolutely fine." said Eliott, even though tears dripped off his eyes, while he faced upwards fake-smiling.

"What happened?" asked Casey, feeling sorry for Eliott; seeing him in that vulnerable condition all alone by himself.

"Nothing at all..." said Eliott, trying hard to hide his emotions.

"Ok, don't tell me but. I'm not letting you drive in this state..." said Casey as she doubted Eliott's concentration on the road.

"No, I am all fine." said Eliott denying to Casey's statement.

Casey neglected to hear another word, and opened the door putting her hand through the open window, and dragged Eliott out of the car; closing the window and the door; locking the car.

"So let's take today as your pamper day..." said Casey funnily.

"What! No..." denied Eliott to the offer held by Casey.

"So we go to the cinemas driving you through the peaceful rain!" told Casey as she went on ignoring Eliott's denial.

Casey decided to make Eliott's mood better through pampering him as if he was a cute little baby boy which made things sweet.

"You like rain or walking under the rainy sky?" asked Dexzart.

"I do. Very much." told Stella as she put her hand out in rain.

"Any movie you'd like to watch in particular?" asked Dexzart.

"Umm no. You?" replied Stella as they peacefully walked.

"I have no idea, let's see." replied back Dexzart in a sweet tone.

It rained; rather stormed, yet things seemed cutely messed up.

"Do you like sweet or regular salty popcorn?" asked Casey.

"Salty." replied Eliott hesitantly, which seemed quite cute.

"Me too!" said Casey as the drive with the storm went peaceful.

"Why can't I stop thinking about Eliott, Is he even alright?" thought Stella as things quieted down except the rainfall.

Eliott was mad at Stella yet he couldn't stop thinking about her.

"How can she do that, I couldn't even imagine." thought Eliott.

"Stella stop! cause you literally saw Eliott and Casey together!" thought Stella as she heated up a bit, but she was rather sad.

Stella didn't know whether to be sad or mad about seeing them.

The rain and the storm defined exactly what both Eliott and Stella were feeling; sad like the rain and mad like the storm.

"Alright Eliott, we're here, but don't get out yet." said Casey.

Casey got out of the car then she held the door open for Eliott.

"Thank you, but you really didn't have to do all this." said Eliott.

"I decide if I had to or not, right?" replied Casey in a funny way.

"Well, you are not wrong." said Eliott keeping the funniness.

"Allow me." said Dexzart as he went forward to hold the door open for Stella making things a bit funny, to light up her mood.

"This surely was unnecessary, but thank you." said Stella funnily.

"I suppose that's a compliment." replied Dexzart with a laugh.

"So, what do you want to do first?" asked Casey as they got in.

Just right after Stella entered, and was walking backwards as she closed the umbrella talking to Dexzart; she bumped into someone accidentally.

"Sorry, sorry." said Stella; while turning to face the person.

"No, I am sorry." said the other person, cause he was walking backwards as well while talking to another person.

But right after they turned, they were shocked to see each other.

"Yeah exactly, you!" said Stella nonchalantly in a harsh manner.

"Yeah you!" said the other person raising his eyebrows in anger.

"Happy Time Together, Casey." said Stella; rude yet politely.

"Have a good time, you two!" replied back Eliott in irritancy.

The two turned themselves back, and grabbed the other two's hand, and harshly walked away expressing extreme rage towards each other by acting as if they didn't care about seeing each other.

"Drring!" loudly rang the doorbell of Minsie's house.

"Stella?" called out Minsie expecting her to be at the house then.

"Let's ring the doorbell again, Stella might have not heard or maybe she's upstairs." said Minsie in her mind to herself.

Before, Minsie would ring the doorbell again, a hand patted at Minsie's shoulder as to calling her, so she turned back to check.

12

THE SUDDEN NEWS

"Hello!" said the person in an excited tone approaching the guy.

"Oh, hello! Jenna!" replied the guy keeping the excited tone up.

"It's been so long!" said Jacob in a loud happily dramatic tone.

"Yes it has!" replied back Jenna in the very same dramatic tone.

The sky's lit up by the sun but it wasn't the brightest of the days.

"Jennifer?" asked the lady as Jennifer stood by the glass door.

"Yes, Miss Winsent." replied Jennifer opening the door to enter.

"Good morning, Jennifer, I need something done by you." told Miss Winsent in a loud clear tone; which seemed as a command.

"Alright, I am here to assist." replied Jennifer in a helpful tone.

"Then, please take a seat and hear out the task to be done." told Miss Winsent pointing at the opposite chair; gesturing her to sit.

Jennifer then sat down on the chair in order to hear out the task.

"Cases of people missing have been rising high." told the news.

"This makes the city a whole lot perilous." said Stacy to herself.

Stacy had the T.V turned on, while drinking the morning coffee.

"Hello?" questioned Lesohn receiving a call on the landline.

"Hello! It's me Telvina." said the person who called Lesohn.

"Hello, Jacob?" said Stella blandly as the call got answered.

"Yes, is everything okay?" asked Jacob; suddenly receiving a call.

"Yeah, yeah. But have you seen or spoken to Minsie since yesterday??" asked Stella in a worried manner; as to being tensed.

"No, I haven't seen or spoken to her since 2 days." told Jacob.

"Oh, okay. Sorry for disturbing you." said Stella worrying more.

"No, it is absolutely fine." replied Jacob in a loud positive tone.

"Thank you!" said Stella, as she hung up the call to Jacob.

"Dexzart, did Minsie say anything about taking more than a day?" asked Stella as tension rose after Minsie not showing up.

"No, nothing about taking more than a day. In fact, she said she would be back soon." replied Dexzart as he was worried as well.

Minsie always stuck to her words, and if she said she will be back soon then she would have been, but she hadn't and that is what made things immensely tensing to both Stella and Dexzart.

"Any other friend of Minsie's; she might have gone to visit?" asked Dexzart trying to figure out the disappearance of Minsie.

"Should I call him?" questioned Stella to herself in her mind.

"Perhaps not, it's quite impossible for the probability that Minsie have gone there; to his place." thought Stella intensely.

"N-no, not really anybody; she might have visited by ghosting us…" told Stella quite certainly; having tiny amount of doubt.

Time was passing, but there was no sign of Minsie; unusually.

"Hello?" said Stacy as the call got answered by the person.

"Yeah, Stelnet speaking, how may I help?" replied the person.

"Stelnet, it's me Stacy speaking!" told Stacy enthusiastically.

"Oh you! Stacy!!" screamed Stelnet out of great enthusiasm.

"Jacob?" said Stella instantly; answering the unexpected call.

"Yes, Stella turn the news on." said Jacob in a very intense tone.

"Alright." said Stella, instantly getting tensed; taking the remote.

"Wait, what the freak!" blurted out Dexzart as he turned to see the news, seeing which literally terrified both Stella and Dexzart.

"Yes exactly!" said Jacob in an intense tone as the tension rose.

"I think we should immediately go and file a missing report in the police station!!" told Stella loudly in a worried intense tone.

"Ok, I'll be heading there right away!" told Jacob over the call.

Stella and Dexzart ran to Stella's car and got in. All the three had headed to the nearest local police station, from Minsie's house.

"What!" screamed out Ms. Franklin turning around facing Stella.

"Why didn't you inform me earlier?!" demanded Ms. Franklin.

"We weren't confirmed till this morning and we had no idea about the news." told Stella emptily, in am extremely fast pace.

"Well, I have no idea if you have even properly heard the news or not, cause how can you not be horrified!" said Ms. Franklin.

"Please calm down, and we are terribly horrified." told Jacob.

"Sorry, sorry. This sudden news of Minsie disappearing literally shocked me to such an extent…" told Ms. Franklin apologizing.

The room contained a serious tension, which was expressed through silence present. Everybody went quiet for a while, and started thinking what they should be doing next to find Minsie.

"Let's go inform the police right away! Or else it would be too late." said Ms. Franklin breaking the silence in the room.

"But Ms. Franklin, we already informed." told Dexzart timidly.

"Alright great, but what did they say?" questioned Ms. Franklin.

Earlier then, Stella and Dexzart went to the police station and Jacob had joined them within minutes, the three had rushed into there. Jacob had asked where to file a missing report, and afterwards Dexzart told the police that they wanted to file a missing report. Stella then had told them everything thoroughly and pointed out any important detail that she could remember of, after which they left from there and headed towards Ms. Franklin's place.

"They told us that they'll waste no time, and start searching for Minsie immediately, and told us not worry." explained Jacob.

"Okay, even though we informed police and they'll be searching for her, can we not sit back and wait, and instead go by ourselves too to search for her?" demanded Stella in a loud tone.

"I think Stella's right, we must go search for her." agreed Jacob.

"Yeah that'll definitely be the keen take at the moment. But we all have to stick together, cause you see it's dangerous out there so let's head out in only one car; my car…" said Ms. Franklin.

Everybody else agreed and the four exited Stella's house and headed towards the car. After everybody got in, they started to discuss where they should be going, cause they had to be organized, so that they could search as many places as possible.

"This a secret mission so I would not want you to tell anybody anything about any of this, or else it'd be trouble." commanded Miss Winsent as she swiped the card-key to unlock the door.

"Keep your mind at peace." assured Jennifer that she'd not tell.

As the automated door unlocked, the two walked into there.

"The amount of people going missing is increasing involuntarily" said one of the police officer in a worried manner.

"It is indeed, very significantly." replied another police officer.

The tension in the whole city was rising as more and more people started to vanish in Riverside, California; one by one.

"We'll first head to the highlands." told Dexzart accordingly.

"Ok, before we head to anywhere, do you want to inform any other friend of Minsie about this?" asked Ms. Franklin.

"No, there isn't anybody else that close, to inform." told Stella.

"And also the probability of us actually finding Minsie is very low so informing anybody else would be idiotic." pointed Jacob.

"Alright, if you people say so." replied Ms. Franklin sighing.

"Feels like this city's going crazy." said Telvina dramatically.

"It indeed is, cause see the rates of people missing is rising rapidly so it's a matter to worry about." replied Lesohn seriously.

"Yes, absolutely." replied Telvina as her talking tone got serious.

The sky was pitch dark even though it was afternoon; storms were up ahead waiting and growling like dark creatures as Stella and the others reached the highlands of Riverside, California. "Oh god, it'll start storming pretty badly." pointed out Dexzart.

"This could be a great obstacle in our search." said Jacob tensed.

"Indeed, so do we continue or pause for now?" asked Stella.

"I unfortunately have to phrase this, but I suppose we shouldn't at the moment." told Ms. Franklin emptily; about her decision.

"We've to move fast, quick!" told Miss Winsent as she walked.

"Yes, alright!" replied Jennifer as she ran to catch up with Miss Winsent's pace, while the storms growled loudly up head.

"We've to think critically." told Ms. Franklin opening the door.

"What do you exactly mean by that?" asked Dexzart curiously.

"I mean like think about where she had been that day, or was there anything suspicious in her actions, or maybe somebody stated to have enmity with her recently like anything that might possibly lead to Minsie disappearing!" explained Ms. Franklin.

"I see, maybe we could go take a look at Minsie's house, to see if we can find any hint at all; regarding this?" suggested Jacob.

"Yes you are absolutely right, and also in the meantime try to recall any hint yourselves, specially Dexzart." told Ms. Franklin.

They started to head out to Minsie's place to check for any hint.

"Wait." said Stella out loud, stopping the rest from going out.

The three turned around to face Stella to see why she stopped.

"Actually, you guys go continue cause I need sometime to be alone by myself, alright?" told Stella in an exhausted tone.

"Yeah alright, sure, you stay here, we'll go ahead." replied Jacob.

The three then headed out as Stella closed the door for them.

Stella went upstairs to her room as slowly tears began to fall off her eyes; her hands suffocating her; as she cried unstoppably.

"It's hurting me a lot, I am in severe pain, but I can't express it to anyone at all, which torments me even more." thought Stella.

Stella's eyes were bright red as tears fell, and her nose started to turn red, while she tried her best to stay silent with her hands covering her mouth, as she suffocated crying.

The four had to pass by Eliott's house on their way to Stella's house, and to Stella's grief; she had seen Casey's car parked out there which gave Stella chills, and she had held her grief since.

Stella felt her heart slowly breaking; each and every moment she saw Casey out there with Eliott; where she was supposed to be.

Stella held her head against the divan; sitting on the ground trembling as she cried her sorrow out with her bright red eyes.

Jacob and the others reached Minsie's house, while it stormed.

"I'll head upstairs to check and you two check here, alright." guided Ms. Franklin closing the door as they entered the house.

"Yeah sure, go ahead." replied Dexzart, while Jacob nodded.

Ms. Franklin quickly went upstairs to check for anything that might lead to the conclusion of that mystery, on that note.

A while later, Stella was in the bathroom speedily washing her face as she settled down after vigorously crying her heart out.

"I really went to another topic while my focus should be actually on Minsie's disappearance." thought Stella; reminding herself.

"Actually what might have actually caused Minsie's sudden disappearance?" thought Stella deeply; questioning herself.

"I actually first should check Dexzart's room cause he'd been living the closest to Minsie, and he's just an acquaintance, and he's not even from this city, and that indeed leads to suspicion." thought Ms. Franklin deeply as she headed to Dexzart's room.

"I'll check the living room and can you help checking the kitchen, specially the drawers please…" said Jacob; guiding.

"Yeah sure, I'll go check right away." agreed Dexzart instantly.

The two went into opposite directions and started opening the drawers and cupboards in there, to check for any hints available.

"Nothing important seems to be here, but I'll check the files and papers and anything at all that points to the situation in any way…" thought Ms. Franklin, while hoping the others take long.

Jacob was opening the drawers one by one, and thoroughly checking each of them, which seemed like an endless process.

"Hello?" said Jennifer as she answered a call from someone.

"Yes, when'll you be here?" asked the person on the other end.

"It'll take some time here, but I'll be there soon." told Jennifer.

"Alright." replied back the person emptily hanging up the call.

"Who was it?" questioned Miss Winsent as she turned around.

Jennifer then whispered the reply into Miss Winsent's ears.

Stella was collecting some stuff; some documents and some other things carefully into a plain large black office-handbag.

"Nothing seems suspicious in this room." said Ms. Franklin to herself as she stood at the entrance of the room viewing it.

Ms. Franklin the left the room after putting everything in place.

Dexzart was done checking the kitchen so he came by to help Jacob check in the living room, which sort of made things easy.

"Were you able to remember any hint that might have been passed during your conversations with Minsie?" asked Jacob.

"Not really, but I am trying my best." told Dexzart hesitantly.

The two then continued checking on some documents in there.

"Okay, I'll meet you up in a while." said Stella over the call.

"Yeah alright, I'll be waiting." replied back the person in the call.

"Ms. Franklin!" shouted Jacob seeing something; perhaps a hint.

Both Ms. Franklin and Dexzart rushed hearing the shout, to see what happened. Ms. Franklin ran her way downstairs, while seeing Dexzart going out, which she followed thinking that the sound seemed distant so probably came from outside or so

"What?!" questioned both Ms. Franklin and Dexzart; confused.

"See here I might have found a hint…" told Jacob with relief.

"Finally!" Ms. Franklin let out a quiet scream getting bit of relief.

"Wow, what is it?" asked Dexzart quite seriously facing Jacob.

"Yeah, come see." said Jacob asking to come forward to see.

Both Dexzart and Ms. Franklin moved forward; to see the thing.

"Look here, do you see some hollow shoe heel sketches on the pavement." said Jacob gesturing with his hands at the sketches.

"Yeah, what about it?" asked Dexzart as he bent down more; to see the sketches more clearly, trying to know why it's pointed at.

"This seems to be rough sketches indicating that somebody was pulled from here forcefully." told Jacob quite like a detective.

"Do you try to mean Minsie was-" said Ms. Franklin without finishing her sentence as she was interrupted by Jacob's reply.

"Yes, Minsie might have been pulled." said Jacob interrupting.

After collecting stuff into the bag, Stella locked her house door, as she left the house, heading to her car in the parking lot. She then entered her car, and headed to somewhere; fully prepared.

"What the hell!, that sounds like danger!" said Dexzart; shocked.

"It does…" replied Jacob entirely worried yet in a calm tone.

"Now that indicates us to speed things up from here on or we're inviting more trouble." said Ms. Franklin aloud as tension rose.

"Yes, indeed." replied Jacob in a worried voice; quite seriously.

"I'll call Stella to tell this." said Ms. Franklin proceeding to call.

"Yeah, please do, cause she has to know all this." said Dexzart.

Ms. Franklin called about three times, but it didn't get answered.

"She isn't picking the call…" said Ms. Franklin getting irritated.

"Never mind, I have to call other people." added Ms. Franklin.

Ms. Franklin went over to a side to call, while Jacob and Dexzart thought Stella will call back; when she notices the missed calls.

"Hello, Ms. Franklin speaking." said Ms. Franklin; introducing.

"Oh hello Ms. Franklin!. Any problem?." replied the person.

Ms. Franklin then proceeded to tell everything after which she called another person, and asked both the people to come help, which they also insisted on cause they got worried about Minsie.

13

The Missing Puzzles

"Alright, let's search for any other hints available after which we will go meet the police and ask them about their progress to this far." told Ms. Franklin; quite taking the lead at the moment.

"Alright, noted." replied Jacob, as they all headed back inside.

All the three then started re-exploring their zones, for any more hints that could join up to solve the equation held at the hands.

"Hmm, I feel like there isn't anything else left to be searched in here." thought Ms. Franklin; closing the drawer beside the bed.

"I think we're done…" said Ms. Franklin walking downstairs.

"I do think so, but why isn't Stella here yet?" questioned Jacob.

"I have no idea, but let's head out to the police station and we'll ask her to come join us over there, alright?" asked Ms. Franklin.

"Yeah, I think that'll be alright." agreed Dexzart unhesitatingly.

Then Jacob agreed as well, and the three left the house locking the door. They then walked to Ms. Franklin's car heading to the police station as all the three got in; closing the car doors.

"This seems like a long ride…" said Jacob with a deep meaning.

"It really does seem like one, but we must keep going without any sort of hesitation, for it leads to our ultimate destination; we are willing to reach in any manner possible for us." told Dexzart.

"That deeply answered it right." said Ms. Franklin; as she drove.

The sky started to turn darker as the hour neared evening, though it was already raining lightly, before evening appeared.

"Hello?" said a person in a questioning tone as they neared.

"Hello, how are you?" replied the other in a greeting manner.

It was raining, and the weather hadn't been constant for hours.

"So, why are we here now?!" asked the person quite confused.

"I called you here for something quite serious." told the other.

"Right, I don't think it's safe in anyway to be out here in this weather!" emphasized the person; quite weirded out & irritated.

"Listen before you blabber, please!" said the other one calmly.

"Alright fine, then let's hear you out..." replied the person as lightning struck with an enormous blast in the ears of the two.

The weather seemed to takes turns quite furiously and untimely.

"It is hard to say to you but with utter apology I will have to say that we've found some dead bodies of some females." told the police officer, as he felt sorry for the people searching for them.

"What!" blurted out Dexzart as he heard the melancholy news.

"Can you tell us of what ages they were?" asked Jacob worriedly.

"Umm, not exactly, but their age group might be considered of university students…" told the police officer quite nonchalantly.

"That's some tensing info right there…" pointed Ms. Franklin.

"It certainly is, and I hadn't expected such an info..." told Jacob.

"We've to find Minsie, she might be dead by now, or in the death bed; not dead, so we can still save her!" pointed Dexzart.

The three looked at each other gesturing that they had to hurry before time runs out, so they rushed to the car in no time at all.

"Hello! Ziezta." screamed Casey in immense joy running to hug.

"Hello!, How're you?!" asked Ziezta keeping up with the joy in the conversation as she got struck by Casey's strong joyous hug.

"It's been so long since we've met!" said Casey with excitement.

"It really has, I can't express how much I've longed to meet you, and this is really an euphoric present for me." expressed Ziezta.

"Well, I am extremely glad to hear that, and I have to say; I am feeling the same cheerfulness in me like- oh god." told Casey.

The two then proceeded to continue chatting, as they've met after such a life-long pause, which had boosted the excitement.

"Can someone tell me where Stella is?!" asked Jacob furiously.

"I have no idea! seems so careless of her..." said Ms. Franklin.

"I think we shouldn't take this negatively, like she can actually be doing something important." conveyed Dexzart calmly.

Stella still had not contacted the three yet, it was pretty angering in the situation held at hands; as someone's life was at stake.

"I need you to do two things for me." requested Stella; guiding.

"Okay, yeah sure, but what are they actually?" asked the person.

"So, you are going to have to collect really important info about two things, but you'll have to do it secretively." explained Stella.

The entire sky was dark enough to be mistaken as night, while it was verily evening, the birds were gone aback to their shelters for safety for which every life urges at each and every moment.

"You have no idea; what have had happened in life!" said Casey.

"Tell me!, I am willing to hear it all out, like please." said Ziezta.

"It's a very long story, but the past months' one are by far the most drastic one to have been in." mentioned Casey opening up.

"So let's hear that out first, I guess." suggested Ziezta; friendlily.

"I guess, but let's just go sit somewhere; Starbucks?" said Casey.

"Yeah, sure, I think that's the closest from here..." said Ziezta.

The two then proceeded to walk to Starbucks to chat peacefully.

"It has been long enough, I think we should go check my house before going to search for Minsie..." suggested Ms. Franklin.

"Yeah, true, now it's actually worrying me." told Dexzart tensed.

"Yeah, sure, let's drive to there quickly though." agreed Jacob.

Stella hadn't been answering any calls and there was no sign of her, and in that situation it was pretty worrying & quite angering. So, they had to stop midway and set off back to Stella's location.

The night was about to appear as every street lights got lit, and the entire human race's main attraction at the sky became moon. Some sat by their windows, lighting up cozy lights listening to soft music that charmed one's ear to absolute desired tranquility.

"Things change so drastically, one can't even tell why, or how it has, while you still got to keep going with the flow." said Casey.

"Yeah everything becomes different as time passes." said Ziezta.

"Just like how lovers turn into hater. Hearing such stories drains your heart in ways, while in the same way it glorifies your heart to hear the vice-versas; it's all so much messed up." said Casey.

"So, two and a half months ago, we had this summer vacation arranged by our university to a secret place and we all were asked to join. Most people including me were hovering over the news, but some of us seemed to not care much about it, and it was showing clearly and that seemed a bit off as they're usually enthusiastic and as per the description of how the program was going to be carried out; felt would be interesting to everyone including them, but as they weren't; made it crystal clear something was up, and I had instantly thought that I had to find out what, which is what I had been putting quite effort into. I had my eyes on them the whole time, I had noticed that there might've been some sort of a clash between them, and that they were sort of separated while previously they all seemed to be pretty good group of friends, so I thought of finding out the cause of the clash; which seemed a bit of a hard task but I was determined. Days went by, they were still like that; all that time, it was two days before our trip, one of them; Minsie, had already requested a ton of times to not join us into that vacation, but the management didn't agree so she had to go, which seemed to be upsetting for her. Then it was the day before the trip and we all were asked to come help pack things up in the university and we all went, and to our horror we heard that-" comprehended Casey openly, as she got interrupted by the staff.

"Here is your order." told the staff handing over the croissants and coffees to them, which smelled of absolute delicacy to them.

"How can Stella be this careless in this sort of circumstance." said Ms. Franklin; quite irritated, as they neared Stella's house.

"Hold on." said Miss Winsent, as she quietly searched for a file.

"Yeah, sure." replied Jennifer; standing as she waited heedfully.

"Check this file, please." said Miss Winsent handing her the file.

"I don't think she is here; although she had said she'd be." said Ms. Franklin after ringing the doorbell for the hundredth time.

"Hello!" a voice came as the door got unlocked from the inside.

"Looks like she is…" said Dexzart in a pretty surprised manner

"Stella, where have you been?" asked Jacob instantly; seeing her.

"Nowhere, I was just about to leave." told Stella pretty calmly.

"Why haven't you answered our calls?" questioned Ms. Franklin.

Stella had just entered the house from the back-door; while she heard the doorbell ringing and she answered it right away. Luckily, she managed to make it seem she was already at home.

"Umm, my phone's battery was dead." answered Stella instantly.

"See I told you it isn't much of a big deal." pointed out Dexzart.

A call interrupted the conversation, as the phone started ringing.

"Hello." greeted Ms. Franklin politely as she answered the call.

While Ms. Franklin was on the call, the others chatted amongst them about what had happened while Stella wasn't there & etc.

"Stacy?" blurred Stella in complete surprise, as Stacy pulled over.

"Alright so, let me tell the names of who I'm talking about as it might actually completely shock you." told Casey; dramatically.

"Yeah please, cause I am extremely curious to hear." said Ziezta.

"Stacy?" asked Dexzart confused as he and Jacob turned behind.

"So it was actually Stacy, Minsie, Jacob & Lesohn, part of it was also Eliott and Stella." told Casey as Ziezta frowned upon her.

"What the hell is she doing here?" asked Jacob in a harsh tone.

"Eliott!" shockingly blurted Dexzart seeing Eliott pullover there.

"What Eliott-" said Stella turning to her side in complete shock.

"Hello, how are you?" asked Ms. Franklin in a greeting manner.

"Not really good hearing the sudden news." said Stacy nearing.

"Yeah right, we shouldn't waste another minute and set off right away, alright?" said Ms. Franklin looking around to everyone.

"I forgot something inside." blurted out Stella trying to deceive.

"Yeah, let them go sit over and we'll be joining in." told Jacob.

"Alright." said Ms. Franklin agreeing, as she pointed to the car.

The two then walked to the car and got in fixing their positions.

"Who the hell called them?" demanded both Stella and Jacob creating a jinx, as the two turned around to face the others.

"I-I did." said Ms. Franklin in a confused tone due to the shock.

"So a bit of back story, Minsie and Lesohn were rumored to be dating in the first year of university as the pair got along quite well, which I had witnessed myself too but they never confirmed to the rumors. Then on the second year, due to some reasons Lesohn didn't appear to the university up until two and half months ago when he just suddenly showed up, and he was again getting along pretty well with Minsie, which was pretty crystal clear to whoever was observant." told Casey; explaining in detail while Ziezta listened fixedly to her and reacted accordingly.

"Why would you ask them to come over?!" asked Stella angrily.

"I mean I don't notice any problem in that." said Ms. Franklin.

"Continuing, the day before the trip we were thrilled to hear that the trip day was changed. Believe me, Minsie was celebrating, while us who wanted to go were sober, but to our delightfulness the trip day changed to that day. We were shocked to hear that but happily, not Minsie though, later I found out that she had planned to not even appear the next day; which was the day set for the trip but to her misfortune she was there and she had no choice but to go. We all went into the buses carrying our stuffs which we'd already been bringing for the previous three days. So Minsie and Lesohn were set to sit together, while Stacy and Jacob were set to sit together. To my pleasure, I was sitting with Eliott but I was actually set to sit elsewhere, but Minsie had asked to change seats with Stella, and Jacob had also asked to change seats, so it was arranged for Stacy to sit with Lesohn, Minsie to sit with Stella, and Eliott to sit with me…" said Casey nonchalantly smiling.

"There is! There are problems and it was important for you to discuss with us before asking them over, even if not me then at least the others…" cleared out Stella angrily in a quite loud tone.

"Okay, so I had instantly suspected that something was going on between Jacob, Stacy, Minsie and Lesohn, but I hadn't known what or why. Fast Forward to the end of the road trip; where everything was jolly with us but not with those four and surprisingly Stella didn't even have time to bother about Eliott sitting beside me… although it had sparked later on. Anyways so we got off the buses and we were told that we'll be staying in camps and each camp must have 5 and that the names were already listed…" said Casey glaring at Ziezta, sort of eye talking.

"Well, although I have no idea why you'd be saying all that; I seek apology from you all and sincerely request all of you to come to the car, cause this is no time for any of the idle quarrel we're getting into." said Ms. Franklin seeing the situation held.

Stella and Jacob walked with harsh steps in irritancy, while Dexzart walked normally thinking to himself how the situation was going to escalate; then; it seemed it wouldn't be near good.

"So, where're we heading to?" asked Stacy showcasing wariness.

"I've got some files retrieved from a friend of mine." told Stella.

"Oh, really?" blurted Dexzart in surprise as she hadn't told of it.

"Yeah, and those are investigation files, and there are some suspected places where they are thinking the cases have taken place, while there are also places where the dead bodies were found so I think it'll help…" said Stella explaining the contents.

"That is absolutely incredible of you!" complimented Stacy.

"So as you might've already guessed what the listing said, it read Stella, Minsie, Lesohn, Stacy and Jacob, quite like putting oil onto fire. I had seen the frowning on their faces which was weirdly delightful, so we were even told the places we were going to do the camping, and we were just instructed onto how we'll be carrying on the next steps. So we all went to our designated places and started putting up our tents, coincidentally my camp was set to be beside the five's camp, and trust me, it was hilarious how they had to attempt a thousand times before succeeding, and let me tell you it was not normal in anyway, they've been the best of the students." told Casey dramatically.

"So we can actually head to 5th Clevic Street." said Stella guiding.

"Yeah sure, we will be there in no time." assured Ms. Franklin.

"It is killing me to be in the same car as Eliott." thought Stella.

"Wish I was anywhere but in the place as Stacy." thought Jacob.

"Thank god, the two didn't blast in here." thought Ms. Franklin.

"Alright, so by the way, Eliott was in the same group as me and as you may already know that's definitely not what Stella would like to hear or see, but that time it didn't spark the bolt that much… Honestly, I do love Eliott cause I have nonchalantly fell for him and I had no intention in that, but I have never wanted to destroy what Stella and Eliott had or has. Anyways, we'll talk that out another time. I was about to go to for a moonwalk on the first night while I heard Stella and Minsie talking; from which I totally understood what had happened and it seemed saddening. Day or two passed just in the same mannerism, till that day when something quite unusual happened; Minsie got separated from her group, later it was known that it was because she was just trying to keep a distance from Lesohn…" paused Casey taking a sip of her coffee while Ziezta bit on her croissant.

"I think it'll be a good idea if you could let us quickly inspect Minsie's house so that we have some clues on the state of this hotrendous situation…" demanded Eliott in a keen mannerism.

"I do think that'll be alright, but be quick." agreed Ms. Franklin.

Ms. Franklin had instantly steered to the road to Minsie's place.

"Wait, how's the light up?" screamed Dexzart in terror as they were nearing the house; and it came at sight with the lights on.

"Umm, maybe, you forgot to turn them off." commented Stacy.

"No, I clearly have seen him turn each light off." told Jacob.

"Minsie was being chased by a tiger…" told Casey horrifying.

"Whoa what!" instantly commented Ziezta; horrified; hearing it.

"Do you think any burglar broke in or something?" asked Stacy.

They got off the car, walked to the house finding the door open.

14

THE CRYSTAL RAINDROPS

"Misses, I would unfortunately have to ask you to leave, as our shop is about to close as it is already closing time." told a staff.

"Really sorry for the inconvenience caused." apologized Casey.

"Why is the door open?!" frowned Dexzart in horror; instantly.

"I don't think it's any burglar or something." commented Stella.

"Yeah, seems like a pre-planned nuisance." said Ms. Franklin.

They all then slowly walked in, with much wariness, being quiet.

"Let's just go our ways for now, I'll meet you later." said Ziezta.

Casey had insisted Ziezta to come over to her house but Ziezta didn't agree, so they went their ways, waving byes to each other.

"You, here?!" screamed off Jacob in pure shock; entering there.

"Take a look at this file, it might quite be useful." said Jennifer.

Miss Winsent then caressingly took the file and started checking.

"Are you alright?" asked Stacy soothingly nearing the kitchen.

"What has happened?!" asked Jacob; horrified into the situation.

"Alright, now calm down…" said Eliott trying best to comfort.

"Yeah take a look over here this seems quite fishy." said Jennifer pointing at a part of the file with a finger indicating something, which Miss Winsent then closely & deeply analyzed for a while.

"Minsie?" said Stella in complete shock, as she ran fast towards the kitchen; deciding to comfort Minsie by giving a tight hug.

Minsie wasn't uttering a word as she was in absolute downpour.

"Good morning!" said Stacy placing the coffee beside Minsie.

"I've prepared you breakfast as well." told Stacy; gracefully smiling as she turned back facing Minsie after placing the coffee.

"How are you, Minsie?" asked Stacy; losing her smile, falling absolutely emotional, after all, they'd been friends; a long while.

"Things haven't been okay since a while, and I couldn't expect things to be any worse like now." told Minsie quite expressively; about to be crying, that was the first time she had spoken then.

"Yeah, it can be clearly seen how much you're going through, sorry if anything I have previously done wrong." said Stacy.

"I have done injustice to such a close friend and I can't be more shameful and sorry for that which I did." said Minsie desolately.

"It's alright, after all, if friends don't understand you then who would?" said Stacy smilingly reassuring that she will always be by her side no matter what; as a friend in need is a friend indeed.

Minsie fell sober, as tears filled up; showing the pain she had been holding in but one thing was up; that it wasn't just about a single thing but several, every tear revealed each wound she had been hiding, had scarred long ago, but kept off-sight for longer.

"Stella?" said Stacy approaching; quite fast paced, worried faced.

"Yes? Any problem?" asked Stella as she arranged the dishes.

"It's insane how things change, weeks ago Stacy and Minsie just hated each other over the events that occurred." thought Stella.

"Come to Minsie, she's literally drowning in tears!" told Stacy.

"Oh god. Badly again?" frowned Stella as she ran toward Minsie.

"Good morning." greeted Jennifer as she knocked on the door.

"Please bring yourself in." replied Miss Winsent smiling to greet.

"Thank you, so shall we continue?" asked Jennifer, walking in.

"Yes, of course, sit down first." told Miss Winsent, facing at her.

"See I've extracted some information and I need you to see anything that's following up." told Miss Winsent, as Jennifer sat.

Jennifer then took the files that Miss Winsent was handing her.

"Minsie, I'm urging for coffee so let's go grab up coffee, freshen up alright?" told Stella just after sometime of comforting Minsie.

Stella pulled Minsie off bed and helped get to the washroom and then left to change clothes herself after what she'll bring her car.

"Alright, do we tell the police about this or not?" asked Dexzart.

"I think not, first we've to let Minsie open up before informing the police, cause we have to first know what actually have had happened before we take any further actions." suggested Eliott.

"Yeah that's probably the right thing to do now." agreed Stacy.

"Alright then, let's just wait until she opens up, and not inform anything about this to the police." said Ms. Franklin; agreeing.

Stella then brought Minsie to the car and left to the coffee place.

"Can we have one Java Chip Mocha and a regular Frappuccino, and packets of Dipped Madeleines and Madeleines?" told Stella.

That order has been all-time favorite for both Stella & Minsie…

"Uh we shouldn't have told Minsie any of this." said the person.

"No it's good that we let her know or else she would've been in more pain than she's now." replied another person thoughtfully.

"See, you really have to tell me what happened." insisted Stella.

Minsie seemed pale and diverted in her own thoughts, thus she wasn't being that responsive and instantly fell into tears at times.

"Alright tell me later, but please do not cry." said Stella politely.

"My aunt." uttered Minsie a crying voice as she had been crying.

"Your aunt?" asked Stella softly; turning confused by the saying.

"Let's prepare Minsie a decorative dine at home." said Dexzart.

"Yeah, it's a good idea, we can work on it." replied Stacy in glee.

"So why not start off now?" said Ms. Franklin, facing smilingly.

Everyone started to think of what they'd be doing for the night.

"Shortly we'll have to visit these sites before anybody else reaches there." mentioned Miss Winsent in a commanding way.

"Yes, I absolutely agree." replied Jennifer looking deeper at it.

"Yes, my aunt; she is absolutely sick." told Minsie as she cried.

"Oh I see, I am really sorry for it, but could you tell me what exactly happened, why did you suddenly disappear, and where were you all this time?" asked Stella softly in a sad tone.

"I'd returned to the house, early that evening, but I didn't find you two, so I went to a place for some work. I had stopped at the red light, when suddenly a call popped up, and I was happy to see that name appear, so I joyfully picked up the phone. But, the voice instantly triggered me. It was sober. It wasn't the person whose name had appeared. I was fully shook; as I wasn't expecting such a sober voice, cause that person's mostly joyful, so I'd already got the wild guesses going. I instantly asked; 'Is everything alright?'. After a long pause, the person said that my aunt was… *battling death*. It gave me a series of shocks, and I fell into tears. I did not waste a minute and went to the airport, while on the way I bought the flight tickets. I just couldn't feel a breath of peace after hearing about my aunt. I was very much focused into that, so I hadn't even thought of telling anyone. I wasn't even able to handle myself. I had my whole face red from crying as I boarded the flight." told Minsie as tears poured off.

"Oh god…" said Stella sympathizing; deeply focusing to Minsie.

"Can I handle the decoration at the entrance?" asked Dexzarr.

"Ok, of course, let us know if you need help." said Ms. Franklin.

Ms. Franklin was preparing the savory items for dinner, while Jacob was preparing desserts for the night, Stacy had decided to decorate the dining space and the living room, Eliott had selected the theme and helped with planning the whole thing up.

"What?!" slightly screamed the person, hearing the other person.

"Yes, I myself was shocked that we hadn't known earlier; maybe we should go check on the issue?" suggested the other person.

"Yeah I'll call you when getting out." agreed the person rushing.

Wind was blowing in a soft manner, while birds flew chirping.

"Stacy, could you help me bring the flowers?" said Ms. Franklin.

Everyone over there had all their hands working enthusiastically.

"Umm what did you find when you reached there?" asked Stella.

"As I reached the airport over there, I found my cousin there waiting in her car for me, which made the journey even easier and faster. As I reached over to my aunt's house, I got out of the car running inside to my aunt's bedroom. When I entered the room. What I saw made me fall even worse. I saw my aunt sitting on the bed all pale, while previously she'd always been very beautiful indeed, but then at the moment she was looking ill, more ill than I had expected. I had never seen her face look that way. Her face was good at showcasing that she was indeed in her deathbed. But… she still had her smile put up widely as she saw me arriving. I can't explain how sober I felt at the moment. I had all the memories flashing up right in front of my eyes. Tears had filled my eyes, but I had put good effort in holding them in…" described Minsie falling into tears midway.

Stella patted Minsie on the shoulder showing sympathy, while hearing everything out in details brought tears up in Stella's eyes.

"When'll they be back?" asked Stacy doing her work fast paced.

"Hey, I am getting out now." told the person locking the door.

"Alright, I'll be getting out right away." replied the other person.

"I am not sure when they'll be back, but I assume it won't take long, so they'll be here any minute." told Ms. Franklin, hurrying.

"Umm, can we return now, please?" asked Minsie in uneasiness.

"Yeah, sure." said Stella grabbing their stuff as the two stood up.

The weather seemed rather gloomy; than pleasant or unpleasant.

"Hey." said the person waving as she finished parking her car.

"Hello." said the other person quite softly; getting out of his car.

The doorbell rang aloud, right as Stacy did the finishing touches.

"Turn the lights off." whispered Stacy, moving the ladder away.

Dexzart then tiptoed to the switchboard to turn all the lights off.

"Hi?" questioned the person from behind as he reached there.

When Minsie turned around followed by Stella, and the person stood while the other person who came with him just walked up beside him facing her purse putting the car-keys in and faced up.

"You?" saying he looked beside to face the other person and looked back at Minsie with a completely surprised reaction

"Yes, her." replied Stella softly in an entirely confused tone.

Meanwhile, Jacob had opened the door behind and he too stood completely confused and surprised seeing the entire weird scene.

"What?" asked Stacy confusedly as she walked to behind Jacob.

"I think you might want to check this file too." pointed Jennifer.

"Alright, get some follow up info about this one." replied Miss Winsent handing Jennifer a file while taking which she talked of.

"Did you people invite them over?" asked Stella as she looked inside at the decoration held in the open air as the light was on.

"Ah, We were here to find out about Minsie as we thought she had been missing, which we had found out earlier today." told Casey justifying, which explained a part of the confused scene.

"Yeah we're here for that;" said Lesohn "well, not are; were.".

"Oh…" sighed Minsie subtly diverting into her own thoughts.

All the people over there except of Lesohn and Casey were off the confusion; as Casey's statement explained why they were present there, why nobody knew and why this scene occurred…

Lesohn and Casey was later invited in by Ms. Franklin, as she appeared to the entrance and saw all them standing she had asked them to enter including Lesohn and Casey. Dexzart was already present there and then when Ms. Franklin asked to enter he had told them that to come in and they'll explain everything.

"Please, make yourselves easy." said Ms. Franklin handing juices.

"I am really confused, can someone explain, please?" said Casey.

"Umm Minsie suddenly appeared yesterday night." told Dexzart.

"No, actually she was at her aunt's place, because her aunt was severely sick, which she got to know all of a sudden." told Stella.

"That explains a lot…" blurted Eliott as their confusion got rid.

"Sad to hear about that." said Lesohn showing sympathy Minsie.

"Does he really care about me?" a thought hit Minsie instantly.

Everyone has sat down onto the dining table in order to have dinner; as Ms. Franklin had asked them to have it then. Most of them complimented the food; specially the desserts Jacob had made got a good amount of recognition. Afterwards they started to get up from the dining table; one by one, and took on drinks.

"So, do we inform the police about all this?" asked Stacy leaning back at the countertop sipping on a cool soft drink; facing Stella.

Moon was off to take leave as the Sun had started on it's entry.

"Uh, Minsie, you'll have to come, as to prove them." told Stella.

Minsie hadn't wanted to go, but Stella insisted as to prove to the police. The two had gotten inside the car leaving for the police station, after which Stella decided to go into a bookstore nearby.

"It's totally fine, we're glad to have served you." said the police.

Days have passed, things remained pretty much the same; Minsie was in sorrow, Stella was trying to help Minsie heal, Eliott and Stacy had been visiting quiet frequently for Minsie, Dexzart and Ms. Franklin were trying to keep up with everyone, and lately Lesohn and Casey were trying best to help out as well.

"Good morning, will be waiting in the car." said Stella peeking.

Going to Starbucks had gotten quite frequent as they loved to.

"Uh, a Java Chip Frappe and a Double Chocolaty Chip Crème Frappuccino, please." said Stella; as the only change they have been doing is going to different locations than one; far or near.

The two had thought of visiting a quiet faraway library that day.

"Let's go to that aisle." said Stella; pointing at one of the aisles.

"Minsie, are you alright?" asked Stella while they were looking at the books, but Stella faced Minsie from her side noticing tears.

"My aunt…" sobbed Minsie "after my parents died; when I was really young, my this maternal aunt fostered me, carresed me through each stage of my life, but I had done nothing for her, she was basically everything my mother would've been to me."

Hearing that instantly brought a load of crystal teardrops to Stella's eyes, as she hadn't known Minsie was an orphan on top of it; that that aunt on her verge of life is Minsie's foster mother.

"Trust me, I can't comprehend, but I can feel what you're going through, this is immensely difficult of a phase to be facing, all I can say is; sometimes you've to be tough to withstand such difficulties, even if it keeps striking you, you have to stay firm, I know it is verily hard but you have to stand it." told Stella with dreary weepy eyes as she couldn't hold but cry out all the crystal teardrops, as she gathered all the apt words to tell Minsie.

Stella helped Minsie get to the car as she was entirely dreary with all the thoughts seizing her mind. On the way to the car Stella had quickly picked up some books which'd be helpful to Minsie.

Stella herself was drearily teary after realizing what Minsie was going through; which to her felt immensely painful and hurting.

"Umm, Minsie why did you come back?" asked Stella nervously, after some time when things had settled down in their minds; hoping to not hear that her aunt had already passed away then.

"Ah," Minsie replied after a long pause "my cousins told me to."

"Huh!" confusedly exclaimed Stella, as she drove slowly "Why!"

"They believed I am sensitive and I wouldn't be able to tolerate if anything happened to my aunt, in front of me." told Minsie.

The evening had started to appear along with a guest; storm. It had covered most of the sky as it lightly rained crystal raindrops.

Stella and Minsie quickly walked to their porch as they stood there unlocking the door, while at the meantime a call loudly rang by Minsie's phone, for which she moved to answer the call.

At the very moment, Casey & Lesohn were slowly running up to the porch, in order to not get wet under the stormy dark sky.

Ms. Franklin hearing the knob moving; went up to the entrance.

The knob was stuck and Stella was trying the best to open the door, and just as she unlocked the door, there was a sudden noise to which she realized Minsie had fallen onto the ground, while it started to rain heavily as the storms roared piercing ears.

"Minsie!" screamed Lesohn as he & Casey quickly ran up to her.

Stella turned around, as she and Ms. Franklin too ran to Minsie.

15

THE TRANSITION

"Just leaving." said Minsie over the phone call as she exited her house stuffing her bag with the utmost essential items of hers.

Casey entered the lobby as she crashed into Eliott; accidentally.

"Oh here you are." said Stella as she saw Minsie walking to the entrance, where she was standing, and the two entered together.

Just as Stella entered inside, to her disturbance she found Casey and Eliott; eye locked, extremely closely stood by each other.

"Wow!" said Stella in a sharp, exotic tone of voice in irritancy.

"Wha-" Minsie began to say turning to see the two "Oh god."

The sky was fresh & brightly lit as the morning had just begun.

"Hello, everyone." said the professor as he entered in the class.

"He is the professor?" everyone in the classroom murmured.

"Did he newly join?" thoughts covered the entire classroom.

"Silence, please." said the professor "Let me clear out all of the confusion held in your heads by having seen me, is that alright."

Silence took over the classroom as all the students cooperated.

"Yes, I have newly joined the university and I have been swiftly assigned for psychology & literature." explained the professor.

Everybody got answered by one short sentence of information.

Stella and Minsie were walking to the cafeteria as their classes got dismissed. Stella had ignored seeing Casey & Eliott sticking to each other; as she had more valuable things to put focus on.

"Hello!" said Stacy as she, Eliott and Casey came to join them.

"Hello." greeted back Stella as she moved giving space for them.

"Good morning." said Jacob not noticing Stacy there with them.

The conflict amongst them seemed messed up; as Stella had no problem with Lesohn & Stacy but had with Eliott & Casey while Minsie & Jacob had problems with Lesohn & Stacy but not with Eliott & Casey although Minsie too didn't like Casey, for Stella.

"Hello, everyone." said Lesohn in a cheerful tone as he sat with them, putting a file onto the table, which was held in his hands.

"What was your last class?" asked Casey sipping onto her coffee.

They slowly began chatting amongst themselves; sipping coffee.

"Hi, I'm Nikert." said the new student approaching the other.

"Hello, I'm Xiwielle." told the other new student by courtesy.

"Freshman here?" asked Nikert in a soft tone; trying to confirm.

"Yeah, you too?" replied Xiwielle as she piled up all her binders.

"Yes, here for mostly literature…" replied Nikert accordingly.

"Oh wow, kinda same, ha-ha." said Xiwielle with a sound smile.

"Oh great!, so we'll be often meeting in classes." stated Nikert pointing funnily as he eyed Xiwielle raising an eyebrow; smiling.

The weather seemed to be cheerily chilled with soft wind blows.

"Hello, how are you?!" greeted Ziezta as she saw Casey pullover.

"I am alright, you?" replied Casey; smiling, as she got down.

"I am fine too!" answered Ziezta "By the way, I got you coffee."

"Good morning." greeted Jennifer as Miss Winsent entered in.

"Quite early today?" asked Miss Winsent; placing the documents onto the desk as she walked in to sit onto the chair by the desk.

"Actually, we have to perform an inspection to retrieve some of the information needed." pointed out Jennifer; a bit worriedly.

"Oh alright, show me the documents first." said Miss Winsent.

"Let's hear out the rest of the story?" requested Ziezta insisting.

"Oh yeah, alright. I was saying…" Casey started to say "Minsie was being chased by a tiger, which just as all of us noticed; we went immediately to that spot. You won't believe that tiger was not only a typical tiger usually seen; it was indescribably huge. Some of us earlier had wanted to go for rescuing Minsie, but right as we had a glimpse of it we all had gasped out of terror. Also we had immediately called for professional help but unfortunately it had said it'll take some time, and the picture held in front of our eyes was in an extreme condition which needed instant action or god forbid something immensely horrifying might have happened, which we didn't want at all."

"Oh god, that sounds terrifying." commented Ziezta; horrified.

"These are all of the documents." said Jennifer handing the last.

Miss Winsent took the file, as she checked onto the other files.

"Hello." greeted Stella as she and Minsie entered Minsie's home.

"Hi, how are you?" replied Dexzart as he lifted a cup of coffee.

"Yeah, I am fine, you?" said Stella closing the door behind her.

"By the way, there is something we've to talk about; later on, alright?" added Stella as she began to go upstairs after Minsie.

"Yeah alright, sure." replied Dexzart casually; sipping the coffee.

Stella walked upstairs while Dexzart sat by the kitchen counter.

"This book is actually nice, cause of the language it possesses is worth putting time upon, thanks for picking it up." said Minsie.

"It's fine, by the way, I told you it'll be a nice read." said Stella.

"Alright so," continued Casey after the short pause "we all were standing right there with our eyes locked onto the ongoing scene, we all were honestly horrified to even think what the next thing was about to happen, cause it was as if we were helpless."

"Listening to this, itself has me dying inside." expressed Ziezta.

"You know the most intriguing part about reading this book is?" said Minsie "This book pretty weirdly relates to our current life."

"Really?" replied Stella "Cause it sounds really weird to hear..."

"Oh, hello..." said Xiwielle as she noticed Nikert was there too.

"Hello, so we're meeting again.." replied Nikert enthusiastically.

"I guess so..." said Xiwielle as a smile fully brightened her face.

"By the way, what are you here for at this time?" asked Nikert.

"Oh, I believe exactly what you are here for." replied Xiwielle.

"So, you're here to talk with the management?" guessed Nikert.

"Yes, yes." said Xiwielle as she approved it as the correct guess.

"Nikert, please." a voice called out from there interrupting the two's spontaneous conversation which was flowing quite well.

"Sorry, I'll have to go." told Nikert as he started to walk there.

"Yeah sure, go ahead." said Xiwielle as she waited for her turn.

"Umm, ok so after all that we had been still waiting for the experts to come for rescue but at that point it felt it was too late. The tiger was right in front of Minsie to which it seemed that it was preparing for a rich lunch." continued Casey fixatedly at it.

"Do you know where we're supposed to go for the extra music classes that are held specially for the freshmen this year." asked the person approaching another, who was sitting over the end.

"Umm, I am also searching for that…" told the other person.

"Oh…mind if I join you up in that search?" asked the person.

"Of course not, though your name?" replied the other person.

"Kelvac, and yours?" answered Kelvac as they began walking.

"Oh, my name's Fiera." said Fiera as they walked to a signboard.

"Wait, let's see if this is the place." said Fiera noticing the board.

"Yeah," replied Kelvac following Fiera "also, cool name, huh."

"Oh thank you, yours is too." thanked Fiera, as she stopped.

Fiera and Kelvac then checked the board, and went inside there.

Casey and Ziezta had exited the coffee place they were situated at, and decided to go on a chill drive as they finish the story left.

"So let's put on some music?" suggested Casey as they got in.

"Yes sure, though put on something soft." said Ziezta; buckling.

"Yeah alright, I was thinking of putting that too." mentioned Casey; buckling up her seatbelt putting on the soft music radio.

"I also have something intriguing to tell about, after you finish." mentioned Ziezta while the music started playing by the radio.

The music was soothing and emotional, which surrounded the environment entirely; deeply conquering control to the hearts.

"Alright, as we stood at the verge of the scenario where either someone goes and saves Minsie, or she uses her last words. It was badly intriguing, it had me terrified to even witness that; but some of us were holding aback Stella while she was weeping as she denied to stay back and go save Minsie but unfortunately she had already been late to the scene and that too injured, so we couldn't at all let her go. For a moment, I decided to go seeing the situation I couldn't hold back and as I went three steps forward I saw something verily odd. It was someone. Someone was there. A guy had stepped up to there. He was there right between Minsie and the wild animal. I had a moment of utmost shock; seeing what I had, cause it was very brave to walk up to there. At the moment I had tried to remember any guy who would do that as not Eliott nor Jacob was there as they were the ones who went uptown to bring rescuers, so who was it? I had questioned myself and then I looked sharply at the guy to notice it was nobody else but Lesohn. Honestly, true love can never let you hold back grudges during a time of immense need. That bravery itself showed love can cause you to be selfless to another extent," descriptively told Casey as she drove, but her mind focused absolutely onto the happenings of that very day.

'Have you hurt someone someday? Or did they took you wrong? Have you ever tried to confront?..." played the song.

"Yes, what may I help you in?" asked the person from the end.

"Umm, do you happen to know about the extra music classes held for the freshmen of this year." asked Fiera assisting Kelvac.

"Minsie!" blurted Stella loudly "We've to go to the university."

"Oh…" said Minsie confusedly; hearing it suddenly "wait why!"

"I forgot something really important over there." told Stella.

The two ran up to the car quickly taking some necessary stuff along the way as Stella mentioned that the important thing must not be found by anyone, or else it'd be bad, so they stormed out.

It was afternoon, the weather was chilly and the sky's all ivory.

"Casey!, we should go fix this mess up before anything further takes place, cause see what you know; she doesn't, and if we are able to bring back something pure, which has been driven apart just cause of some absurd misunderstandings, then who can be any superior than us!" stated Ziezta firmly as she faced Casey.

"Yeah, you're verily right, we should hurry, I think." said Casey.

They steered back to the path leading towards all their houses.

"That was a pretty awkward scenario right there." said Kelvac.

"It really was, I believe." said Fiera as the two walked out slowly.

The two were peacefully walking towards the exit while two girls stormed inside, making them unbalance quirkily out of surprise.

"What the hell was that?!" blurted Fiera in absolute disturbance.

"Let's go check, maybe something's wrong." suggested Kelvac.

Fiera nodded as they quickly but controllably followed the two girls who had gone inside storming leaving low to no trace at all.

"Do you know where they can be?" asked Ziezta; rushing softly.

"I have no idea but we should go check first." suggested Casey.

Fiera and Kelvac were looking for the two as they happened to lose trace due the pace of the two, which indeed was verily wild.

"Oh god, let's go check." said Casey as they got down their car.

"How may I-" said Dexzart "Oh you... what brought you here?"

"Is Minsie here?" quickly asked the two storming into the house.

"Is there any problem?" asked Fiera as they found the two girls.

"Umm no, absolutely not." said Stella trying to hide the object.

"Actually we had forgotten something, so we came to take it from here." Minsie keeping things quite discreet but still weirdly.

"Oh. We actually saw you rush in, so we thought whether or not something was wrong, so we came to check." explained Kelvac.

"Oh, it's fine, thanks for intending to help." said Stella instantly.

"By the way, I am Fiera." told Fiera introducing herself to them.

"Ok, we can go check over there, alright." told Casey rushing.

A girl suddenly stormed into the room where Stella and the rest were situated. She sounded as if she had been running for days.

"Hey, hey," questioned Kelvac immediately "are you alright?"

"No listen, I have no idea where-" gasped the person suddenly.

"Oh god!" screamed Fiera as she immediately moved forward.

Casey and Ziezta just reached the university after hell of a rush.

The weather seemed to cool down as evening was approaching.

"Yes, hello." said Ms. Franklin receiving the call "Wait, what!"

"Hello," replied Jacob answering the phone call "immediately?"

Lesohn had just came home from some work after university.

"Hop in, quickly." said Jacob as he reached near Minsie's house.

"Oh, thanks for coming." said the person as he hopped inside.

Jacob seemed to be hurrying as he drove faster than ever before.

"Stella?!" exclaimed Ms. Franklin right as she entered over there.

"What happened!, why're you in a hospital?" asked Ms. Franklin.

"Stella?" called out another voice from the end approaching her.

"Wait, I'll explain." said Stella as she turned to see both of them.

"We're actually waiting for her consciousness to return." told Casey as she faced her side to notice them questioning about it.

"Wait, whose consciousness?" asked Dexzart in absolute horror.

"Umm, so what happened is we were in the university while out of nowhere a girl came storming, and she was just about to say something, but she gasped and fell to the ground as she fainted and so we immediately came here." explained Fiera thoroughly.

"Oh my god, ok that's pretty messed up." commented Jacob.

"Did she say anything at all, before she fainted?" asked Dexzart.

Kelvac and Fiera shook their heads signing to a no; at Dexzart, to which everyone over there sighed in worriedness and unease.

"Let's meet the doctors to see what they say." said Ms. Franklin.

"I just did." said Minsie as she came & joined the conversation.

"What'd they say?!" asked Jacob furiously in absolute eagerness.

"They asked us to wait here and they'll inform us." told Minsie.

Everyone were worried thinking what that would open them to, but they still had to have patience. Some of them stood there, while some sat down in twos including Jacob and Ms. Franklin.

"Life's so weird, right? Like it transits from here to there; sad to happy & happy to sad in no time." thought Ms. Franklin aloud.

"The transition of life is pretty absurd. It moves so quick that at times it's arduous for our minds to keep track." replied Jacob.

"Life's a risky rollercoaster; going through various phases, ups and downs, which you have no choice but to ride..." phrased Kelvac dramatically in a poetical tone, as he arrived with coffees in hand; in front of Ms. Franklin & Jacob, and joined their chat.

Hours were passing by, as they all waited there for information.

After quite some time; during the midnight, there was a call from a doctor, as they told that the girl had came back to consciousness, but not even a long while that she went back to unconsciousness with murmuring just a few words before going unconscious although the few words were enough to shock one.

"Should we call Stacy, Eliott & Lesohn?" asked Dexzart rushing.

Minsie had gestured a bitterly no; noticing which Casey instantly went to talk to Minsie about the things for which she was there.

"Minsie, may I have a moment with you?" insisted Casey tensed.

Hearing what Minsie was a bit weirded but she agreed and went.

"I have not much idea about your issue with Stacy and Lesohn, but I wanted you to know about which I have known." told Casey "I actually am in a mutual class with them and we were assigned for a project and they two were paired into a team..."

"A project?!" gasped Minsie in utmost shame, guilt and shock.

16

THE FORMATION

"Yes they'd been working at a project, and also Lesohn was the one for whom you are standing here; today…" told Casey softly.

"What do you mean?" asked Minsie, though still just as shocked.

"Umm…" said Casey pausing in the middle "he saved you from the verge of death, which you were at because of the wild tiger."

Minsie didn't utter another word, and dashed out of there in no time, which did surprise and brought suspicion to the remaining.

"What just happened?" asked Dexzart instantly in utter surprise.

The atmosphere was quite intense due to all of the happenings.

"Who could be here now, at this hour?" thought the person.

The doorbell was being rang vigorously which seemed strange.

"You! Here! Now?!" exclaimed the person in complete surprise.

The other person said no word but hugged him tightly, and fell into enormous tears which intensified things seizing the time.

"Minsie, are you alright?" asked Lesohn feeling too intimidated.

"I am really sorry for everything." uttered Minsie fully in tears.

"It's okay… but you don't have to be." told Lesohn patting her.

"I really love you, Lesohn." said Minsie as she drowned in tears.

"I-" hesitated Lesohn but said "I love you more than anything."

The moment seized as Minsie's tears poured heavily and Lesohn felt deeper in love with her, as he too started to deluge in tears.

"She isn't answering;" told Stella calling again "any of the calls."

Casey had wanted to tell but she didn't, cause Stella took charge.

"Good thing Ziezta is here, she'll help handle the rest." thought Casey; sighing in relief seeing Ziezta go over to Stella to tell her.

"But, Minsie was the only one who heard this girl." said Stella in a soft tensed voice, when Ziezta pleaded her to calm down a bit.

"I have a good news." told a person smilingly as she came there.

All of them sighed in relief and hurriedly went over to the room.

They all kept quiet as they slowly and silently entered the room.

"I have to go." pleaded the person helplessly as tears fell off her.

Fiera insisted and sat down beside the girl trying to comfort her.

"Miss, please don't cry," said Fiera, very selectively choosing the words "see, we're here to help, but you've to calm down & tell."

Hearing that, the girl tried to calm herself down from crying out.

"Think we should be hurrying." said Stacy seeing Eliott park by.

"Yes, I believe." said Eliott quickly getting off; shutting the car.

The two hurriedly walked towards the entrance, and into there.

"M-m-my nephew is missing." said the girl in quite a weak tone.

"And y-you know the news out nowadays, right?" added the girl.

"Yes, we do." gasped Fiera "I am afraid to ask, but since when?"

"I can't remember properly; even how I got here." said the girl.

"Let's contact the police." suggested Dexzart in a typical way.

"I had done that," told the girl "but they were taking too long."

"What should we do then?" a thought captured all their minds.

They all were called from outside to exit the patient's room.

"What happened?!" asked Stacy breathing heavily, as she came.

"You ok?" asked Stella confusedly "And who called you here?"

"Yeah, yeah, I am fine. And Dexzart did." told Stacy while Eliott arrived and all the others came out of the patient's room.

Stella looked back at Dexzart as she subtly signed asking why, to which he signed toward Ms. Franklin; meaning she had asked to.

Kelvac & Fiera started to explain Eliott & Stacy everything out.

"I'll be back." said Stella not particularly to anyone, and left off.

Stella accidentally bumped into someone exclaiming "You two!"

"That sounds like we have to do something!" exclaimed Eliott.

"Yeah us…" said Minsie feeling a bit awkward at the situation.

"We've to do something or else this'd be worsening." said Stacy.

Stella, Minsie & Lesohn arrived as they saw others sit worriedly.

"Oh, you are here." said Ms. Franklin seeing the trio come over.

The weather seemed misty as the clouds subtly covered the sky.

"I think we've to have a keen planning." pointed Miss Winsent.

"I believe; we must." stated Jennifer thinking deeper and deeper.

"Before that we've to go somewhere." mentioned Miss Winsent.

Jennifer nodded as she proceeded to ask where they'd be going.

"Are we the only people here?" asked Xiwielle as she walked in.

"Perhaps, maybe." opined Nikert as he walked in alongside her.

"Umm no there are two other persons." answered the professor.

"See, we've to do something about this; cause I am really done of hearing more and more news about more people having gone missing or found dead. Cause it's hurtful and shameful to hear all that; because we are to protect people and if we can't do the least act of protecting them; then we don't at all deserve to be here." said the person to the people there, in utmost frustration.

"Yes. I think we all can agree to that." replied one from there.

"Alright, we'll be having some new officers assigned with us on this particular mission, so that we can solve this more quickly. And I have designated a handful of tasks for each of us, but I would like you to check it and suggest any changes if needed." said the person in charge; quite politely trying his best to be nice.

They all understood that it was of immense hurt to find dead bodies lying around of all innocent people and not being able to stop it; even after so much time passing by and all the effort put

"A quest?!" exclaimed Minsie as the person shared their idea.

"Yes, a quest, which we could carry out by ourselves to solve this issue or sit down and watch people die." stressed out Fiera.

"We'll have to work a lot onto that." commented Stacy pointing.

"Yeah we must work on that thought, or else it'll be a matter of moments that we run into the webs." said Stella in a deeper way.

Thoughts started to capture everyone's mind after hearing Fiera.

All of them then sat down; thoroughly thinking about the idea.

"I actually totally agree with the idea." told Stacy as she stood.

"I think, I too agree to go for the idea." said Kelvac as he stood.

One by one; almost everyone agreed except particularly Jacob & Stella who were suffering through indecision as the two kept silent; sitting down noiselessly, while the others did opposite.

"I would love to volunteer to help save lives as people's lives are immensely precious; but not alongside Eliott…" thought Stella.

"I would like protecting the lives' at stake, but I am unable to do anything while I'm around Stacy." mourned Jacob in his mind.

"I have no idea what I should do; cause I can't go against my friend who has supported through my worst, but I also can't leave people by themselves to die." a thought captured Minsie.

"I must be deciding quickly or else it's going to be too damn late." thought Stella hastily as she stood taking the hardest steps.

A person literally threw Stella aside while she was hastily walking which triggered Stella when Stella noticed it was Casey Zyenkett.

"I'll be back." said Stella as she passed by the others right there.

Stella straightaway went to the bonny garden beside the hospital.

Stella had sat on an open bench, while a man sat beside her and approached, which actually seemed perfectly normal to Stella.

"Any problem miss?" asked the man as he sat positioning right.

"What do you do; when you are more than willing to serve for something good, but some personal stuff hold you back entirely; encapsulating you from doing the good?" Stella held a question, which indeed intrigued the man seeing the question's depth.

"Well, let me first state that it's a great question." said the man quite eager to answer "Life is pretty complicated, sometimes it puts you in those types of situation; where you can't let go nor let in. Trust me sometimes just for other fellow lives you have to jump into the ocean you've always feared to even walk beside."

Stella's main sufferance from indecision was because of Casey; the moment Casey walked past and she realized that Casey too was there; it triggered her more than anything previously did.

The sky tended to get mistier with time, but yet signed of clarity.

"The man's conveying was subtly of immense depth." thought Stella to herself as she walked in there with a bunch of thoughts.

"Thank goodness Stella's here." thought Minsie as Stella came.

"Hey, I-" Stella was about to say but a nurse came calling them.

Everybody had hastily went over to the place they got called by.

"Are you alright, now?" asked Kelvac as he entered in the room.

"Yeah, I think physically I am stable; now." told the girl "but perhaps not mentally and/or emotionally cause of the events."

"Listen, as we told earlier; we are more than willing to help so you have to keep going strong." told Ziezta leaning forward.

"We actually want you to open up, so that we're able to help you out; or else it'll be tough to help." told Jacob approaching softly.

The girl listened and nodded alongside, but she still was going through mental stress and anxiety thinking where her nephew was, what state was he in, whether or not he was scared, and etc.

"What's your name first?" asked Dexzart in very a keen manner.

The girl's words were enough to melt someone down absolutely.

"There's still time, but not everyone get's time." said Stella as she stopped right as they all walked out of that girl's room.

Everybody turned back glaring at Stella to complete her saying.

"I am absolutely onto this." declared Stella as it intensified stuff.

They all had surprised looks on their face as it came unexpected.

"I want to introduce you to our new team members; Stella and Mileyn, who'll be given much authority." announced the officer.

"Alright so; we'll have to have a keen plan first." told Dexzart.

"We have no idea what amount of time we have left on our hands, so we better hurry." commented Eliott as they sat down.

"Yes, right." said Lesohn "What I think we should first do is map out what we'll be doing in the quest, which will be helpful."

"Also, I think the first thing on our list should be writing down some questions that'll be needed throughout the quest," said Minsie putting up a keen thought "which we'll ask Giwelyev."

"Yes that is a keen idea," said Kelvac "we should definitely work on it as it is quite essential to know some stuffs before we start."

They all sat down sipping coffee, as they gave out their thoughts onto the quest they'll be carrying out within a very short while.

Things were quite intense at that point as seriousness increased.

"It's insane how things change so quickly…" told the person.

"But no matter how far you've travelled, the titbits of the past can still sometimes cover the sky up-head." said the other person; meaning it in a deeper context; quite the confusing one.

"True," said the person "and it rains heavily when there are some particular clouds; seeing which tends to brings you to the passed times that were either immensely awful or awesome."

Eliott reached his house just a few moments ago. He picked out a book off the shelf where his collection existed quite organized.

"We've been through storms, tangling through the sparse lands of groundcovers; holding us back..." sang Nikert playing the piano as Xiwielle played both the part of the audience and aide.

Stella sat by the wide window of her room, giving sight to the starry sky, as she thought of how adverse life was and could be.

"I know this has been rough." sang aloud Nikert rhythmically as he caught up the melody "Is that why it has always felt tough."

Fiera sat down by the piano in her hallway as she began to sing.

"I can sense the breeze." sang Fiera melodically; playing the piano "Like we used to feel the tingles; run up our sleeves..."

Casey leaned onto the chair as she positioned herself into the world where fairytales existed, and all the things she had ever pictured before started coming to life as she set her eyes closed.

"Were we able to confess, had it ever been easy cause where have we been all along..." sang Nikert as music took over.

"Now it's a turning point of the voyage held." thought Minsie.

"When it ends, will we be blissed or displeased?" rendered Fiera.

"Life can get tough, but it can never feel tougher when things end but the memories still live." thought Stella staring at the sky.

"Is this the end, will it ever conclude happily?" sang Nikert as his eyes filled with tears which through melodies was expressed.

"Stepping into the woods she felt breeze take over." read Eliott.

"How can we ever forget; the moments, which still torments… why have we been through them?" melodically sang Fiera softly.

Casey's imagination rose to be orthodox as it took over reality.

"Why'd we have to always imagine? Why can't it ever be all true? Why?" sang Nikert as the volume rose accordingly to the music.

"As she went deeper into the woods; she felt the wind blow and the sky chant, to which she thought whether it'll be storming or raining." read the book held at Eliott's hands as he dived into it.

"Will tranquility be the end, or will it be belligerent?" sang Fiera.

The music felt more than pleasant and the accompanying of the wind had created the perfect tranquil & emotional environment.

The birds were chirping as they flew in the misty skies overhead.

"Good morning." said Stella as she just arrived at the hospital.

Everybody else greeted her back as she went over joining them.

"We're short on time." mentioned Dexzart as he too sat down.

"Yes, we are, so I think that let's go ask some useful questions that come up to our minds now, to that girl." suggested Jacob.

"Yes, I think so too, but let's first just suggest some questions before going and asking them to her, alright?" advised Minsie.

"What's her nephew's education institution?" suggested Fiera.

"Who's her nephew's parents and where they are?" said Eliott.

"Where she last saw him or where he was supposed to be at and whether or not he wasn't?" suggested Lesohn quite thoughtfully.

"What he likes to do or go and etc." suggested Kelvac confused.

"Ask her to give us her nephew's photo, what's his name, what's his age and etc." said Casey keenly as she looked onto the mere but most useful basics that they'll verily need for their quest.

"Just to clear things out with you all, the quest isn't only about finding the girl's nephew, but it is also to find the cause of all the people going missing and saving all of them." pointed out Stella.

"Yeah, you're right, but these information about the girl's nephew might lead us to the main reason of the people going missing and being found dead." explained Kelvac quite keenly.

"Not only that, our first lookout should be for the girl's nephew cause we definitely don't want him dead." said Fiera softening.

"There isn't much time, he is gone missing for quite a long while so we should actually hurry!" pointed out Minsie gesturing that they should go right away to ask the things and start the search.

"Listen, Stella would be the main guide for this mission as that is what the authority has asked for." informed the person for the rest to obey Stella's upcoming orders on the mission they held.

"I hope I am able to carry out this honour properly and I respectfully seek apology in advance if I make any offense to any person within our team and for any mistakes." mentioned Stella.

"And I'll have to unfortunately announce my leave for the rest of the mission as I have some other urgencies." told the person.

Casey and the rest proceeded to go to the girl to ask their questions and had decided they'd act onto the quest immediately after the questions have been answered; as they're short on time.

"May we go into the patient's room?" asked Fiera quite politely.

The nurse turned as she told something that none had expected.

17

The Quest

"What?!" Stella let out a slight scream as the shock took over.

"What do you mean she left?" demanded Jacob immediately.

"She had left earlier this morning, as she had shown gradual improvement in her health; the doctor didn't restrict her leave either." mentioned the nurse, continuing to do her own work.

"How can that happen?" asked Fiera in horror, to the others.

Some of the other visitors stared at them confusedly as the amusement of suspense took over as they felt eager to know the rest of the story as in how the situation rose to its current state, which indeed rose some questions which're to be fully avoided.

"I'm still just as mortified getting to know that." declared Casey.

"It is mortifying to hear such a thing in such a way." said Fiera.

"Ok, let's open the note she had left for us?" requested Dexzart.

"Dear helpers, thank you very much for helping, I won't lie I· desired any sort of help and was glad to find yours." read Stella.

They drove through the mountainous roads under the light rain.

"Continue, what happened?" questioned Fiera cause Stella had stopped in the middle of reading as she was glaring at the note.

Stella passed the note putting her hand to the behind, which was a simple gesture asking someone else to take it and read instead. Casey took and passed it back to Fiera as she asked to volunteer.

"I am sorry having to tell this, but I'll have to leave cause I can no more sit back and watch, however if you actually will and go to really help out on this search then you'll find me along the way as I'll be on the similar if not same; path." read Fiera aloud.

"That makes me wonder whether it was a good idea to split into two different groups for two different purposes or not." said Dexzart in a soft timid voice as surprise took over all of them.

"According to our base plan, let's first go to Meleander's, okay?" said Jacob as he read onto a note with the raw plan they'd made.

"Yes, I believe they'll be able to give us some info." said Kelvac.

"I am pretty sure; Kelvac and the rest are astute enough to go by the plan while redesigning it along, don't worry they'll be just fine. Also, if we cross our paths then we'll have them join us." said Casey in an assuring tone to her absolutely silent audience.

Silence portrayed their confusion and unsureness on the matter.

"Hello, may we ask some questions?" asked Lesohn, stepping in.

"Umm, sure. Follow me." replied the lady as she started walking.

"Do you think it'll be alright?" whispered Minsie within the five.

The other four nodded while they walked by; following the lady.

"So how far are we from Devlic Highs?" asked Casey tilting out.

"I believe we're pretty close." told Fiera as she held the map up.

"Wait, wait, stop!" slightly yelled Stella looking out the window.

Everybody got confused and looked where Stella was staring at.

"Oh, god!" said Casey as she quickly unlocked the car door getting off while others gasped watching her get off ferociously.

Seeing Casey get off despite of being detained by them, Dexzart quickly got off followed by Fiera and the rest in a hurtling way.

"Casey don't go any near!" commanded Dexzart nearing Casey.

"Miss, we wanted to ask you some questions." said Minsie as she knocked onto the open door while the others stood behind.

"Yes, please come in." replied the lady, staring at a document.

"Omg, are you okay?" said Fiera following down towards Casey.

As they got down astonishment took over in utter incredulity as they instantly put their hands over their slightly opened mouths.

There was a moment of absolute silence due to the utter shock, after which Dexzart quickly grabbed Casey dragging her out of there as his senses came back, a moment later the rest followed.

"What brought you up here?" asked the lady facing up at them.

"Do you know the Ennocels?" asked Lesohn sitting down stilly.

"Perhaps you mean Giwelyev Ennocel?" said the lady squinting.

"Yes, yes we do." said Minsie aloud immediately in sort of relief.

"We wanted to know few details about her." added Jacob softly.

The lady looked back up; giving a soft expression of surprise.

"What'd I just see?" said Stella in a pale tone due to the trauma.

"I didn't at all expect that." worded Fiera keeping the pale tone.

Others talked even if little about the thing but Casey kept silent.

"Too bad, we couldn't retrieve information." said Stacy walking.

"Now, do we have any other targeted places from where there is a higher certainty of retrieving info?" asked Minsie as wind blew her hair strengthfully while the five were walking up to the car.

"We've to put our minds into thinking…" replied Jacob sharply.

The sky was hazy while it lightly rained in the mountainous sites.

"Have we reached Devlic Highs?" asked Casey sounding empty.

"Yes, we have reached but it'll take a min to park." said Dexzart.

"Perhaps, we can take rest then." suggested Fiera not mindfully.

"I believe we're running out of time." stated Casey in a harsh manner, as she hastily unlocked the car door readying to get out.

Fiera got frightened by that behaviour; realizing she was wrong.

"Are you sure?" asked Kelvac as the five stood outside a door.

Everyone else nodded, seeing which he rang the doorbell slowly.

"How may I help?" asked the person as she held the door open.

"We really need you to do us a favor." said Lesohn persuasively.

"And what sort of favor?" demanded the lady all of an instance.

"Will it be safe to go?" asked Dexzart as they neared the place.

"We have no other choice." pointed Stella speculating the place.

Stella and others silently stepped in; one after the other. As they entered they could hear the creaky wooden floor and see few spider webs, while it stood absolutely dark, as everything seemed to disappear into the dark; more and more they went into there.

"Really?" said the lady in surprise to the fact that they really reached up to her asking for help on such a thing; just as the five were done explaining what of a favor they had needed from her.

"Yes, please, if you don't help us at this then the lives at stake will have no chance of being saved." requested Kelvac urging.

"I understand, but how may I trust you when you're asking me to not inform the police about any of this?" demanded the lady.

"See if we were to lie; we could've just more than easily acted to be police personnel and come up to you…" said Minsie "but we did not, we chose to come up to you being just brutally honest."

"You have a point and you're more than polite, so I shall agree," said the lady "but I'll put up a deal; you've to sign some papers."

"Follow me." said Casey taking the lead as she had the best night vision, which enabled them to go in there with ease at not alerting of their arrival which flashlights verily would have done.

"Not a single noise as we proceed." whispered Eliott ordering.

Everyone nodded as they continued tiptoeing into the building.

"Yes, Giwelyev Ennocel." replied Jacob as the lady questioned.

The five had signed on a simple contract, which said that they'd asked or rather persuaded the lady for the info for good means, but if any mishappening occurs then they'll be held responsible, which they unhesitatingly had agreed and signed onto to actuate.

"That seems quite skeptical." said Kelvac as they drove through.

"It does if seen in the basic view but if you look at it in a more critical way then it makes more than just sense." added Minsie.

Minsie and the rest were at the midst of popping deep thoughts.

Casey gasped putting her hands on her mouth saying "Oh god!"

"What happened?" said Fiera walking up to behind Casey, followed by the rest as they all gasped in absolute astonishment.

"What a mess..." opined Dexzart whispering "people must have taken shelter over here that tells we have to be more cautious."

"Check quietly if you can find any clues over here." asked Stella.

Everyone nodded as they immediately went checking onto stuff.

The room looked as if someone had stayed there recently, but it was noticeable that the stay have had been temporary in order to take shelter during the night, which made stuff more mysterious.

"She was literally a pianist quite renowned." pointed out Stacy.

"But only known by her name and not appearance." said Minsie.

"Could the missing of her nephew be connected to her métier?" Lesohn raised a question into all their minds as it led to theories.

"That could explain a lot but not with certainty." opined Kelvac.

"True, so why not let's find more info about her métier by using the info being seized in our hands?" suggested Stacy teasingly.

Everyone glared at Stacy as minds brewed out various thoughts.

"Should we go check out the rest of the place?" asked Dexzart.

"Sure, but be careful & vigilant, and most of all do not make any sort of sound while keeping an eye for any prowlers." said Stella.

Dexzart and Fiera noted as they went in and about the building.

"I think visiting any institution she had before performed would be a good idea..." suggested Jacob although he thought deeper.

"Actually, but we'll have to search one first." mentioned Kelvac.

"We can dig up newspapers for any articles about Giwelyev..." pointed out Minsie as the others amused the idea she had given.

"Have we reached the attic?" whispered Dexzart as the two suddenly stopped constantly climbing the wide creaky stairs.

"I suppose…" said Fiera "cause it's been forever on the stairs."

"Keep an eye for watch." told Dexzart as they went in tiptoeing.

Fiera nodded as the two went onto opposite sides of the place.

"Do we have to wait till the morning?" asked Kelvac sighing off.

"Not at all, I have an aunt who is obsessed with musicians, and she keeps newspapers which mostly contains information about musicians, which may also include pianists." told Jacob instantly.

"Oh great!, but are the newspapers of date?" questioned Minsie.

"She has all newspapers ranging from the first day of earth up till now…" said Jacob figuratively as the others sighed in relief.

Kelvac began driving right as he was told the address by Jacob.

"Fiera, quick, come take a look at it." called Dexzart whispering.

"What the hell?!" exclaimed Fiera as her eyes widened in shock.

"Come with me, right now!" commanded Casey as she came running; breathing heavily, to where Stella and Eliott were inspecting the things; hearing which the two turned around to face Casey then looked at each other as they quickly went over.

"Do you happen to know Giwelyev Ennocel?" asked Jacob as all of the five were looking throughout a pile of recent and ancient newspapers, sat beside even more piles of newspapers.

"Giwelyev Ennocel…?" said Jacob's aunt as she tried to recall.

"Yes I do, and I also have some articles talking about her; she's a really good pianist and quite renowned." replied Jacob's aunt.

Jacob's aunt went over to a specific part of the newspaper piles.

"Stella, look at this." said Dexzart as he ran getting off the stairs.

Stella, Eliott and Casey instantly looked to their side where Dexzart and Fiera came from; hearing Dexzart's loud whisper.

"What? A ukulele?" responded Stella as she noticed Dexzart had a ukulele in his hands while Fiera carried a bag along with her.

"Yes..." said Fiera a bit hesitatingly as the two reached the three.

"Although it's just a ukulele, this place doesn't seem like a place to have a brand new one..." pointed out Dexzart widening eyes.

"That seems quite unusual..." said Eliott instantly as he heard

"Like who might have had a need to bring a ukulele up to this place or even anywhere in Devlic Highs." opined Fiera seriously.

"You people, have look at this, this is stranger than what your mind must be capable of taking now." ordered Casey loudening.

The four others turned around to face Casey moving slightly forward to see something they weren't prepared for at that time.

"Do you think it'll be open now?" asked Stacy getting in the car.

"I believe it's nearing the closing hour but let's try." said Kelvac.

"Is h-he d-dead?!" shuddered Stella as the four backed to senses.

"I have no idea..." swallowed Casey enclosing her lips in terror.

Eliott bent down to take a look at the body checking if it's dead.

"How long till we reach there, cause time's passing fast?" asked Stacy as some of the others too gestured agreeing to her query.

"We're about there, don't worry." assured Kelvac immediately.

The others sighed in relief hearing Kelvac and sat back waiting.

"Could the ukulele have anything to do with this person?" asked Fiera as they checked onto the body bending down; examining.

The others shrugged gesturing that they didn't know if or if not.

"Seems like someone had been here before us." said a lady in a harsh tone as she let go of a thing in her hand verily in irritancy.

"Can you please drive faster…" requested Stella as they tried to bring the body back to consciousness but kept failing to do so, which brought increment to their panic due to the uncertainty of whether the person was alive or was their body laid without life.

The atmosphere seemed quite panicking as tension rose all over.

"We need information about Giwelyev Ennocel." told Lesohn.

"I sure would have given but you're no police." replied the lady.

"We are sort of what private detectives are; to whom you would have given the information almost immediately." argued Stacy.

"We can guarantee you that there won't be anything harmful done by retrieving these information." offered Minsie coaxing.

"And how do you mean to do that? questioned the lady intently.

The five then explained that they could sign onto an agreement.

"Emergency!" screamed Stella as they reached the hospital; after which the hospital crew came out rushing to take the body over.

"Put on the oxygen mask quickly!" told a crew to another one.

"Put the thermometer and check the temperature." told a crew.

The scenario over there was full of panic and rush as the focus went onto the patient and all the surrounding felt absolute silent.

"Alright then, I agree to give you information." said the lady signing the paper and the others sighed in relief but not totally.

"Can you start by telling us basic details on Giwelyev Ennocel?" requested Kelvac, as all of the five went onto analyzing each and every word of hers to retrieve any sort of clue that'd help find.

The lady started to tell out basic details about Giwelyev, as she gradually escalated to tell intriguing information about Giwelyev.

"Ma'am, you'll have to stay outside as only hospital's crews are allowed to go inside, please accommodate." said a hospital crew.

The five nodded as the crew went into the room with the body.

"Pressurized?" blurted out Stacy as they frowned hearing things.

"That is substantially cruel." commented Minsie as she shook.

The lady continued; reacting with just facial expression to them.

The five were hearing stuffs they hadn't at all expected to hear.

The five noted down every important point said; in there heads.

"That was bizarre!" said Stacy loudening as they got in their car.

"Ok as to what she had said; I think we must be heading to our next destination." pointed out Minsie as she sat in buckling up.

The weather still remained misty although the rain had stopped.

"Did you hear him say any thing before he went unconscious?" asked Fiera as they stood dreaded outside the room with no sign of any crew or any information about the person they'd brought.

"He didn't go unconscious in front of me…" said Casey loudly.

18

The Traces

"Immediately?" asked Minsie frowning; over sudden phone call.

Everyone else stared at Minsie; eagerly listening to what she said.

"They have asked us to go over to where they are." told Minsie in a pretty worried tone as the others got worried by seeing her.

"Is there any complication?" asked Lesohn resting his hands on Minsie's shoulder giving her company while the others set their attention towards Minsie as it seemed the news wasn't too good.

Previously, Minsie and the other four with her had went onto a place the lady had talked about; in order to retrieve information.

As they had reached the place, it had seemed quite shady to the five, so they had decided to subtly go over to the place; as they had felt the absolute need of that subtleness in order to proceed.

Minsie had said when the door had opened "Hi, Ms. Twenfizel!"

"How may I help?" had asked the lady in an irritated way which had triggered Minsie a bit but she had ignored; as they had to be as subtle as possible during the process of that part of the quest.

"You must know; Giwelyev?" had asked Lesohn backing up her.

"Yes, but what about her?" had replied the lady almost instantly.

"We're her acquaintance and she had asked us to help her out." had said Minsie quite subtly carrying out right as to the planning.

The twos actions had seemed as if they'd been wanting to sit in and talk to the lady, so she'd asked them to enter, before she'd continued the conversation as an act of courtesy and etiquette.

Minsie and Lesohn had instantly agreed onto going in; as they had been trying to get in; in order to accomplish their mission.

"Hopefully we'll succeed on this mission." had thought Minsie.

Meanwhile, Stella and the rest along with her had been worriedly waiting outside the operation theatre eagerly wanting to know what'd been happening inside there but silence had felt louder.

"Would he be dead or was he already?" had questioned Dexzart in immense horror on his face as he had faced the room infront.

"I can't tell if he'd survive, but I am pretty sure he was alive as if he wasn't then they would've told us on arrival." had told Casey.

Nikert had sat by the piano as he had started to sing "Maybe you are at a place where you feel unsafe, but you have to believe you'll be facing tranquility soon, but no matter how long it takes you've to keep the faith in yourself; no matter how tough it is."

The soft melody had felt melancholy but still quite guaranteeing.

Dexzart and the others had felt sober hearing Casey's statement about the person being alive but uncertain about continuing to.

"Things get rough, but you'll have to keep holding strong." had sang Nikert soothingly as the harmony had took over the place.

Minsie and Lesohn had been acting absolutely like a couple; in order to make the lady think they had been just casually there & not for any sort of inspection, which they actually had went for.

The lady had owned a musical institution designated to minors.

Minsie had been noting the lady's actions since her appearance.

"I feel like we're doing something wrong." had said Stacy softly.

"Don't think it that way, cause we're doing this just to save lives and nothing other than that." Kelvac had reassured; getting in.

"Start searching; right away." had led Jacob analyzing the room.

Stacy and the two had sneaked into that lady's house in order to get information without being noticed by staying totally discreet.

The three have had separated by going searching onto three different sections while keeping conscious not to make sound.

"Be sure to carefully inspect each and everything and also put everything back into place the exact way it was." had told Jacob.

"Alright, this is gonna be a tough task…" had thought Kelvac as he'd started, at first he'd analyzed how it was kept in order to be able to put them back right where it had been before touching it.

Each one of them had been observant while caressing the stuffs.

"These are some details on some sort of group plan." had said Stacy to herself "how would this have anything to do with him."

"Oh, a diary." had thought Kelvac as he had found and dusted a diary written by someone probably taking classes in that place.

The three were quite keen onto doing their job over in the place.

The three had seemed to find a lot of stuff over there which had felt confusing as if whether or not that had been a clue, cause some had felt very much like a clue but then it hadn't been one.

Stacy had seemed to look onto everything spreading them out as she had been putting out the stuffs one by one checking it quick.

Jacob had been taking out only some of the objects which he'd felt that it had needed further inspection or had been a real clue.

Kelvac had been doing his part quite organized as he had been checking one thoroughly and putting back if it hadn't felt a clue.

"I feel like I heard something…" had blurted the lady off-topic.

Lesohn and Minsie had eyed one another in despair biting lips.

Casey have had found something quite too absurd not to be of importance, for which she had immediately taken it and as she had been about to go show to the others she had tripped onto an object creating a sound; not too loud nor too soft either.

"Oh god, what'll happen now?" had thought Minsie sobbing in.

"What, what sound…" had said Lesohn tensely; trying to make the lady believe that there had been no sign of any sound at all.

The lady had faced upwards saying "No, I feel like there was…"

"N-no, I haven't heard a single thing." had told Minsie quickly.

"Are you sure?" had said the lady getting up "I think I should go up and check, you two can remain seated and I'll be back soon."

"Oh gosh, we'll be dead if she finds them." had thought Minsie.

Minsie had eyed Lesohn subtly signing asking what they should be doing next in order to not had gotten caught by the lady.

Lesohn had shrugged subtly; gesturing that he had no idea what.

Two of them had felt as if they had been dying or about to had.

The group of five had been at stake to have gotten caught then and there which would have meant them failing their full quest.

All out of a sudden; there was a very loud banging sound which had came from behind the lady while she had been walking to the staircase in order to go upstairs and check to clear doubts.

Stella and rest had been eagerly waiting for any news from the hospital crew about the person; but they hadn't gotten any at all.

Each and every passing moment for the five had been feeling like a honed knife being kept at their neck, with pure uncertainty of when and whether or not the knife would had been struck.

The minds of the five had been absolutely dull due to tension.

They had sat right outside the room fixedly staring at the room.

"Stella… Is Ms. Stella here?" had called a hospital crew; exiting.

"Stella they're calling for us I think." had said Fiera immediately.

The five had quickly got up as they had rushed toward the crew.

"Yes me, I am Stella." had said Stella as she had put her lips in and out in nervousness reaching in front of the crew over there.

"Oh alright, umm…" had said the hospital crew "the boy you had brought in an urgent medical need is happily out of danger."

They all sighed in relief, but the crew hadn't seemed to be quite jovial which they normally should have been; and that had triggered the five cause they almost immediately had known that not everything had been alright so the news hadn't been for joy.

"Is everything alright?" had asked Dexzart turning a bit worried.

"Umm.. " had said the hospital crew "yes, but the thing is that the patient isn't conscious yet and will take quite some time to get back to consciousness which isn't to be too stressed about."

"Oh…" had blurted Fiera as her voice had softened in shock.

The others too had been astonished as the news had uplifted them but suddenly had also down-lifted them in just a matter of mere minutes which had seemed quite sentimentally brutal.

"Do you feel better?" had asked the lady softly; facing at Minsie.

"I'll be fine, it's alright." had said Minsie hinting it hadn't been fine, but also keeping the politeness of not totally worrying her.

Minsie have had slipped over a spill of some sort of liquid on the ground and that have had created a loud banging noise, and the lady have had turned around and have had came running to help seeing which Lesohn have had felt both very good and bad; as he have had known that if Minsie haven't had fallen then the lady would've had already gone upstairs and caught the others.

Minsie have had been laid down onto the couch while the lady have had gone to bring up a first-aid kit, while Lesohn have had been patting on Minsie's shoulder and eying signing to being safe as the others haven't had been caught by the lady then.

"Did it hurt too bad?" have had asked Lesohn sympathetically.

"Anything for the mission." have had whispered Minsie smiling.

The lady have had been walking back toward Lesohn and Minsie carrying the first-aid box she had gone to bring for Minsie's scar.

"Thank you." have had said Lesohn seeing her arrive to there.

"Not to mention." have had said the lady sitting besides Minsie.

"I think tea had been spilt by someone." had guessed the lady.

"Yeah probably." had said Lesohn; jumping in glee in his mind.

"Thank god they hadn't heard us." had whispered Stacy sighing.

"But we'll have to be more cautious now." had opined Kelvac.

"Yes right." had said Jacob, and as he had said it a music book had fallen off his hands and the three had stared at each other.

"You know what, I'll go and check upstairs as I think something is wrong." had said the lady as she'd gotten up, and had started walking towards the stairs in a quite fast pace and sly suspicion.

"Oh no! Please don't go!" had shouted Minsie in her head; cause if it had been said aloud then it'd have had made her suspicious.

Lesohn had looked at Minsie making a face of feeling failure.

Minsie had managed to get up softly and had poked Lesohn; for him and her to go follow the lady as that'd had been less killing.

The two had rushed onto catching up with the lady's pace; while she had already gone midway on the staircase quite quickening.

"Oh no!, I hear footsteps probably on the stairs towards us!" had said Stacy in absolute horror while the rest cried in despair.

"Uh, you two could've stayed aback." had said the lady smiling.

"No, it's fine." had said Lesohn trying his best to sound normal.

To their fortune the staircase was quite lengthy; so it took time to climb up all the way to the top where the sound had came by.

"What do we do?" had thought Minsie while climbing the stairs.

The more they had been nearing the place, the more it had felt despair & sensed failure to complete the mission; nearing them.

"We have to do something!" had whispered Stacy in full tension.

"Yeah!, or else we will get caught!" had exclaimed Kelvac flying.

"Can't think of anything! Omg!" had said Jacob hitting his head.

The three had by then completed climbing up the stairs and had been standing right outside of the room as the lady had been about to open door and go in to find Stacy and the others there.

"Should we be waiting here?" had said Fiera looking at others.

"Yes, maybe…" had opined Dexzart tilting his head to the side.

The five had been still seated in front of the person's room as the crews had been preparing to shift the person to another one.

"I think we should go continue onto our quest." had said Eliott.

"But how can we leave this person on his deathbed?" had demanded Stella sounding a bit sober due to being sympathized.

"But there might be more people out their battling death and if we stay back for one person then they'll die." had argued Casey.

"I think Casey has a point." had commented Fiera breathing in.

"But what if there is none out there, and while we might be of any help this person needs and later we find him death because we weren't here to help…" had said Dexzart sympathetically.

Stella and Dexzart had been sober ever since they had seen the person in that condition and had felt quite sympathized at them.

"See Stella & Dexzart, I understand, and it's normal to be quite sympathized towards the injured, but this isn't the hour of being sympathized rather it's the hour of being fierce." had told Fiera.

"Yeah, Fiera is absolutely right cause we need to destroy this issue from its roots and not a stem after the other, cause it will regrow in no time; and never end." had explained Eliott softly.

"And don't forget we were here to do that, and not the latter which the police too are doing and that's which had us bugged." had mentioned Casey quite piercing right into the twos mind.

The two had been looking down as they had dived into their own thoughts, while the others had been waiting for their reply.

"I think it's about time we leave." had said Minsie with a smile.

They have had been on the top floor where they had been about to be caught; when Lesohn and Minsie have had clenched their teeth in absolute horror but the lady have had opened the door seeing which Lesohn and Minsie have had closed their eyes.

The lady have had entered the room after opening the door, and she have had went in; to check, which have had put Minsie and Lesohn a bit in relief, but they knew that wasn't it, it'd felt more and more panicking the more the lady went in and checked onto thoroughly with each time a place she have had started to check feeling like a knife being put on their necks and each time she haven't had found anything feeling like the knife being put away.

That have had continued for a while, up until the last spot left where Minsie and Lesohn have had their eyes set on as the lady have had proceeded to check and the panic have had took over, but then to their surprise the lady have had turned around facing the two as she have had proceeded to tell that she had been done and that there haven't had been anybody in there.

Lesohn and Minsie have had been astonished to hear that lady; but also happy thinking that they have had been fortunately safe.

The three then have had been climbing downstairs all in relief but for two different reasons & not one reason; very unusually.

"Come on, stay for awhile." had said the lady showing courtesy.

"Yeah, we would have loved to, but it's getting late." had said Minsie in a soft and polite tone while Lesohn had been nodding.

"We didn't even have a proper conversation." had said the lady.

"It's alright, we'll come again sometime; to have one." had said Minsie letting out a little laugh while the others too had smiled.

Stella and Dexzart have had been convinced to go and then had been going towards the parking lot where their car had been at.

"I think going right away was the right decision." had said Fiera.

"Yes, absolutely…" had replied Casey as she had been walking.

The five had reached their car while talking but Dexzart and Stella had been substantially quiet pretty much the whole time.

"Where should we be heading though?" had asked Fiera softly.

"That is actually what Stella tells every time." had pointed Eliott as the five had been getting into the car closing each one's door.

"But I don't think Stella is in the state of telling us." had said Fiera facing up at Stella sitting with a face empty of any colour.

"You can take my bag and check for the documents." had told Stella as she had put her seatbelt on while pointing at her bag.

"Alright." had noted Fiera, as she had headed over to that bag.

The others had shook their heads noting onto Stella's words as they had been waiting eagerly for the address they had to head.

"I can only see some of your personal documents, your id and some of your notebooks; over here." had told Fiera searching.

"Check onto the next section, I am pretty sure it's there." had told Stella gesturing with hands, and then she had faced forward.

"Wait!" had exclaimed Dexzart breaking his silence as the rest instantly had stared at him trying to figure out why suddenly out of nowhere he had screamed as if to recalling something useful.

"The bag!" had continued Dexzart "The bag we found in the attic of that building might have that person's id card which can help us in the quest and it might as well have his personal diary!"

19

The Unveiling

"Did you guys not go?!" had demanded Minsie staring at them.

"No, we actually did." had replied Stacy looking back at Minsie.

"I don't even believe." had said Minsie as it had been too absurd of a thing to have been believed by anyone standing at her place.

"No, actually we did go to there." had told Jacob facing in front.

"Even if you did, did you leave quite early?" had asked Lesohn.

"No, not at all." had told Kelvac with a slight grin while driving.

"Then you must've heard us coming upstair?" had asked Minsie.

"Yes we did and that felt horrifying both times." had told Jacob.

"I am really confused, if you have had heard us then you should have gotten caught by now." had commented Lesohn instantly.

"Yeah so how did you even get out of there?" had asked Minsie.

"Oh, that's a long story." had told Stacy seeming quite dramatic.

"Well, we still want to hear…" had told Minsie raising eyebrows.

"Yeah, actually tell us from the very start what happened in that place." had wanted Lesohn as Minsie too had nodded agreeing.

"Alright so what actually happened is that we were inspecting as quietly as possible and we made sure that not a single thing was audible." had begun Stacy as the two had been eagerly listening.

"We three were searching on three different sides in order for it to be as quick as possible and it had been." had continued Stacy.

"Yeah it was going pretty well; as we were finding so many stuff but it kept getting confusing as to if a thing was important or not, and so we kept stuff we suspected on one side and stuff we felt were related to our quest on another." had added Kelvac.

"Then I had found something too important to be kept silent of and proceeded onto showing it to them, but as I turned around there was a spray paint on the floor and I tripped over it and it created quite a noise that gestured of trouble." had told Stacy.

"Yeah, also that spray paint had been kept by her. Anyways, so when we heard that; we turned to face each other, and that is when we heard footsteps, and we soon realized it was the lady who was probably coming upstairs." had told Jacob horrifying.

"Was about to." had told Minsie as she had been then and there.

"Oh..." had said Kelvac continuing "so suddenly we heard noise of something banging loudly and we instantly felt that it was the moment we start to clean up so I asked Stacy and Jacob to start clearing things up, as my one was pretty organized so I didn't have to think much of it, so what I did was proceed to clear up Stacy's part as it seemed to be the messiest of all of our parts..."

"The banging noise was of me falling." had told Minsie shying..

"Oh... so when he came he started to put all the things I had put aside as I had thought it was quite important but I didn't notice him doing that, cause I was focused at clearing the other part so as he didn't know he continued to put every one of those things back inside." had mentioned Stacy sighing in discomfort of reliving the moments of those triggering actions had done cause of her unawareness and unpaid attention to the important stuffs.

"So then I was done clearing up my part, and then I looked at Kelvac's part and found it already cleared up and then I looked over to the two almost done clearing, so I told them that let's leave listening which Kelvac heard and poked Stacy calling her as well, and she had quickly put the few remaining thing in her hand and we proceeded to leave the same way we had entered before." had told Jacob as he had held his hands onto the seats.

"And when we were mid-way to our exit I realized that I had nothing in my hands, so I asked Kelvac if he had taken the stuff I had set aside to take, and he & Jacob signed a no to which I was totally thrilled and I immediately asked them to go back and take those stuff, so we went back up." had continued Stacy; stiff.

"Yeah, and as we were up Stacy found the things weren't out, so she immediately went rushing to that part of the room and started looking in for those objects, and while we were in the search I heard footsteps again, but that time it felt like it was closer and faster and a lot." had told Jacob quite feeling the chill.

"Yeah probably; as it was me, him & that lady." had told Minsie.

"Alright so then I instantly went onto the exit and thankfully it was already set in place; as we had just came in, and I was calling Stacy out for her to hurry although it seemed she wasn't done, and then the footsteps felt nearer than ever, and I quickly went back and grabbed her, and rushed towards the exit, and holding her tightly I jumped down." had told Jacob quite frighteningly.

"So what about Kelvac; cause when the door got opened by the lady no one was there…" had questioned Lesohn quite instantly.

"Fortunately the second time we got up we had asked Kelvac to go to the car and get it started so that we could be ready to leave upon you two's sign, and that was probably a good decision as if he was there we'd be caught." had told Stacy; breathing in relief.

"Yeah you're right…" had commented Lesohn eying at Kelvac.

"Alright, I have a question," had said Minsie garnering attention "so, were you all able to retrieve any information at all or not?"

"Ah, yes that." had said Lesohn signing to concurring to Minsie.

"Yes, we were, but I am uncertain of how useful it'd be for the quest held." had said Jacob making a face showing uncertainty.

"Oh, then tell us in details what you've found." had said Minsie.

"Yes, so that we can tell if this mission succeeded or not." had said Lesohn trying to uplift the rest from the harsh seriousness.

"Okay, so I found this notebook which pretty much describes a lot on how the class of that lady was taken and it also talks onto how each and every student had seemed during the classes and I thought this could be quite helpful." had told Kelvac in detail.

"Can you read a page or two from there?" had adjured Minsie.

"Sure, it says 'It is Tuesday, the tormenting Tuesdays that I have hated ever since, it is the day I have to go to that music institution on Frekent Avenue, the horrifying nightmares fail in front of this institution, no matter what anybody says that place can ever be called good if not okay. So, it is about time that I leave for that terrifying tertiary service as my mom had gone to the car, and she'll be here any minute ringing the loud horn. So, honestly I can't even blame anyone at all; as if anyone is to be blamed then it is me, cause I was the one that urged so badly to get into a music institution and that place was one of the most renowned of all, so I didn't even hesitate when it had been suggested to me, but I regret now looking back my decision with low if not any inspection at all; cause little did I know this place was a graveyard; not the fantasy garden full of flowers that I had thought of." had read Kelvac assiduously with a dramatic tone.

"Seems quite a bit harsh of a place although I wouldn't disagree that this had been written too exaggerating." had posited Minsie.

"Yes! I concur at it. And shall I continue?" had replied Kelvac.

"Yes, please go ahead." had replied back Lesohn immediately.

"I know this wasn't what anybody would be expecting seeing how great the place was or is being called; and that bugs me quite too much. I am on my way to that place, but the streets today feel emptier than it usually is and that is pretty triggering to me if not to everybody. Although, I am feeling concerned I do not have much time to go and research onto why it is this way. Few moments had passed, and now here I was; inside a car standing outside a mental asylum -I can't find a better way to describe it. Alright, I had entered unwantedly into this place and am sitting in the middle of the ongoing class, we have to maintain the rules very properly which seems triggering, but fortunately we are allowed to check onto our musical notes and our notebooks; so I am able to write onto this diary without being caught and insulted in front of the whole class. Actually it is of embarrassment due to us being humans but not due to the people in there seeing; as they seem to be nothing but mere robots doing their given task, though one boy stands out as he is sort of what is referred as blessed with talent." had read Kelvac.

"And yeah that's it I think…" had said Kelvac closing the book.

"Like is that all?" had asked Minsie being a bit confused at him.

"No there's more but I think it's good to stop." had told Kelvac.

"Oh alright, but what about Jacob?" had replied Minsie fronting.

"Oh yeah so I've found bunch of ids and an attendance list of the students who took particular classes." had told Jacob shortly.

"Oh that seems really useful." had commented Kelvac instantly.

"Wait, you people said you were hurrying when the lady came the second time, and then Jacob grabbed Stacy and jumped down and all that, right; then was Stacy able to get the thing you had gone back to get?" had very intriguingly questioned Lesohn.

"Yeah were you able to get it?" had said Minsie arising curiosity.

Curiosity had risen as Minsie, Lesohn and Kelvac stared at them.

"Yes, yes!" had begun Stacy smiling "I was able to get the stuffs. Right when I heard the lady putting her hand on the knob I very quickly grabbed the thing, but I thought it was too late and then I felt like some sort of strong pleasant force was striking me as it swept me along its way while I lost control of myself and went."

"Jacob's played a big role in here." had opined Kelvac instantly.

"You're probably right!" had said Minsie smiling "But Stacy, what information have you found from there after all that..."

"Good question," had replied Stacy "so I actually found some bizarre stuff and I am pretty much certain that it's helpful for our quest. I found a diary and that tells a lot, I found a photo album and a photo frame but both containing absolutely unalike photos, and lastly a note intended for someone which seemed to be very recently written and probably was about to be given..."

"Oh that's extremely excellent of you!" had commented Lesohn.

"Yes absolutely," had said Minsie "and can you please show us those things now, cause I can't keep patient now that I heard of them as those can be seriously important to the quest or maybe even literally be the thing that leads us to the finishing of it..."

"Yeah sure, it's at the back over there." had said Stacy pointing.

"But before all of that," had demanded Stacy "I want you two to tell us what you guys have noticed or even found inside there..."

"Alright let me tell my part up, I actually focused onto how the lady was behaving and all that, and it felt quite strange; cause she seemed quite benevolent towards us; meaning maybe towards every visitor," had told Lesohn "although I did notice her being quite malevolent whenever moved onto a topic about her pupils, seeing which I could only conclude that she is a nice person, but much of a strict person when it comes to training or teaching..."

"Oh…" had commented Kelvac "sounds quite understandable."

"Yeah, and what about you Minsie?" had asked Stacy curiously.

"Alright, this might sound quite outré… so sit stiffly or else you might fall…" had told Minsie "Umm, I actually got that lady's to do list and stuff she notes down; in a notebook; from there…"

"Wait, do you mean you took it?" had asked Jacob immediately.

"Yes, I did." had said Minsie as others had been staring at her.

"Wait wha-" had blurted Stacy "you couldn't just literally take something that was hers and that too which she probably uses daily as she would most likely notice that that thing is missing..."

"No, see what happened is I found the notebook quite near a trash can, and fortunately somehow I had a similar pocketbook or let's say the same looking, so I replaced it with her one and threw it inside the trash can." had told Minsie raising curiosity.

"But, what if she takes it out of the trash can?" had asked Jacob.

"Don't worry I executed that issue as well," had told Minsie "as the pocketbook with me had writings but less than hers so what I did is scribble orderly and then I spilled tea on it to blur it up."

"It still feels absurd to me how we had found a ukulele in that place and that too newish if not brand new." had opined Fiera.

Stella and the other four had been going to Devlic Highs; again.

"It is strange and I can't tell why it was there." had said Dexzart.

Dexzart and Stella have had been sober but had managed to come at the normal state of mind; difficultly but still had done.

"Alright, we're about there." had said Eliott informing the rest.

Eliott then after a few moments had pulled over while the rest alertly waited readily; for him to gesture to get down of the car.

"Alright, so do you remember where it was." had asked Casey.

"Yes, I do." had said Fiera as she got down and went forward.

All of the five had gotten out of the car proceeding to entering the building in front of them, where they have had departed to.

"Tell us which way to go." had told Casey turning toward Fiera.

Fiera had entered before the rest, and had been roaming around.

"I can't remember, this feels like a maze." had expressed Fiera.

Everyone had heard her and had went in and about the place in search for the place they have had left the stuff at, but the building had been more than huge; the hallways & passageways all empty and silent, and quite looking of the very same built.

"Oh god, this is really confusing." had said Fiera "A-am I lost?"

"Here!" had called out a voice afar and everyone else followed.

"What? What here?" had questioned Casey reaching the caller.

"I found the bag!" had said Dexzart showing the bag smilingly.

"Great! Open it!" had advised Fiera coming "see what is in it."

"Uh, it has a book and some other things." had told Dexzart.

"Can you find any id?" had said Stella as she had just reached.

"No actually, I see none." had told Dexzart looking into the bag.

Stella had squatted down tilting her head to check into the bag.

Everyone else had been staring fixedly at Stella's hands' motion.

"Wait!" had screamed Stella saying "this book has a name on it."

Casey had quickly squatted down reading out "Eitvern Seloiht."

"Oh, can you read what's inside that book." had requested Fiera.

"Sure, I'll read the last thing he wrote…" had said Casey as Stella had handed her the book "Dear Diary, I have been taking part in various activities, and today I'll be going for one that is quite new to me and also quite too important at the time. I haven't had an opportunity to do this sort of something before, and I'll lack words if I go to comprehend how excited I am. So what really am going to do is going for a camping in order to connect with nature while playing music, and I'm not alone onto this adventure as I have my friends and acquaintances coming. I will continue writing how this trip goes cause it's exuberating…"

"Continue reading please..." had said Fiera as Casey had paused.

Casey had turned the page reading "We are almost here at the highlands -honestly we chose the one we found easiest access to. It is about dusk and we've already set out our camp, and this is a mesmerizing feeling to sit with a favorite instrument looking out the sky viewing the magnificent twilight as you play the music. I have been pretty much occupied so have now set out to explore the surroundings while the others are in the camps having rest."

"Wait, so it means he wasn't alone here?" had pointed Dexzart.

"That means he wasn't the only one endangered!" had narrated Casey in a quite dramatic tone as she had helped the horror rise.

"Yes, that means we've to rush to saving them!" had told Stella.

They all -as they have had heard Stella- had faced each other as they signed that approval and had literally ran rushing to search.

The five had separated into separate directions individually into the deep dark dreaded woods of the highlands they had been at.

The woods had seemed quieter than the vacuums as nothing but silence had been present and none but horror had been at sight.

The five had been thoroughly searching and shouting out asking whether or not someone was there; without fearing of getting caught by any sort of danger out there waiting for their arrival.

Much time have had quite passed since they have had started the search, but yet no one had been to be found and thus they were going deeper and deeper into the woods, and that too separately.

As Dexzart had been walking; he had been hearing footsteps near him other than his which had felt as if someone had been secretly spectating. He had went silent. Suddenly a thing struck!

"You!" had said Dexzart sighing in relief while walking slowly.

"Yes me..." said Casey slightly smiling, walking next to Dexzart.

"You literally had me dead!" had told Dexzart staring at Casey.

"I found no one and lost my path but saw you so." had told she.

"Sounds familiar of a case." had said Dexzart letting out a laugh.

"Ah!" had came a very loud & horrified scream from the woods.

20

Finally Decoded

"I can't say for sure if there's any complication or not but surely something is up cause Stella and them asked us to reach the site they are at without wasting a moment." told Minsie very tensely.

"Oh alright, that was quite unexpected of a call…" said Lesohn.

"Alright, let's head quickly!" told Jacob ordering fully in tension.

The five were headed toward the place Stella had asked them to, and there was nothing but silence in the car as they drove flying.

"Can anyone of you think of a single good reason we could have been called for?" Stacy raised a question as they stared emptily.

"Can you?" asked Kelvac sounding despair as his voice lowered.

"I will have to unwantedly say;" told Stacy "no, I cannot at all."

All of them were in deep thought as they already knew that the call had hinted on something drastic coming their way real soon.

"For instance, we can only hold up, till we reach there and find it out, ourselves." blurted Jacob fixedly staring at nothing at all.

"I hope nothing unwanted blocks our way…" said Minsie softly.

Things quite started to feel more haunting every passing minute.

They all sat there thinking of thousands of possibilities why the other group had called them; all of a sudden, and spoke nothing but just gave a hasty message that they had to be there as soon as they could, and that too in their first call; breaking the silence.

"Is this the place?" asked Stacy seeing the car become stationary.

"Should be." said Kelvac timidly, stopping their ride completely.

They all got off the car as they walked to in front of it encircling.

"So, we don't know where exactly the place is but Stella had told it's deeper into the woods." informed Minsie looking at the rest.

"Alright, noted." replied Stacy as the five started to walk inside.

The environment was covered with uncertainty and pure silence.

"Ouch! Sorry." said Minsie massaging her eye with her hand as it covered her entire face; as she had bumped into someone.

"What!" screamed Stacy loudly as she saw Minsie and the other.

Minsie quickly put her hand away as she screamed "You here?!"

"Pretty sure you were more unexpected here!" said the person.

"Jennifer, why would you be here?!" demanded Stacy instantly.

"First of all why did you enter in a restricted place?" asked Miss Winsent in a quite harsh manner and tone while the five stared.

"Mind if I ask why did you?" demanded Stacy loudly; arguing.

The five had no idea about that area having any restricted entry.

"I perhaps have to let you know that we're part of FBI, and we do not abide by the restrictions on entry." told Miss Winsent.

"F-F-FBI?!" Minsie let out a scream as she was totally unaware of Jennifer being a FBI agent while other thought came flashing in her mind which made her more horrified at the situation held.

"Do you mind to tell us why you're here?!" asked Miss Winsent.

"Jennifer can we have a moment with you?" asked Minsie softly.

"Do you have any issue talking here?" demanded Miss Winsent.

"Perhaps if Jennifer finds our conversation appropriate she'll tell you…" said Stacy out loud in a hard tone as the rest stared her.

Jennifer eyed Miss Winsent, and she eyed back in approval, and they moved aside to talk, while Miss Winsent remained standing.

"You never told you were a FBI agent!" said Stacy dramatically.

"Let that aside, why are you here for, is anything wrong?" asked Minsie as absolute tension rose among her and her companions.

"No, we are here just for some inspection." told Jennifer softly.

"What sort of inspection?" asked Stacy as others stared fixedly.

"Before all that, tell me why are you here?!" demanded Jennifer.

Minsie and the other four told accordingly in details about how, why and what for they were there while Jennifer listened fixedly.

"Oh god, that's messed up!" said Jennifer as Minsie completed.

"It is." said Lesohn as they all sighed thinking of it as a whole.

"I hope you allow to keep moving." requested Kelvac politely.

"I'll go tell this out thoroughly to Miss Winsent." told Jennifer.

Jennifer then went on to tell Miss Winsent out; being selective with her words, while the others waited where they had been at.

Jennifer then a while later came as she said "We can let you go but only if you agree upon a deal between us or else we cannot."

The others widened their eyes in shock as they asked what the deal was, to which Jennifer said "Keep updating on everything."

"Hello," said Xiwielle as she entered the place "how are you?".

"Hello, please come in." said the Professor as Xiwielle came by.

Nikert joined Xiwielle shortly as he too entered alongside her.

"Aren't they here today either?" asked Xiwielle as she walked in.

"This was supposed to be part of a routine check!" shouted Stella as the others looked down as absolute guilt covered them.

"Sorry ma'am we lost track of it." told her group member softly.

"How can you lose track of this, this is nothing voluntary that you can forget!" said Stella "If this had been done routinely I can say with certainty that there isn't any way track can be lost."

"I am sorry we'll keep clear of any such mistake." told a person.

All of them walked quietly toward the place they were headed at.

They had forgotten out on a routine check and it seemed not only a problem creating towards Stella but also to the cause they were supposedly to do the routine check for, and it'd be drastic.

"I want you to separate into different teams, while I'll go by my own." guided Stella "Remember you've to be quick cause we're already late by I don't how long, but also be cautious as this area is more than just danger so I want each one's eyes widely open."

Everyone there noted as they separated into different groups.

"I hope nothing bad happens." told one of Stella's personnel.

"It is our bad we didn't inform her about this while we were the ones held responsible to inform her about all these sort of stuff, and if anything bad even occurs it shall absolutely be our guilt; and I can't keep sane knowing that, cause of what messed up stuffs had happened here previously." replied another personnel.

The two sighed in despair as they quickened their walking pace.

"I'd rather be poisoned than to be leaving out on an important task that needs to be done constantly without any manner of interruption..." thought Stella as she walked searching the place.

"Yes, hello, Stella speaking..." said Stella receiving a phone call.

"Stella, you'll have to return to the headquarters immediately!" said the phone caller in a serious tone making things too intense.

"Is there any sort of problem?" asked Stella getting bit worried.

"We'll clear those queries out upon your arrival." told the caller.

"Alright, I'll be right there shortly." told Stella; deciding to leave.

Stella immediately went back her path as she rushed out leaving.

As a matter of rule; on Stella's absence no one was allowed to carry out any decision which both bugged and put Stella at relief.

"Did you search the left side?" asked the person taking account.

"I have." told the person nodding as he reached to the person.

The two proceeded onto their path as they checked thoroughly.

The search going over there, was being done without any pause.

Minsie with the other four too were searching along their way.

Diversity could not be told between the separate search teams.

"May I go check this side?" asked Kelvac pointing at his right.

"Alright, we'll be here so return to here." told Minsie; guiding.

"Listen, I think that sides are all clear and there's no sign of Fiera's group there so we should be moving front." told Lesohn.

Minsie, Lesohn and Stacy went towards the front while Kelvac and Jacob moved to the left in order to search for Fiera's team.

"Might they be in any danger?" asked Stacy as she got worried.

"I really hope not," said Minsie thinking deep "but there stands a high possibility of it, so that's why we need to rush on finding them; so if they are in danger we can get them out of it quickly."

"Right." said Lesohn as all of their pace became even hastier.

"I think we should return." told Kelvac as the two were walking.

"Yeah alright let's go…" replied Jacob as they two turned aback.

The two quickly returned through the path they had went in by.

Eliott had been walking alone but he could hear some noise out in there although he was at the part of the woods that's nowhere near where humans inhabited nor was there any sign of a visitor. He felt like he was getting surrounded. He couldn't tell what was surrounding. It felt more and more captivating. He stopped and stood there. The feeling didn't diminish. Every passing second it felt even closer. He couldn't think of anything but of the noises.

"Is someone trying to trap me," thought Eliott "or is it wildlife."

The noise within the silent atmosphere of the woods gave chills.

Footsteps could be heard due to dead leaves on the forest floor.

"Eliott?" called out a soft voice from behind Eliott; guessing.

Eliott turned around with closed eyes as he nervously bit his lip.

"Y-yes?" said him nervously as he began to open his eyes slowly.

"Where's everybody?!" asked the voice as it got louder & clearer making it easy for someone to hear and recognize the speaker.

"Minsie?" said Eliott toning voice as his eyes got fully opened.

Minsie nodded as she and the four with her too stared at Eliott.

"Where are the others?" asked Stacy stepping forward to Eliott.

"The others are here," told Eliott "we had divided into solitary teams. But why're you all here cause you're not supposed to be."

"I thought you knew," told Minsie "Stella had suddenly asked us to come here and that too really quick, for some sort of reason."

"Is Stella alright?" screamed out Eliott loudly in absolute horror.

"We don't have any idea, do you not know what happened?" replied Kelvac as the others eagerly waited for Eliott to answer.

"No, cause when we divided everything was alright." told Eliott.

"Can you tell us from the start what happened?" urged Minsie.

"Uh, we had come over here because of the information Stella had retrieved somehow where this place was mentioned, so we came for any clue then as we were on our way you won't believe what we saw; on the way, Casey had suddenly asked to stop the car and to our astonishment it was a wolf eating something, but by the time we were about to figure out what it was eating; Casey had already got off the car and we rushed behind her and i-i-it was l-literally a human being eaten, and we stood there absolutely freaked out," explained Eliott thoroughly "although we were a bit on the upper land than the wolf; Casey was literally standing inches away from the wolf. We would have had brought the body with us but it was too late, so Dexzart quickly grabbed Casey and dragged her out of the scene and after a few moments of trying to decide whether to call for help to get the body off there or not; we followed them and went out of that scene empty handed as we didn't want to let more people die."

"Oh my god!" said Stacy "before we waste time any further; let's go find Stella and the rest; cause they could be in utter danger."

"Yes, please, let's go and I demand everyone to stay together!" told Lesohn as everybody stood listening and nodding duly.

"I have to leave but you can stay to practice." told the Professor.

"Do you happen to know which direction they had gone when you people dispersed into individual groups?" asked Stacy softly.

Eliott nodded showing although he felt numb and mournful in.

"Times may seem parlous, tasks may feel onerous." sang Nikert in a soothing and melancholy manner "but keep holding tight."

The group of six piloted by Eliott was searching thoroughly and hastily for their fellows as they might be imposed by nightmares.

"I believe through the horrors will you fasten yourself." sang Nikert as melody covered the atmosphere while tears got shed.

"Here!" blurted Kelvac as the others followed his voice rushing.

"What?!" asked Minsie reaching Kelvac followed by all the rest.

"Here, I think this is Fiera's…" told Kelvac showing the object.

"Omg!" said Stacy as she ran down the path while others quickly ran behind her asking her to slow down but failing and rushing.

"Could they have been chased by a wolf or something?" asked Kelvac as they all ran quite synchronously down the steep path.

As they neared the end all their hearts were throbbing heavily not due to the running but to the fear of what they were going to find down there whether or not it'd be pleasant or too drastic. They were having thoughts of thousands of different sorts of possibilities the others had asked to arrive forthwith; off silence.

Eliott was running hastily looking at the ground and as he found Stella's feet feets away; he ran harder in pleasure to knowing she was standing all alive and as he went nearer he closed his eyes hugging Stella tight; striking as a lightning as tears filled his eyes.

"No matter how drastic things get, remember it might all be well at the end…" sang Nikert playing the piano quite harmonically.

The rest five came a little later and they too got happy finding everyone standing alive; safe and sound, but as their senses came back they heard ambulance sirens and as they turned to the sound they felt it was nearing them then they quickly turned back towards Stella and the rest; looking at what's behind them.

To their horror they saw Stella, Fiera, Casey and Dexzart standing lifelessly and behind them stood a grassy field full of possibly dead bodies seeing which numbed each one of them.

Eliott too came back to sense and as he reared from hugging Stella he was petrified to see the drastic field behind him & her.

"What atrocity occurred here?" blurted Lesohn moving forward.

Stella and the three alongside her were so lifeless that they were facing difficulties to have their senses working or to even react.

The ambulance came and instantly went to working as they too were astonished to see such an enormous amount of bodies laying down onto that huge field almost lifeless if not lifeless…

"We found this and called instantly." told Casey in a numb tone.

Minsie and the others with her shook their heads understanding.

"Were you all able to figure out what happened…?" asked Stacy.

The four were still completely stiff and so were the other six.

"Nope." said Stella shaking her head as she breathed in gulping.

Minsie and the five with her turned back at the field dolorously.

"I think we had delayed too much." expressed Fiera sighing off.

"You still saved a lot of lives." said a hospital crew reaching out.

All of them turned to face the hospital crew as her words eased.

"And Ms. Stella, I have to happily tell that the patient you had brought other day became well really quickly." told the crew.

"Who?" asked Stacy as the rest five too eagerly stared listening.

"Before all that, what about Giwelyev's nephew?" asked Casey.

Minsie and the other four looked at each other disappointedly.

"We weren't done with the quest…" told Minsie quite guiltily.

"We had found an ill guy through whom we got the clue of these others might being here." told Casey in a lifeless voice.

"Did you not find anything with him?" asked Lesohn instantly.

"We found a ukulele…" told Dexzart sighing in total despair.

"A ukulele?!" said Stacy as the other four with her stared at her.

"Actually we found a diary of Giwelyev's nephew talking about playing ukulele…" told Kelvac getting quite a bit enthusiastic.

"Oh, we also found a journal along with that boy and there was a name but the surname wasn't Ennocel." said Stella informing.

"Wait!" yelled Fiera "remember Giwelyev blurting out 'sister'?"

"Do you try to mean that;" said Stacy garnering all the attention "the nephew's her sister's son so the surname wasn't Ennocel!"

21

THE DIVERSITY

"What could've caused these deaths?" asked Fiera facing a dead.

"Could this be any sort of animal attack?" pointed out Dexzart.

"I believe not but might these be cases of... murder?" said Stella.

All of them went silent for a moment; hearing Stella's statement.

"No, not at all..." said Casey breaking the silence "these are not cases of murder in any manner due to what I detected by now."

"And what makes you say that so surely?" asked Eliott instantly.

"Alright so, I've noticed that the person we found getting eaten by the flesh-eating wolf had definitely died before these people here, and I don't know if you noticed or not the boy we found sick or let's say almost lifeless had written the date in his journal and from that we can surely say these were dead later. And we can also notice that some of these people are still alive, and if a person was to kill so many people they would've been professional so they would have never killed people in such a slow method; cause he/she too would have known that they would get caught if it's this slow and not only that; serial killers will never make such a mistake. And also the fact that we'd not found a single similar fingerprint throughout our whole search proves my point in an even better manner..." explained Casey.

"I would have to agree with Casey; as the method these people were intended to be killed is quite slow and another thing is that none of them looks struck, injected or strangled." told Lesohn.

"So what might've caused them this very fatality?" asked Stacy.

"It is hard to identify." told Lesohn pressing onto a dead's hand.

"Could it have been done by snakes or anything?" said Dexzart.

"I suppose not; as I mentioned previously nothing seems to be pierced or injected into the body as there's no mark on the body by the injection of anything…" told Lesohn as others listened.

They all went into deep thought as they tried to figure out what had caused those sicknesses; while they stood right at the scene.

The dead and sick bodies were being taken by ambulances, but then all the ambulances were gone and they were going to be back after some time as they ran out of enough ambulances to take all of the bodies cause the hospital had no idea that there was that many bodies to be taken before arriving at the scene…

"Though was it caused by any sort of poison?" asked Dexzart.

"I can't tell for sure but let me inspect them a bit." told Lesohn.

Lesohn began to inspect without any hesitation; as it was only them and the fatally sick over there; cause the hospital crews were gone due to taking all the other bodies out of that place.

Meanwhile; some of the rest nine helped nurse the alive bodies.

"Everyone come here please!" called out Lesohn quite loudly, as all the others began to rush up towards there one after the other.

"What it does is make people faint after a short period of time, and then it takes over the whole body, but fortunately it's a slow process." told Lesohn demonstrating by gesturing with hands.

"Yet can't tell what caused that?" asked Fiera, as Lesohn denied.

"Now, we need to find out what have caused this." said Lesohn.

"Could that have been anything related to this environment?" pointed out Stacy as the others stared fixedly listening to her.

"That is a good estimation!" exclaimed Lesohn as others looked.

"It could have been caused by the climate." told Lesohn smiling.

"Do you intend to mean it could've been caused by the climate change?" asked Stella enthusiastically as everyone else observed.

"Omg that is the closest take!" said Lesohn "why didn't it hit my mind all this time cause that's one of the only valid possibilities."

"Oh, that is the reason!" blurted out Minsie as she was amused.

"Even though I am saying that's the closest call, it still remains uncertain cause we'll have to examine." told Lesohn elucidating.

"But that's not quite possible…" said Fiera hearing some sirens.

"Oh yeah if the bodies are all taken then it'll be hard to identify the actual reason." told Lesohn getting upset onto that matter.

"But we can take permission from the hospital to go there and examine for observation purposes." told Stella uplifting moods.

"We need to research theoretically as well." told Stacy pointing.

"Yeah that's true cause theories might help give us a boost onto the examination." told Lesohn approving with Stacy's statement.

"Why wait on doing such a well intent work." pointed up Eliott.

"I think Stella, you should go ask the hospital for the permission while we continue planning our next steps." requested Minsie as the ambulances went stationary, and the siren stopped slowly.

"Yeah sure, I'll go ask, you people carry on and I'll be right back alright…" said Stella as she walked in a quick pace to the crews.

The nine were discussing stuffs when Stella returned from there.

"What'd she say?" asked Stacy immediately as she noticed Stella.

"She said that she'll go ask the hospital management and that we'll probably get the permission; as we helped save all these people's lives, so it's sort of bound to." explained Stella smiling.

"Oh alright, that's great!" said Jacob as everyone else smiled too.

"Also we should hurry on onto our next steps, cause we have to solve this issue as soon as possible." told Lesohn informatively.

The rest nodded listening to Lesohn; fixedly staring right at him.

"Ok so we've to first go to a library and search through as many stuff about climate change and those related to it; as possible." guided Lesohn while the rest nodded; widening theirs eyes fully.

"Does anyone know a library where we can get most scientific information from?" asked Jacob as everyone departed the field.

"We can go check out the city library…?" suggested Dexzart.

"Yeah, that's probably the best place." said Casey sighing lightly.

"Alright then, we can go the exact seating setting we had carried out our whole quest." told Minsie holding the car door all open.

"Yeah, that." said Stella as they all got in their cars accordingly.

The field had been cleared off of any bodies while the ten left.

"I can't think of the diversity between a case of crime and a case of science; cause that's too heterogeneous." told Fiera sitting in.

"It surely is, cause both take such different paths." said Dexzart.

"Yeah but that is how life is; absolutely unexpected." said Eliott.

The ten had reached the library, as they got permitted to enter.

"Ok, so what's next." asked Stacy as they gathered in one place.

"Well, there are more than one section for science over here; so we'll have to divide up into groups for each section." told Eliott.

"Yes I suppose, but we'll have to leave out physics." told Stacy.

"Yeah, only check on chemistry, biology or biochemistry based on the basic knowledge of what climate change is." told Lesohn.

"Just for a recap, climate change is any kind of harm imposed onto the nature; which is being reflected by the climate; and it is caused by pollution, littering and etc." told Eliott informatively.

The ten then parted into different groups as they went to the different science sections in the library seeking eagerly for info.

"I think as we're in the chemistry sort of section; we should focus onto pollution and all that." said Casey as Stacy nodded.

"Yes, I believe so too, hopefully we find something." told Stacy.

All of them reached their sections as they began taking out and reading books off the shelves; only which they felt as important.

The ten quickened onto garnering as much information as it was possible, and filtering out what they really needed and vice versa.

"I have to answer a call." said Stella as she went a bit to the side.

"Hello" said the phone caller "I wanted to let you know that you were granted permission to observe the dead bodies but you have to remember they don't wait long for dead body visitors..."

"Alright, we will be there real soon." told Stella hanging the call.

"Is there any problem?" asked Eliott as Stella walked back there.

"No, just got told that the hospital permitted us to examine the bodies, but we won't be waited for long." told Stella going hasty.

"I'll go inform the others." told Eliott closing the book he held.

"No it's fine, I texted." told Stella stopping Eliott grabbing him.

Stella hastily let go of Eliott as she got into her senses. The two still had complications but had decided to abide by the situation.

"Stacy, quick!" called out Casey quietly "see what I have found."

"What?" asked Stacy coming rushing with a book in her hand.

"Here are some books with brief explanations of the gases causing climate change ..." told Casey, as Stacy got intrigued.

"Summarize the thing for me; please." requested Stacy seriously.

"So there are several gases affecting the climate which is emitted by us humans." explained Casey thoroughly yet shortly "these gases are produced through industries as in factories and all that, although these are also produced naturally by the nature but that is the mere amount and not excess, which humans are imposing. These gases are referred to as greenhouse gases, and these cause the greenhouse effect which is the trapping of heat in earth from going into the space where it should be; and that's the problem."

"You mean enhanced greenhouse effect?" corrected Stacy siting.

"Why enhanced greenhouse effect?" asked Casey in confusion.

"Cause greenhouse effect itself isn't harmful rather is vital for us to live but the thing now with the excess levels of emitting of the greenhouse gases is that it's enhancing greenhouse effect which's trapping heat more than it's necessary." explained Stacy.

"Oh, alright." said Casey "I suppose that's bad for our future."

"So see the excess greenhouse gases caused by us humans can itself harm us to the extent of killing us." explained Lesohn.

Minsie and Lesohn sought the biological aspect of their topic.

"How can it literally kill us?" asked Minsie while picking a book.

"We've to breath at least about nineteen percent of oxygen, but if the air is polluted by so many other gases than oxygen then we would suffer to breath and eventually die." told Lesohn quietly.

"Oh so it's basically like taking out water from a fish's aquarium, and replacing it with oil and then it won't survive." said Minsie.

"Yeah that's true." told Lesohn as he proceeded to read further.

"Also the heat is melting glaciers, so it's slowly causing sea levels to rise," told Fiera "actually to be said it is rapidly causing not slowly; if compared with the previous eras earth faced before."

"So if the sea levels keep rising the land may drown underwater. And also it can cause glacier-turned-water to evaporate and slowly create more water vapors i.e. clouds than that're originally existing and that can cause flood by excessive rain." said Kelvac.

Fiera and Kelvac were on the aspect of chemistry on that topic.

"It can actually be prevented!" said Jacob garnering Dexzart's interest as he focused "as it's mainly caused by the industrial pollutions through factories; causing them to stop using those sort of harmful chemical can cause severity of climate change to reduce by a lot which would be quite helpful and besides that we can also do the simple act of reducing plastic consumption by altering that with something not harmful to the environment."

"It's quite peculiar for anybody to even think of such an action, rest aside applying that into daily practice." blurted out Dexzart.

"I think we shall go to the hospital quickly!" told Stella intensely.

"Yeah, time's passing; let's go call the others up." advised Eliott.

The two quickly went to the others to inform about leaving to the hospital; as the hospital wouldn't wait too long for them all.

After informing all of them, they gathered and decided to leave.

"I hope the amount of information we've in our hands help us complete our benevolent quest." said Minsie getting in the car.

The ten after some time reached the hospital, and straightway went to a room to examine the dead bodies, and sick too.

"Here, this is a body you can examine." said the nurse guiding.

"Kelvac and I will go check the ill people and also talk up with the doctors about the patients, alright?" told Fiera, requesting.

"Yeah sure you two go while we examine over here." told Stella.

Fiera and Kelvac left instantly, while others started to examine.

"How are you feeling now?" asked Fiera reaching to the patient.

"Better than earlier, but I still feel suffocation." told the person.

"Oh. . . can you write down how exactly you feel in details on this paper?" requested Fiera handing over a paper hearing him.

"It seems a bit difficult to identify." told Lesohn as he observed.

"Keep checking and see if you could tell or not." opined Casey.

Lesohn got back to checking the dead body while others looked.

"It seems like they all are still having a hard time to breath due to the event but what have caused them this complication?" said Kelvac as he and Fiera were walking over to the other patients.

"People, you keep checking and I'll catch up later." said Eliott.

"Why, where are you going?" asked Stacy as the others looked.

"I am feeling a bit nauseous, so I'll return in awhile." told Eliott.

The others nodded understanding as Eliott left out immediately.

"Okay, so what complication do you see in them?" asked Fiera.

"So I think after all the observation and results; it looks like they must have been suffering to breath, and the other thing is some sort of thing was intoxicating them slowly." told a doctor briefly.

"How may have this occurred?" asked Kelvac as Fiera nodded.

"It looks as if something they inhaled had caused them to feel nauseous and later made them faint and later disable them from breathing properly, so as they couldn't breathe they eventually faced a harsh death." concluded Lesohn after observing a while.

"Isn't there any exceptions, like death not particularly due to suffocation?" asked Fiera while Kelvac and the doctor listened.

"Uh, good question, yes there were a multiple who died due to some sort of heart rate imbalances." told the doctor mindfully.

Everyone was stuck tightly onto the act of finding the reason why and how those people were intoxicated or have faced death.

Things started to intensify as they moved further and further into the investigation, and that too quite rapidly as they hasted.

Things started to become more and more intriguing and mysterious as they tried to solve the question held at the hands.

"We've to keep examining for longer." told Lesohn informing.

"But do we have enough time to do so?" replied Casey instantly.

"Hey, I'll go check on Eliott; he hasn't returned yet." said Jacob.

"Yeah, it's been a while..." commented Casey as others nodded.

"What could've caused this intoxication...?" blurted out Lesohn.

"Wait, wait, could that've been caused by any greenhouse gas?" asked Casey pointing out while Stacy too nodded widening eyes.

"Not sure, but it could have." told Lesohn looking at the body.

"Could methane have caused it?" asked Minsie immediately.

"No, methane itself is not harmful at all." pointed out Stacy.

"No, it can actually be harmful..." told Dexzart in an instance

"But, how would that be possible?" asked Stacy in confusion.

"You said it yourself; methane on its own isn't harmful, but when it mixes up with other gases it can be toxic." told Minsie.

"But how exactly can it cause death?" asked Casey; astonished.

"Methane when mixed with other gases causes asphyxiation; which is done by displacing oxygen, and that may cause trouble to breathe; although it's a slow process and it shows some symptoms which is basically nausea; but it often goes unnoticed until it is extremely hard to breath and the person does eventually die in no time." told Lesohn explaining thoroughly.

"Wait, so it could actually have been methane released from the permafrost due to melting of it; causing the deaths!" said Fiera as she and Kelvac just arrived to notice them discussing all that.

"Yes, yes it could actually have been that!" screamed Lesohn.

"People then Eliott?!" said Stella as they all stared at each other slowly getting what Stella meant, then getting shocked in horror.

22

Unlocking Treasures

"Will he be okay?" asked Stella as absolute tears filled her eyes.

"Calm down, he'll be alright." reassured Minsie trying to calm.

"What happened! How is he?" asked Stella seeing Lesohn come.

"They're giving him pure oxygen..." told Lesohn reaching Stella.

"Oh, is it because the complication was created by methane displacing oxygen so providing the oxygen would help him with breathing?" asked Minsie while softly patting Stella's shoulder.

"Yes exactly that." told Lesohn as he nodded softly; looking out.

Stella, Minsie and Lesohn stood in a balcony, while the rest were inside the building standing in front of the room Eliott was in.

Earlier, Stella had pointed out Eliott might had been affected by the methane, then the eight had gone rushing to Eliott, and had found him struggling. They had gotten more worried and without any other word or any wasting of time they had asked him to go check with the doctor; which he had denied saying that he would be alright, but Stella didn't agree and forcefully had made him go to the doctor, and the doctor had told that he needed immediate care so they had rushed and had put him on a stretcher and had taken him to a room that had been supposed.

Slowly the tension had rose as Eliott's condition had been getting severe every single passing moment; and had indicated a possibility that he might've actually died which had been horrid.

Everyone then were told Eliott would be well soon, but not that he was out of danger which horrified each & every one of them.

"I shouldn't have let him go that day…" said Stella as tears shed.

"I think we should carry on." said Xiwielle; drinking some water.

"Which day?" asked Minsie softly "What are you talking about?"

"The day before you went missing." told Stella melancholically.

"What happened that day?" asked Minsie; not having any idea.

"The memories acquired might make you feel sober at times." sang Nikert melancholically as harmony soothed the weather.

"Eliott came that day and found me and Dexzart, but I think he had come to search for you but didn't see you there so he left. He'd probably took me and Dexzart wrongly." told Stella softly.

"Oh." said Minsie empathizing "why'd he take you two wrong?"

"I hadn't been answering any calls as my phone's battery was dead, and he probably had called a million times…" told Stella.

"You know at times life stands in such a way that it does make you feel guilty, but it also makes you realize how other things were or even something you had mistaken earlier." told Minsie.

"Yeah…" said Stella shedding tears "but the thing didn't end there cause me and Dexzart had gone to the cinemas, and Eliott was there too, and we had bumped into each other and instead of clearing things out with him I turned off in a very harsh way."

"But why?" asked Minsie really softly "why did you act harshly?"

"Cause I had seen Casey and Eliott together earlier that morning and I was sort of really mad," told Stella regretfully "and also in the mall where we went for the cinemas, but what I really didn't think is that I could have mistaken them the exact way Eliott did seeing me and Dexzart, but during this quest I realized he and Casey had nothing in between them, and that really is mortifying and I can't feel more guilty not being able to say sorry to Eliott."

"Umm, sometimes we all make mistakes and that is why we are humans, but once we realize then nothing but apologizing is the way we can make up for our mistakes..." told Minsie reassuring.

"But as I said earlier I am unable to say sorry; cause there's no more time left…" said Stella as tears constantly fell off her eyes.

"Sometimes it's impossible to let go off our memories." sang Nikert in a very soothing tone; playing the piano melodiously.

"Don't lose hope, he will hopefully be alright." assured Minsie.

"But there is no crime in hoping it's not the end." sang Nikert.

"Why," cried out Stella softly "like why did I not see all the wonderful memories I had with Eliott, why had I seen a glimpse of something not even true and hated him for it, why did I not love him for all the precious moments he had provided me."

Minsie lacked words to speak and patted Stella; shedding tears.

"Stella, quick, come immediately!" called out a voice from afar.

Stella and Minsie turned around hastily wiping their tears as the two quickly walked if not run toward the person who had called.

"What happened?" asked Minsie as she stopped reaching there.

All of them were gathered into one place, as Stella and Minsie reached them absolutely tensed due to being suddenly called.

"The doctor said that Eliott is back to consciousness and he is absolutely out of danger." said Kelvac in a happy tone; smilingly.

"Hi, Good morning!" said Stella in a joyous tone, as she walked.

"Good morning!" replied Minsie keeping up the cheerful tone.

Few days had passed since their quest had ended that very day.

Minsie and the other nine had told Jennifer everything that had happened, and the cause for the deaths that had been occurring; and after that going to highlands had gotten restricted, and all the highlands had been told to be undergoing checks for any sick or dead people as quick as possible and it ended their quest.

"Hi, how are you?" said Fiera as she just entered the university.

"Good, what about you?" replied Minsie sipping onto coffee.

"Stella, Eliott was searching for you." told Casey as she came.

"Thank you very much for informing," said Stella a bit harshly "but I wanted to tell you something. Please from now on stay away from me and Eliott, and don't interfere into our lives..."

Stella walked away saying it to Casey and Casey too went away.

"What's between these two?" asked Fiera sitting beside Minsie.

"A story going back to the stone ages." said Minsie figuratively.

"Why not tell it out?" said Fiera facing at Minsie enthusiastically.

"Don't you have any class" asked Minsie raising her eyebrows.

"No I am free at least the first two periods." told Fiera smiling.

"It was a very hasty day as I got dressed really quickly, cause I was quite late on my schedule. I went to the car really hastily, and got in being quite enthusiastic! It was my first day at the high school. As I reached over to high school I could see all the people peacefully going in the high school premises, cause I was able to make it on time, I too went peacefully walking. I was in the classroom and I saw everyone talking to each other, but two girls stood out of the herd and was being the best besties out there, I was thrilled to see such close friends. Then days passed and later I got to know that they'd studied in the same schools since elementary and had been friends ever since. I never had so close friends; specially no friends of that long time." told Minsie.

"Oh okay…" said Fiera sitting fixedly listening feeling intrigued.

"The two were Stella and Casey. A literal year passed that way; I always was wowed to see their friendship. Ok so some events were more than wowing. One of them was when we had an annual event coming by and were preparing for it; as we had to perform on an act. I remember Stella and Casey were going to play roles as sisters and yeah so, each day we would go on practice for our plays, and it was really intriguing to be selected as the lead roles; but actually we were just practicing for auditions so we would only know after the audition if we were selected or not so each of us were working hard to get selected by the auditions." told Minsie pausing to take a sip of the coffee.

"Oh, that sounds really fun," said Fiera "and oh that reminded of me taking part in this year's extra music classes, and I did not appear to any of the classes and I run the chances of being kicked out but Kelvac was with me as well so I think it'll be ok."

Minsie laughed hearing Fiera, as she proceeded to continue on.

"Alright so, after so many days of practicing and all that, we were two days away to the audition so then it got quite serious, it was no more the funny rehearsals anymore as it became the quiet and focused ones. Everyone there was more than scared as every passing minute felt more and more tensing. So it was the last rehearsal before the audition and we all were thrilled, but

Stella and Casey seemed pretty chill; although they too were scared but not as much as the others and me. Then time passed like lightning, and it was the day of the audition and we all were horrified and immensely tensed. Things got intense. They were calling one by one. Then after some time; we all were done with our auditions, but we still couldn't breath in relief cause we were yet to be told who were chosen. Then some time later the crew came to tell out the people who were chosen. But, there was a change of plans as we knew that if we were chosen we'd do the act the same setting we had practiced, but then they said they'd choose who does with whom. We were mortified. Ok so, they started telling out the names and they did not choose Stella but they chose Casey. Although Casey was given a better role; they practiced everything together and put so much effort altogether as a team so Casey was asking to let Stella act with her. Even after all the requesting they did not agree. Fast forward, the event day came and we were on the backstage getting ready and all, then it was Casey's team's turn but Casey hadn't appeared, and there was no sign of her so they had to pick someone, but everyone was already in their own costume then Stella was called from the audience seating to take part as they had no choice, but also the thing was Casey had done just a bit better than Stella so if Casey hadn't done the audition Stella would have been chosen, anyway. So later we found out Casey purposefully did not appear to the event as she knew that the management had chosen understudies for each & every participant." told Minsie.

"They were so good friends?!" screamed Fiera in astonishment.

"Yeah, but there's a lot more to it." told Minsie laughing softly.

"I am here to hear it all." replied Fiera; absolutely intrigued on it.

"Ok so this other time, it was a very peaceful day; actually more peaceful than it normally was. I was a bit late to school that day, but it seemed as if I was the only one there, but it felt all chilled and peaceful so I got kind of happy and was feeling myself. I entered the classroom. I was literally dragged with my mouth being closed by a hand. I had no idea what was happening, and I got really mad. I had actually thought someone was pranking or something like that. I was trying to get out of the captivity of the person but I failed." said Minsie pausing to take a deep breath.

Fiera had her ears and eyes stuck at Minsie; as she drank coffee.

"Later to my astonishment, I got told by a girl and Casey that the whole school was hijacked. I was horrified. I asked how're they not held captive as hostage; and they said that the other girl was talking to one of her friends in school on her way to school, so suddenly that call had been cut off by a scream, which had made the girl suspicious that something had happened, and when she had arrived to school she had found it too quiet, so she had became cautious and had been to figure out that there were people roaming around with guns. Then when Casey had arrived this girl dragged Casey as well; to the hiding spot. I was thrilled to hear all that, and asked what to do next to which they replied that they too had no idea. I said why not call police, and they answered that calling police will put everyone in the school at more danger, cause the people who hijacked had some sort of device which could track incoming and outgoing calls from that area, and if they found out that police were coming then they might kill everyone over there with gunshots…" told Minsie.

"Oh freaking gosh, how'd you even survive?" interrupted Fiera.

"Things were quite intense. We three were the only ones who weren't held captive and all the other were in fatal danger. We three were helpless as we could not make any phone calls to get help, and the whole thing had been done so discreetly that there stood no chance of police coming for help cause they would not even assume such a thing was happening. So after a lot of thinking we decided to take the rescue mission in our hands and so needed to plan accordingly." told Minsie intensely "So as we had planned, it was Casey who had earlier collected details of the people and intellectually put it out in a mapped manner. So what we were supposed to do is first go to release all the animals that had been kept for the upcoming carnival; and there were a lot of animals so it would catch the hijackers' attention, which would make them all come to one place to diminish out the issue. Meanwhile, we were to go and bring all the hostages into one place very discreetly, so that everyone was at one place when we opened the back door, which would take much less time for us to escape. We did all of it, and everything was going according to our plan. But one thing that was missed out that there'd stood a possibility of someone not going to help resolve the animal issue, and it had happened. Fortunately that person was alone in a room so no hostages were there, but on the contrary the unfortunate thing was that he's the head of all the hijackers. He found out. But good thing was that we all were already about out of the place. Bad thing was that Stella had gone to the washroom even before we started to apply our plan. Stella got captivated and the head hijacker pointed a gun at her head, and asked us to get everyone inside, but we denied except Casey. Casey went running, as she stood between the gun and Stella. It was heroic. The head hijacker was about to trigger the gun. But right at that moment the other girl of us three came spraying the fire extinguisher on his face making him raise his hands to his face; by which the gun fell down, and Casey kicked it farther than ever, and after a few moments, we heard police sirens, and we sighed in relief as the police escorted the place." told Minsie.

"Oh god that sounded horrifying of an event…" said Fiera widening her eyes "but I have to say you three did a heroic job, and I think if it weren't for Casey then Stella might have died…"

"Oh, here you are." said Stella as she finally found Eliott "I was told you were looking for me, but it seems I'm looking for you."

"Another thing that happened is when we had gone for a trip set by our school. It was a very anticipated event, and specially I was really enthusiastic for the trip. We were told a month before the day we'd go and trust me you could only hear about that trip in every corridor. We were told what we'd do on the trip, and it sounded so much fun as it was set in the jungles; which we all had wanted to venture. So time was passing with every day talking about the trip which usually was happily conversed, but that day I heard an upset voice when I entered the school, and I was a bit shocked as no one had felt bad about going to the trip; cause it was literally what we all had wanted to do. Then I went nearer as I heard that Stella wasn't going to go for the trip for some reason and Casey was upset and requesting her to go, but as Stella kept disagreeing Casey had said that she too wouldn't go." told Minsie toning her voice "And that news stayed up until some days later Stella agreed to go as she had felt bad that Casey had anticipated the event so much and just only for her, Casey wouldn't be going; hearing which Casey was really happy. So days later we were at the school all prepared to go for the trip as everyone brought their belongings and the buses stood outside the school; creating more enthusiasm to everyone over there."

"Oh wow, sounds like a nice trip!" commented Fiera; listening.

"Just hold on the story isn't over." told Minsie giggling slightly.

"So, we were having a lot of fun on the road as we sang songs together and played different sorts of games and then we reached the place after a long ride. We were told to have our tents set up by ourselves and so did we. Each tent had five people, and in the same way we were divided into groups for the rest of the camp. It was a long trip. About two days had passed, that day we were set to go deeper into the jungles and we were really excited; as we were awaiting to do that. We all got readied for the thing, and were standing out organized in lines as the guide instructed us onto how we were going to carry out the whole jungle journey. It was intriguing to even hear about it, well, at least to me; as I loved adventures. Some time later, we had begun going into the jungle while we heard that Stella was late, but then she joined us up. Time passed as we went deeper and deeper into the jungle, and every second of it was feeling amazing as we saw different wild creatures such as wild butterflies and all that. Things were going pretty well until there was suddenly a pause. We were at the back and something had happened at the front. Moments later we moved front to see what had happened, and heard that Casey had entered a cave and that cave might had snakes; toxic snakes. Everyone was scared, but then Stella came up and was about to volunteer into going into the cave and bring Casey. Stella had went. A lot of time had passed and Stella hadn't returned. Every minute was feeling horrible. Finally Stella had returned with Casey, but seemed like she was injured or something. She had gotten bitten by a snake trying to save Casey from a group of snakes, then we took Stella instantly to healthcare as the snake might had been venomous, but thankfully it was not that severe of a venom and Stella became all alright after a day of absolute rest." told Minsie.

"Oh god, that was thrilling." opined Fiera taking a deep breath.

"Yeah…" said Minsie "I unlocked a lot of treasured memories."

"Yeah you actually did." said Fiera laughing out looking at her.

"Uh, everything had been going that great with Casey and Stella always having each other's back," said Minsie sighing "for about a whole year, which not only was good for them but truly it felt good to even us; seeing them, up until something happened..."

23
TRACKS CHANGED

"What?" said Fiera in confusion and intrigue "something what?"

"Things changed drastically..." told Minsie widening her eyes.

"Oh god, tell me everything up, please!" cried Fiera desperately.

"Actually I will tell you everything out, but I think we are getting quite late to our classes." said Minsie; nervously clenching teeth.

"But I think there is still some time left." opposed Fiera politely.

"Yeah," told Minsie "but it's not sufficient to finish the whole story and it's better to not tell than to tell halfway and stop out."

"Yeah I believe; as I too have to go to the extra music class and it'll take time to quite explain everything to them." agreed Fiera.

The two finished the coffees and got up smilingly greeting a bye.

"Oh, Hello!" said Kelvac politely, greeting Fiera "how are you?"

"Omg, I was just about to go to search for you..." told Fiera.

"Oh, wow, what reminded you of me?" asked Kelvac smiling.

"Uh, you forgot how & why we had met?" asked Fiera giggling.

"Oh, wait," replied Kelvac; recalling "the extra music classes?"

"Yes, yes, the extra music classes," said Fiera dramatically "that we have not attended a single day since we had joined them..."

"Oh god, I had totally forgotten about it." told Kelvac sighing.

Fiera and Kelvac decided to go to the extra music class right after their classes they had then; ended, and explain everything.

"What happened?" asked Stella going and sitting next to Minsie.

"What?" said Minsie facing up at Stella "Nothing happened."

"Looked like as if you were wandering in your own world of thoughts." said Stella dramatically, looking at Minsie; smiling.

Minsie made a face showing disapproval as she smiled broadly.

The period ended as all the students got out of their classrooms.

"So, do you think that professor would be mad?" asked Kelvac.

"I really hope not," said Fiera as the two walked "but he might."

The walked hastily towards the extra music class's room aback.

"Hello, Good morning…" said Kelvac as they quietly entered.

"You two are actually alive." said the professor very sarcastically.

"Sorry for not attending the classes …" said Fiera moving front.

"And why was that?" asked the professor in a quite harsh tone.

Fiera and Kelvac then thoroughly told about the quest, and all the things that had happened within it; as the professor listened.

"Sounds surreal but yet makes perfect sense." told the professor.

"Yes, but we're still sorry not to have informed you." said Fiera.

"It's totally fine cause what you have done was more than humane, and I believe it was the very right decision and I am happy to be able to teach such fierce people." said the professor.

Fiera and Kelvac felt happy to hear that, as they smiled broadly.

“So, you two are Fiera and Kelvac?” came a voice from behind.

Fiera and Kelvac looked finding two people entering the room.

“Who are you?” asked Fiera “And how do you know us two?”

“Oh, we are Xiwielle and Nikert, and we are in this class along you two, although you two hadn’t appeared at all.” told Xiwielle.

Fiera and Kelvac faced at each other, as they again explained all.

Nikert and Xiwielle reacted with pure astonishment hearing that.

“Today’s so peaceful, right?” commented Stella as she sat down.

“Yes, it absolutely is...” replied Eliott immediately; hearing Stella.

“Do you want to visit a place today?” asked Stella smiling softly.

“Sure, why not.” said Eliott smiling emotionally thinking stuffs.

The interaction only within the two’s conversation was able to tell how much they were in love with each other, nothing but pure love between the two, which showed the euphoria of love.

“Where do you want to go?” asked Eliott trying to figure it out.

“Leave that to me, I’ll arrange us the schedule for the whole outing, and you don’t have to worry about it.” mentioned Stella.

“Oh alright, sounds pretty nice.” told Eliott smiling happily.

The connection between the two showed the true meaning of pure love, although there had been complications in between them before, but they had made it out those complicated times.

“Also, I was able to bring out some information about the topic; you had wanted me to.” informed Eliott pretty enthusiastically.

“Oh alright, thanks a lot for that!” exclaimed Stella in happiness.

"Minsie!" called out Lesohn as he approached "I was searching for you since the morning but couldn't find you anywhere here."

"That means you didn't search properly." said Minsie jokingly.

"And what makes you say that?" demanded Lesohn raising eyes.

"I was literally there at the front lobby." told Minsie laughingly.

"Oh, my bad," replied Lesohn "but are you free now to talk…?"

"Not really," said Minsie "I actually have stuff to do with Fiera."

Lesohn smiled a bye as he slowly walked saying "See you later."

Minsie replied back as she went onto the front lobby for Fiera.

"Let's continue." said Fiera as she sat down hastily reaching her.

"Sure, but take a breath first." said Minsie as Fiera smiled out.

"Ok, so after a long time of Casey and Stella being the best of the best friends, there was a huge conflict between them. It was more of a misunderstanding than anything..." told Minsie softly.

"Was it about any boy like now?" asked Fiera listening carefully.

"Umm…, no not even at all." told Minsie, quite surprising Fiera.

"It was more critical than just a random boy ruining a damn friendship of years. It was more heart wrenching. It was about something involving intense feelings. Honestly I felt really bad seeing their friendship break; as the friendship was so powerful that I wanted it to last forever and forevermore." told Minsie explaining in details "So life was going in the same way and then there were also new stuff happening. I had been absent for a month as I had gone abroad for some personal reasons. Then when I arrived back there, I saw nothing remained the same; at least not Stella and Casey. Everything seemed dull than peaceful.

I was absolutely confused on what had been happening so I later that day I asked one of my friend that time. What she told astonished me to another extent, cause I had not been expecting to hear any of that. I was told that one peaceful morning all the high school students were sitting, waiting for the morning class to start; when they heard a person sobbing out loud. That really surprised them as it was all of a sudden. To their astonishment it was Stella crying out so loud as she entered. Seemed like she had not wanted to attend school that day but was insisted to. All the students instantly knew some bad news was on its way. And it actually was. After a long time during recess, everyone gathered up trying to calm down Stella. After a while when Stella went calm, the people asked why she was so sad. And to their pure astonishment a more than tragic news came out of Stella's mouth as everyone around her went fully silent while she shed tears. Stella had told that her dad died. Even wording this makes me feel sad. It must have been a horrifying experience for Stella. But it got even more horrific of an event when during those times even though Casey was still attending school she was not there with Stella during all that tragedy." told Minsie quite sadly.

"But weren't they still good friends?" asked Fiera in confusion.

"They actually were still good friends." told Minsie nodding.

"Then why didn't Casey accompany Stella then?" asked Fiera.

"Alright so I later found an even more astonishing side of the story. It literally thrilled me to get to know all that. I really couldn't believe such misunderstanding in such unfortunate way could take place. I found out that when Stella had been weeping for her father; Casey had been weeping for her mother, but for some reasons Casey didn't get to know that Stella's father had died and Stella didn't get to know that Casey's mother died. I believe it was probably cause the tragic events occurred at the same time so none of the two were mentally stable or in their proper sense to see what was happening in their surroundings. So as to my knowledge few weeks had passed after which both Stella and Casey managed to return to their normal lives. Well, not really normal as everything changed; as the two did not even bother to confront each other as both of them felt emotionally angry that their closest friend hadn't supported them through the hardest times when they had been needed the most. The two did not know each other's part of the story and had from deep within been waiting for at least an apology; but how would that have even be possible. In fact, some of the people knew Stella's part of the story, while some knew Casey's but there weren't anyone who knew both of their stories for some absurd reasons. As time passed, the severity of the situation increased, and eventually lead to the befalling of the twos much precious and long friendship..." told Minsie feeling pretty sentimental at it.

"But when you returned you got to know about both their stories, right?" asked Fiera widening eyes and raising eyebrows.

"Yes, I did eventually." replied Minsie shortly, nodding softly.

"Then why didn't you try fixing the issue?" asked Fiera instantly.

"I did. But I think it was just too late. Once I got to know both part of the stories I found the right times to tell each of them individually. At first, I went to Stella on a peaceful morning, but before I could even start just right after hearing Casey's name Stella gave a horrified look as to signing that I really was that audacious to go up to her to talk about the person she hated more than anything. So I failed to tell Stella as she had asked me to go away. Then on a recess I had went calmly to Casey and started chit-chatting, and it seemed like she was a person who would hear another out, but right as I went onto telling Stella's name, she literally shook and stood, and left without any word.

So I felt that I was too late at the scene to help resolve the case. But I still tried a bunch of other times but I failed to tell each time and they till date are fully untold of the story." told Minsie.

"Ugh, that is really sad to hear." commented Fiera feeling bad.

"Yes, to be honest it was and is a tragic thing..." said Minsie.

"Yeah," replied Fiera in an emotional tone "is there more to it?"

"Yes, there really is a lot more." said Minsie continuing "So days were passing in that way; Stella and Casey turning more than haters. Then there was a huge hiatus of the two as they hadn't appeared to school for more than two years. Then one day I went to school feeling it was just a normal day, but then it was not. Stella had made a comeback after literally two years. I was quite shocked to see her, but wasn't that much of a big deal as she barely was even my friend. We were more of acquaintances. I entered the classroom and sat down as usual; thinking of all the things about Casey and Stella that occurred years ago. Then surprisingly Stella sat down beside me, and I greeted as a courtesy. Then she replied in a friendly approach. She was quite nice. That went good as we two chit chatted about life and all that. From then on; we started to sit together; as one of my close friends was gone forever so I was all alone and so was Stella. We'd usually sit in our recess together as well and have our coffees talking about quite random stuff. Things were going that way for a long time as we switched from acquaintances to friends. Time passed as we started to visit each other's houses getting to know our families even better. We had annual events by school on which we would perform together and everything was going all well as we started to become as friends. Then things went on just in that way, and we became quite good friends. Our families knew us, and whenever we had to go to any sort of outings they'd allow if both of us went." told Minsie.

"So you became friends cause Casey wasn't there?" asked Fiera.

"You could say that, but not exactly. There was no certainty that the two would have been friends if Casey had returned. Though when Stella had returned all of us thought Casey too might return, but there was no sign of her." told Minsie "Ok so, there was this one time we were preparing for an upcoming event, and I & Stella were really excited for it. Then an unfortunate thing happened. I got injured, so I wasn't able to go perform, and to my astonishment Stella came over to my house, and stayed up with me the whole time, while the event went by although Stella had a really important performance that she had cherished. I was fully thrilled to see such a benevolent act by someone. Then and there I knew no one but Stella was a true friend. And that is when we turned into more than close friends and it's going on."

"Aww, that was so cute!" commented Fiera listening closely.

"It really was, thank you." replied Minsie as she smiled broadly.

Fiera was more than intrigued to hear all those stories of them.

"Ok so days went all well like that as we finished high school. We two decided to join the same university and we did as you can see. We actually looked a lot for a good university together, and we eventually found this, and it was the best match for us so we joined in this university. We actually were really extremely enthusiastic for university." told Minsie thoroughly "So it was the first day of university and I dressed well and went. As I entered, Stella did too and gave each other a high-five, as we started to talk with each other. And as we were talking constantly we accidentally bumped into somebody. To our absolute astonishment i-it was Casey! There was a moment of literal silence as we stared at each other while our smiles went away. Casey nor Stella seemed alright to see each other. Stella tightly grabbed my handed and dragged me out of there. And I knew that it was nothing good. Stella's so mad to even see Casey. I stood there trying my best to calm her but Stella wasn't at all calmed down. In fact, she's deciding to leave the university. Like literally leave on the very first day! but I requested a lot and managed to convince her to stay. Times were passing with each moment being brutal. I had then tried to fix their friendships back but wasn't able even after putting a lot of effort into it…"

"Sometimes once the track changes, changing the tracks back is sort of more than impossible." commented Fiera impressively.

"Yeah true. Things started to go even worse. Then one day Eliott appeared. He was actually a really nice guy and we shared a class with him too. Slowly Stella started to fall in love with him; immensely in pure love. I felt good that Stella finally found someone special. But what I had no idea about is that Casey shared a class with Eliott too, and she too had slowly fell in love with Eliott. Then time passed by as the two slowly found out about each other loving the same person, and that resulted in million different conflicts between the two, which made the two hate each other even more. Now the question was whether Eliott would choose Stella or Casey. Trust me it was haunting to be part of those events. Stella would not let a single second go away without the thought that Casey was an extremely wicked person, and probably so did Casey the vice versa. Days went by as the hatred grew more and more between the two, and as they planned to tell Eliott that they loved him. Honestly, Stella would secretly cry at times thinking that Eliott would choose Casey if it was for her and Casey." told Minsie dramatically "Then one day, Stella decided to confess to Eliott about loving him and so she prepared. Garnering all the courage she went and she was about to go she bumped into Casey and to Stella's surprise; Casey too was about to go and tell Eliott that she was in love with him…"

A call interrupted Minsie, but she hung it up without even checking the caller's name as she was too hooked onto the story.

"The two was about to start a quarrel but there came Eliott. The two were thrilled to see him. Even though they were going to tell; they felt scared as it supposedly to be that way. I don't know to refer to this as fortunate or unfortunate, but yeah as Eliott came he looked directly at Casey, breaking Stella's hope and heart. But to both the girls' surprise Eliott had requested Casey to give Stella and him a moment. He then confessed about him falling in love with Stella. And no, it wasn't any coincidence but the thing's that he's about to leave the university." told Minsie.

"Oh god that sounded frightening…" commented Fiera "but then how's Eliott still in this university if he was going to leave?"

"Uh, he had some sort of complication for which he was going to leave. Then there stood Stella who was mourning the fact. So, they went at the airport in order to leave and Stella to say one last goodbye. Actually we thought that's where they're about to have the end. Time passed as Stella felt more than dead over the events. I used to calm her down each time she felt the highs of emotions. After a long time, we went to the university taking it as the most usual day, but we heard the freshmen talking about a new guy that joined the university, which we didn't give much thought upon. Then to our disbelief, it was Eliott. Stella was thrilled to see him as she got shocked and stood there as a statue and then Eliott came over, and hugged her tightly as they both fell into heavy tears and heavily sentimental." told Minsie softly.

A phone call came to Minsie again, as she just finished the long storytelling about a lot of treasured memories from the past.

"Excuse me." said Minsie answering the call while Fiera nodded.

"Wait what?!" screamed out Minsie just as she answered the call.

24

FURTHER ON

"Oh, Eliott!" shouted Stella as she hurriedly walked up to Eliott.

"Oh god, what happened?" asked Eliott as he exited the room.

"Nothing, was just waiting for you." said Stella after scaring him.

"You literally scared me." said Eliott dramatically, as she smiled.

"So, I wanted to tell the details about today's outing." told Stella.

"Oh, alright, go ahead." replied Eliott as the two walked slowly.

"So, get ready by afternoon, and I'll come pick up." began Stella.

The two walked rhythmically, as Stella told the details in a serial

"What, what happened?" questioned Fiera in complete horror.

Minsie was absolutely astonished while she talked on the phone.

Fiera was getting more and more horrified seeing Minsie react.

"Is there anything wrong?" asked Fiera as she got more worried.

"Omg, so you're going to go all of a sudden?!" spoke Minsie on the call while Fiera gulped a heavy breath fixedly staring at her.

"No come on," said Minsie sighing "you can't just go suddenly."

"No, it's just all unplanned but I'll have to go..." told the person.

"Alright tell me where are you at least." demanded Minsie softly.

Minsie gestured Fiera to note down the address and so did Fiera.

"What happened!" asked Fiera seeing Minsie hung up the call.

"A person is leaving…" said Minsie sighing as she felt quite bad.

"Who is leaving?" asked Fiera instantly "Is it a mutual friend?"

"Yes, sort of." told Minsie intensifying "It is actually Dexzart..."

"Oh! What!" blurted Fiera; quite shocked "Dexzart is leaving?!"

"Yes, he is." told Minsie as she searched something in her bag.

"Why?" questioned Fiera in shock "Why is Dexzart leaving and that too all of a sudden like did something happened or what?"

"First of all," said Minsie standing up "do you want to go to the place; joining me up? And I will tell everything up on our way."

"Yeah alright," said Fiera confusedly "but when is he leaving?"

"I think he said" told Minsie picking her bag up "couple hours."

"Couple hours!" exclaimed Fiera as she stood up immediately.

"Yes," told Minsie "that's why we need to hurry up, or else by the time we reach that place; he would already be gone away…"

Fiera hastily took her stuff; knowing they'd to leave right away.

The two then quickly walked out of the university, as they went to the parking lot; where their ride had been waiting for them.

"Show me the address please…" said Minsie as Fiera quickly showed the address; taking out a paper from the bag on her lap.

Minsie quickly started driving right as she read the address out.

"Umm," said Fiera as the two were already on the road; hastily heading to the address Dexzart had given "so now can you tell why Dexzart's leaving all of a sudden without any prior notice?"

"Alright, so as you might or might have not known that Dexzart was here as an apprentice at the place I work, so he was here for already knowing that it would be for a short period of time. But, I believe his time as an apprentice hadn't ended so we have to go check with why suddenly he is leaving." told Minsie in brief.

"Oh, okay, didn't know that at all," said Fiera in awe "feels sad."

The two sighed as they drove through the roads under clear sky.

After a long but hasty drive, they reached the place; near airport.

"Oh god..." sighed Fiera saying dramatically "Dexzart, why did you not tell us that you're going to leave; earlier, why suddenly?"

"Oh you're here too," said Dexzart noticing the two "actually it was just so unplanned, that didn't get time to give prior notice."

"Well," said Minsie as the two reached him "tell us now why is it so unplanned that you were about to leave without even telling."

"Oh," started saying Dexzart "actually it is quite complicated, but umm... I had gone to office today, then it was feeling as a normal day, but all of a sudden a call came as I got offered to work at a really highly renowned place, and I replied to them saying that I'll let them know in a while. Although it felt great of a thing I was still worried, up until coincidentally Mr. Monzelle came and told me that I had worked pretty well and my time of being an apprentice had ended so then I accepted the job offer."

"Oh," said Fiera raising eyebrows "that's great! congratulations!"

"Thank you," said Dexzart smiling "I think I shall say goodbye."

"Yeah, goodbye!" said Minsie smiling broadly facing at Dexzart.

Minsie and Fiera said goodbye as Dexzart took a leave by going into the quick ride that takes people to the airport from there.

"I am outside, please get out." said Stella quite enthusiastically.

Stella had planned that day's outing and as to their plan Stella was outside Eliott's house to pick him, and go to the set place.

"Alright I'll be outside in a moment." told Eliott as he smiled.

Eliott quickly got out, putting on his shoes he had already setup.

"So where are we going to go?" asked Eliott as he got in the car.

"I have told you it's a secret." said Stella smiling mischievously.

"Alright, so I need you to close your eyes." told Stella guiding.

"Oh no, come one, why?" blurted Eliott as he denied playfully.

"See, you have no choice," said Stella as she smiled "and also I need your eyes kept close until I ask to open and am not putting any blindfold on you cause I trust you, so don't break the trust."

"Wow," replied Eliott in epiphany "literally a serious blackmail."

Stella began driving as the two set for their anticipated outing.

The two had harmony in between them and quite much elation.

"How farther?" stated Eliott "it's been quite long sitting here…"

"I really do not have any idea if you would like it…" told Stella.

"Trust me I know whatever it is, it would least be the best, as no one can object that your beautiful mind is put at it." said Eliott.

Stella smiled emotionally, as tears filled her eyes with happiness.

"It is not any farther, we have about reached there." told Stella.

"Oh, good to hear, cause it's frustrating having to close my eyes in this way, while you sit there enjoying the scenery." said Eliott.

Stella slightly laughed hearing Eliott, as she drove a little faster.

"You can get down, but try not opening your eyes." told Stella.

"Alright, so we have reached..." said Eliott smiling "yay, finally."

Eliott slowly got down; keeping his eyes closed as Stella guided.

"Give me your hand." said Stella as she reached him on the side.

"Oh, alright." said Eliott putting his hand forward as Stella took hold of it; leading Eliott to the place while his eyes were closed.

The two walked rhythmically while Eliott kept feeling impatient.

"You can have your eyes opened now…" told Stella ebulliently.

Eliott hastily opened his eyes saying "Oh… this is spectacular."

"Do you like it?" asked Stella smilingly; looking at the scenery.

"Yes, absolutely," said Eliott glaring "this truly is magnificent."

Eliott felt as if words would fall short if gone to explain the beauty held before his widely opened eyes; glaring at it's beauty.

The sky was put up in twilight, while fireflies lightened it in such a manner that human eyes would fall weak to resist it's beauty.

"I can't thank enough," told Eliott "cause I am lacking words."

"Well, I too lack words to thank you for being with me," told Stella in exhilaration "being the fireflies to the twilight of mine."

The two smiled deliberately as they let go of their pain and accepted the happiness over everything they have had together.

"I hope to always stay maundering in the world of yours." said Eliott as his words brought tears to Stella eyes accompanied by a broad smile as she stared at Eliott feeling the mesmeric intensity.

"Hi Good morning!" greeted Stacy as she noticed Stella arriving.

"Good morning, how're you?" said Stella, as she smiled at Stacy.

"Yeah, I am fine, and you?" replied Stacy as she opened her bag.

"Yeah, I am great, thankfully." told Stella giving out a soft smile.

Stella went to get a fresh morning coffee from the canteen there.

Stacy sat there drinking coffee while Stella returned buying one.

"Alright, so I needed to tell something to you all." stated Stella.

"What is it about?" asked Minsie as she reached sitting by Stella.

Eliott, Jacob and Lesohn too were present there along the three.

"I actually want to perform a short thorough research on the climate change, and I wanted to ask if you'd join in." said Stella.

"Oh, a research..." blurted Jacob as he went onto thinking on it.

"Actually, count me in with you." told Lesohn enthusiastically.

"And I am by default in, right…" said Eliott giving out a laugh.

"Also I would like to help." told Stacy slightly raising her hand.

"Great! What about you two?" said Stella pointing at Jacob and Minsie as the two hadn't said a yes or no; while they sat blankly.

"I think Minsie's probably joining…" commented Stacy smiling.

"Yes, I was just thinking whether it's just six of us." told Minsie.

"Yeah, I mean six of us are enough." told Stella opinionatedly.

"Yeah, I think so too." said Jacob as the rest four except Minsie nodded briefly "And also, I think I too am willing to participate in such a fun work; I mean who doesn't like group researches..."

"Alright," questioned Lesohn garnering attention of all "how or what exactly are we going to do onto what we are going to do?"

"Yeah actually," accompanied Stacy as the rest listened "how?"

"Stella knows it all…" told Eliott in a serious tone facing Stella.

"Yeah so," told Stella intensifying the conversation "I had asked Eliott to gather information; about which libraries have the best information about climate change and all that, and so he did. So, we're going to go off to those libraries to perform the research."

The rest nodded listening carefully as Stella explained it briefly.

"I believe we should start off today right after all our classes in university ends." opined Jacob as the others nodded in approval.

"Ok, so we all meet up at the parking lot, after-class." told Stella.

The six then went to their classes accordingly as the bell rang.

"Oh, you're here already." said Stella walking to the parking lot.

"Yes, my class ended the first so…" told Eliott standing there.

The two stood there chatting randomly; waiting for the others.

"Hey, Eliott and Stella." said Minsie as she came walking hastily.

"Where are the others?" asked Minsie as she went and stood by.

"There they are." said Eliott as he noticed the others from a distance; walking towards them as they rushed due to latency.

The rest came joined them as they all got inside the car quickly.

"Ok, so tell the location." requested Stella, as she went to drive.

"Also, I think once we reach there we can divide into different groups in order to quicken our short research." told Lesohn.

The six reached the location shortly and got out and went inside.

"Alright, see what this book says..." said Eliott calling out Stella.

Stella was picking a book from the shelf while she listened too.

"So, it basically says that climate change is increasing threatening massive amounts of lives, most of today's issue such as deaths by malaria, under nutrition and etc. are caused by it." told Eliott.

"And as we know it takes place due to greenhouse gases emitted by humans' industrial activities…" added Stella facing Eliott.

"Most of the activities that emit greenhouse gases are burning fossil fuel, non-biodegradable wastages, and etc." told Minsie.

"Yeah, and cutting down of forests help increase the emission of carbon dioxide; as tress take in carbon dioxide but if forests are cut down then there won't be enough trees to take in the carbon dioxide…" told Lesohn while Minsie listened carefully.

"So, forest fires are effects of climate that cause unhealthy air which is harmful for people to breathe." told Jacob in shock.

"When the unhealthy air is breathed the people can actually face fatal situations, and with less healthcare to be found in those forest areas; huge amount of deaths can be seen." stressed Stacy.

"Everyday activities by commoners can also help cause climate change." told Eliott as Stella eagerly listened feeling guilty for it.

"Yes, and those activities include plastic consumption as most plastic products are left out to be heated naturally; causing methane and ethylene release into the atmosphere which is quite harmful as those are greenhouse gases." told Stella quite guiltily.

"And as we already know that methane can cause deaths which gives symptoms barely noticeable!" emphasized Eliott deeply.

The six were thoroughly reading through the info found there.

"Stella, I think we should switch places and go to somewhere where we can get like articles to read out." told Jacob; reaching.

Stella nodded, as they informed all the others, and went to the place where they could get articles about climate change and all.

"Oh god!" screamed Lesohn "according to some research we have about only some years to fix the issue on climate to avoid the worst outcome of the huge ongoing issue threatening lives."

"Yes, and if by the next few years we do not reduce the carbon dioxide in atmosphere by about forty-five percent then people will face massively bad outcomes…" added Minsie in shock.

"Also, it is also estimated that after some years if climate change continues in it's current path then approximately two-hundred-fifty-thousand death increase per year will be seen." told Jacob.

The six were at the same place as they chatted reading articles.

"And that too just by malnutrition, diarrhea, excess heat and malaria, so there stays other kinds of deaths too." added Jacob.

"Yeah, and also poorer countries and people will face much difficulties coping up with those upcoming harsh outcomes, and as if such a thing actually occurs then wealthier countries will fail to provide aid as they too will be affected by much." told Stacy.

"And yeah, the previous scientific estimates about climate change have already been seen into effect now; such as sea-level rising, forest fire and etc., so it is highly likely that the current estimates too will come into if the issue isn't solved." said Stella.

"I believe we need to know the preventions as well." said Eliott.

"Ok then, let's head to the next destination, right?" said Lesohn.

The six nodded as they again went onto switching their location.

"Alright, so let's go start reading onto the info." guided Minsie.

They went to read info about the prevention of climate change.

"Ok so, there are so simple ways of reducing the severity of climate change;" said Stella; garnering attention of the rest five "most easiest are reducing everyday plastic consumption and planting trees, and all it takes is the will and not much effort…"

"But there will be people coming and saying that what will occur if only they start doing those things." said Jacob deeply; sighing.

"Yeah although everyone and everything starts out small," said Eliott "just like those pretty minds under the very limelight."

"Yeah, also if deforestations are stopped then the increasing of carbon dioxide will also stop significantly." told Lesohn clearly.

"Also changing our sources of energy can help by large means," said Stacy; emphasizing "such sources are solar, wind and etc."

"It could also help if we limit our fossil fuel consumption, and industrial emissions of greenhouse gases and waste." told Jacob.

"An act of recycling too helps by a fair percentage." told Stella.

"Sea and oceans are the largest storage for greenhouses gases, and preserving it by having less unsustainable development activities and stopping overfishing can help trap much of the already emitted greenhouse gases." informed Lesohn loudly.

"Actually all it takes is the will to do so, cause the preventions don't even need that much of effort; so if the will of preventing the issue of climate change is present in good measures then if not diminishing at least reducing the severity of climate change will more than be possible…" said Stella as the others nodded.

25

LIFE

"I believe we should do something to save lives." stated Stella.

The six had departed from the place, and were then in their car.

"What should we do?" said Jacob trying to think of something.

They all felt guilty and sentimental of what was happening to the earth, and the future of millions of little children who then were unaware of what they would be bearing when they grow up.

"I feel desperate to do something for all the lives that are at stake." said Eliott; feeling emotional, as he took a deep breath.

"It's funny how when children are even a bit exposed to getting hurt; the parents try their best to protect them," said Minsie "but now that their whole future, health & all upcoming things' at stake, nobody is even bothering to think of solving the issue."

"It is quite." blurted out Lesohn as he looked out the window.

"We actually have to do something; in order to save all those cute little lives, that now are probably playing with crayons knowing nothing of what is coming ahead of them." said Stacy.

"Yes, they don't even know anything, and by the time they get to know about all those things they wouldn't even be able to breathe anymore..." said Stella as tears fell off her eyes heavily.

They fell into deep thoughts of what they should be doing to save all the lives that would be crying suffocating in the future, and who would have no time to even know what living life is.

"Why not go buy some lives?" said Lesohn as his mood uplifted.

"What do you mean 'buy some lives'?" queried Minsie instantly.

"I mean why not go buy and plant some trees." told Lesohn.

"That's a good idea, let's go put it in action." said Stella smiling.

The six then decided to head to a store in order to buy plants.

"Ok, let's buy some seeds." said Stella as they entered the shop.

"Alright, let's go pick some up." said Jacob going another path.

The six bought plants and seeds in order to plant all of them up.

"We plant them up in our backyards and gardens?" said Stacy.

"Yes, we'll go to each and every one of our house, and help each other plant all the bought seeds and plants." told Stella instantly.

The six drove through the streets in a more than cheerful mood; as they're going to contribute into helping save the planet earth.

"Can you bring bottles of water?" requested Stella as she and the rest were planting the seeds in the backyard of Minsie's house.

"Yeah, sure, I will come right back." told Minsie as she went in.

"Jacob, can you pass me the shovel?" requested Eliott smiling.

"Yeah sure," said Jacob handing him the shovel "here you go!"

They worked together as a team, planting the seeds and plants.

"Whose garden next?" asked Stella in amusement; staring back.

"Your!" shouted them all; loudly, synchronizing with each other.

They felt the joy of helping save numerous lives by doing such an easy and simple act, which just grew humans more humane.

"What else should we do?" asked Stella eagerly, as she drove.

They were done planting all the seeds and plants in their houses.

"Why not visit some public places and collect any plastics on the ground and throw them into recycling bins?" suggested Minsie.

"Oh yeah, that's a great idea." said Eliott as the others nodded.

"Let's first think of some public places and we'll go." said Stella.

The six started listing out some public spots where they'd head.

"Alright then, let's go!" said Stella as they finished their listing.

The atmosphere was filled with harmony and tranquility; as above all was the peace of having the life to save others' lives.

"Oh god, this is way worse than we thought." commented Stacy.

"Well, that's what makes the idea of coming here even better." said Eliott as they all stood by their car looking at the full area.

"So, let's get to work!" said Stella handing a jute bag to them.

The six took a jute bag each, and ran to raid the place of plastics.

"Eliott help me put them into this recycle bin." requested Stella, as Eliott came over to help and then the two slowly poured it in.

"Stacy can you quickly help me up put these in?" asked Minsie.

"Yeah, of course!" said Stacy as she went over to help Minsie.

The sweet thing about group works are helping out the others.

"I am done by my part." told Stacy raising her hand quite high.

"Yeah me too!" said Lesohn very loudly, from a farther distance.

"Yeah, I think we all are actually done here!" shouted out Stella.

"Hey you all, have some coffee." said Minsie, as she brought some pretty glass cups of coffee in a tray; for all the six of them.

After finishing thoroughly cleaning up two different public areas the six came to Minsie's house to take some rest drinking coffee.

"Today was quite a pleasing day." said Stacy in a beatific tone.

"It really was a quite mesmerizing day." opined Eliott smilingly.

"Trust me, I never felt so harmonious." told Jacob dramatically.

"Me neither." told Minsie very blissfully, as she drank the coffee.

"Yeah!," said Lesohn "never knew life could be so magnificent."

"Yeah actually," said Minsie "but what happened to Stella cause she's not saying a word and seems to be lost in her own world?"

"What happened Stella?" questioned Eliott poking Stella softly.

"Oh, nothing," said Stella sighing "I was just thinking that we six aren't enough and we do need more people doing these things."

"Oh…" said Minsie in a really soft tone; as it came unexpected.

"I mean you aren't wrong, but what can we do." sighed Jacob.

The six's mind went into deep thinking mode as they tried to figure out what they should be doing to get more people into saving all those unfortunate future lives that are totally at stake.

"I wish we could get more people into doing all the blissful things we had done to save our and many others' lives." said Stella in an emotional tone as others looked at their coffee cups.

"Yes you are right that'd help a lot." commented Stacy softly.

"Is there nothing that we can do?" asked Jacob softly; sighing.

"I don't think we can get anybody to join us…" said Stacy.

"Besides, nobody would come up to join us in." said Eliott.

"It is quite saddening to think all that." commented Lesohn.

The six tried their best to get out an idea but seemed to fail.

"We have to at least try think a way to garnering all people's interest and make them understand the importance of all these things." said Minsie, as all the six stared blankly right at her.

"But I can't think of a single way that might help garner a lot of people, let aside garnering their interest." told Jacob instantly.

"Wait wait!" screamed Stella as her mood uplifted "I've an idea."

"Oh ok, what idea?" questioned Stacy as the rest waited eagerly.

"So why not set up an event!" said Stella in a quite cheerful tone.

"What exactly do you mean by an event?" asked Eliott instantly.

"Like a program; where we invite a lot of people and talk about climate action and things related to it." explained Stella in brief.

"So, you mean an event where people are free to come, and where we all raise awareness about climate change." said Minsie.

"Oh that is a cool idea." commented Jacob widening his eyes.

"But do you think it would work?" questioned Lesohn; thinking.

"I mean it's a good thing to give a try and besides we can at least put our minds at rest knowing we tried our best." opined Stella.

"I mean, I can't disagree with that." commented Eliott instantly.

Some of them started to think more into it as they took sips of their coffee rhythmically; while sitting on the luxurious couches.

"So, what do you say?" asked Stella looking around the room.

"Alright, even if we all agree, how do you plan to do all that for the 'very event?" questioned Lesohn as the others stared at him.

"Yes: that is quite a valid question." commented Eliott instantly.

The room went silent looking at Stella for a proper answer while Stella went to thinking how to put the whole idea into words.

"Alright, so what we need to do is set a place to do the event, bring out creative presentations about climate change and how it can be prevented, and also invite people." told Stella explaining.

"That is quite a task to be carried out..." commented Lesohn.

"And we will need to think how we will invite the people to be our audience, like you know..." said Jacob as some nodded too.

"Oh, we can put up a huge poster saying all about the event and asking them to join us up for free..." explained Stella instantly.

"Wouldn't it be harmful for the climate?" questioned Lesohn.

"Not if it's made with jute and eco-friendly paint." said Stella.

"Alright, but none would want to join a paid event." said Jacob.

"No, we'll keep it fully free." told Stella gesturing with her hand.

"Wait, what, how'll that be possible?" asked Stacy immediately.

"We all have our earning source, so we can take some from our earning just to help save the lives at stake." said Stella nervously.

"Even if we do I don't think it would be enough." told Minsie.

"Besides it'll cost a lot to book a place for the event." told Stacy.

"Not if we do it in our university premises." pointed out Eliott.

"Okay that's actually a good idea." opined Minsie instantly.

"But, will they even allow us to do so?" asked Lesohn politely.

"Yes," said Eliott "but only if we take permission prior to it."

"Permission?!" screamed Stacy softly as she got a bit shocked.

"Yes, permission," said Eliott "we need to go take permission."

"So why not let's go right away?" asked Stella, as others nodded.

The six quickly got out of Minsie's house and got into their car.

"What if we don't get the permission?" asked Jacob in horror.

"Don't worry, we probably will, cause the thing we are going to do is not any mere event but a huge evolution." stressed Eliott.

The six were in the car as they drove through the path to glory.

"May we enter?" asked Stella, as she knocked on the door softly.

"Yes, please." said the professor as all the six slowly walked in.

"How may I help you?" asked the professor facing up at the six.

"Uh, we wanted to ask permission in order to arrange an event in the university premises." told Stella as the others nodded out.

"An event, what sort of event?" asked the professor looking up.

Stella and the rest five explained thoroughly about what the event was for and they would be doing and all that in full details.

"That is a great idea!" said the professor "and you know what?"

"W-what?" asked Eliott nervously as the others too got worried.

"The university fund will help you out on this absolutely keen idea of yours!" said the professor; as the six shook in pure awe.

"Whoops," said Minsie "that was purely intense in there, up until it changed into absolute joy hearing the fund will help us!"

The six had exited out of there and then were walking to the car.

"Ah, yes it was, and the best thing is that now we are not bound by a tight budget; like we're just few minutes ago." said Lesohn.

"Alright so are we done for today?" asked Stacy facing her sides.

"No, it's not yet the end," said Eliott "the day hasn't ended yet."

"So, what. do we have anything else to do?" asked Jacob softly.

"Ah, we'll have to go check for a poster maker who would make us an eco-friendly poster and also we've to buy some other stuff, so when time comes we're not missing out on them " said Stella.

The others nodded as they quickly got in their cars and set off.

"So you want me to make a poster in an eco-friendly way?" said the person as he got up from his chair and walked left and right.

"Yes, so can you seem to make us one?" asked Lesohn instantly.

"Yes, yes, we can." said the person as the rest sighed in relief.

The six told him the details on how they wanted the poster to be and how big it must be and negotiated the price and set the deal.

"Okay, everyone, bye!" said Minsie smiling happily facing them.

"Yeah bye," told Stella "it was such a mesmerizing journey!"

"Yeah, see all of you; later on!" said Eliott in a tranquil manner.

"Hope to be continuing soon!" exclaimed Lesohn in total bliss.

They all waved each other a sweet bye, as they left after such a magnificent and spectacular day which'd always be remembered.

"Hello! Everyone!" said Minsie as she just arrived over there.

A few days had passed and it was finally the day of the most awaited event of all time of all the people who arranged it.

It was a day that would take the first steps towards saving the lives and future of all the innocent people out there on earth.

"Are the mikes here?" asked Eliott as Minsie showed up there.

"No, no, they are just on the way!" told Minsie smiling broadly.

"People, are we getting late?" asked Stacy from the other side.

"No, the guests have just started to arrive!" shouted out Eliott.

"Yeah, but Stella is still not here!" shouted out Lesohn loudly.

"I thought Stella already arrived…" said Eliott being shocked.

"No, I actually haven't seen her yet…" told Minsie raising eyes.

"Okay, we'll just wait for her awhile." told Eliott nodding lightly.

They went back into checking and arranging all the other things.

Time flew up by an hour and a lot of guests had already showed up, but there was no sign of Stella at all, which was astonishing.

"An hour literally passed, where's Stella?" asked Stacy in horror.

"She should have been here by now." said Lesohn in confusion.

"Wait people, I'll call her up." said Minsie taking out her phone.

"I already did call her up…" told Eliott as others stared at him.

"What did she say then?" asked Stacy as others got horrified.

"No, she didn't receive," said Eliott as the others stared at him with an astonished face "in fact her phone's likely switched off."

The five were extremely horrified due to what was happening.

"Stella's not there either!" shouted Stacy as she came running.

"She's not even there!" blurted Eliott; getting more tensed on it.

Stacy had gone to Stella's house to check if Stella had been there but wasn't there and Stacy had found the whole place empty but what had been more shocking was that Stella's car too had not been there which literally terrified Stacy so she had returned fast.

"Oh god, what will we do now," said Lesohn out loud "we are getting late, and almost all the guests have arrived and are there under the sky waiting for us to actually start the event up..."

The atmosphere felt really horrifying as all the five felt as if they were falling off a very high mountain or hill and were terrified.

"I think we will wait for Stella a bit longer," said Jacob "maybe she is gone for some important work, and she might be here soon, so let's just wait for her awhile and let's calm the guests."

"People I had just contacted Ms. Franklin." told Minsie arriving.

"What did she say?!" asked Lesohn immediately coming front.

"So I told her everything out, and she told she would go and check the house up..." told Minsie breathing heavily "Then she called back after checking. And what she said is...she found a note, which said that it was by Stella, and that she had left and not to worry for her, cause she was truly gone by her own will."

"What?!" said Eliott in an emotional tone in pure astonishment.

"I find their story retaining a taste similar to that of Chamenoy Eraztez." said a guest girl getting out, as she played the car radio.

"Why doesn't it ever sign what might be the end?" tuned radio.

ACKNOWLEDGEMENT

I would love to show my highest gratitude to all who does support nonetheless, to all who supports involuntarily but judges voluntarily. And to all of those people who continue to do that; I would and do pour out utmost love; forevermore.

To all the people, who are always there for others no matter what or where they stand; as long as they're righteous, and to those who still stand by others even if they are wrong; just in order to bring them to the right path; they all have my whole heart and appreciation to them and honestly no act can be enough to appreciate those people...

No matter where I stand, as long as I exist I hope that I never stop appreciating all those who have had shown and been an example by doing the right and spreading all the positivity without expecting anything in return, cause those people deserve more than anything they ever got, get or would get.

Coming Soon...

Just Began...

"I'd rather be part of history than mystery..."

Sadab Mahir

1

THE SUDDEN APPEARANCE

After a long hiatus, Stella arrived at a party in a more than gorgeous dress entering as if she were a royal entering the ball...

Eliott has longed for her more than anything in the past year. Eliott stared at her vividly with nothing but pure love. He then due his surprise slowly walked in front towards Stella, as he broke into slight tears. He smiled a painful smile, as he reached to her, while Stella turned to her right side to notice Eliott. She noticed his eyes filling up with tears as he put on a narrow smile. She smiled broadly seeing him as her eyes too filled with tears.

He innocently biting his lips asked "A long of a hiatus huh?".

"Yes." said she letting out a little laugh; in a quite painful tone.

"Is that Stella!" asked Stacy in an absolute shock as she tilted.

"It is." said Fiera as her voice lowered due to the surprise taking over her completely, as she glared right at Stella; blurring others.

"How long has it been, hasn't it?" blurted out Jacob facing right.

“Stella! Where'd she been all along!” demanded Minsie noticing.

“Stella?!” questioned Lesohn in absolute disbelief facing Minsie.

Stella and Eliott faced each other right in the eyes as they stood feets apart while tears constantly poured down the two's eyes.

Soft music accompanied by piano; playing in there, set the aura.

“Where've you been?” demanded Eliott in a soft nostalgic tone.

ABOUT THE AUTHOR

Sadab Mahir, an indie author just starting on his path hoping to reach the benevolent audience; who has their ear up, no matter whether it's a small or big voice. It's just the start of the journey, and he looks forward to say one day that it's been a long euphoric journey; although it is not certain, there stands no harm in hoping. He just landed onto the path with the new novel "*The End?*", but has his sight onto other upcoming rides; such as "*You know me...*", "*Just Began...*" and etc.

Sadab Mahir would love to have the spectators join him on the road; also using:

Instagram: sadabmahir.official

Twitter: sadabmahir_ofcl

Facebook: sadabmahir.official

YouTube: Sadab Mahir Official